FUCK YOUR THOUGHT EXPE

SDP

SWEAT DRENCHED PRESS

FUCK YOUR THOUGHT EXPERIMENTS & LOVE YOUR DISEASED "*child*"

Cover art by Zak Ferguson

ISBN: 9798871554692

Publisher's Note: WE HATE PAGE NUMBERS.

FUCK YOUR THOUGHT EXPERIMENTS & LOVE YOUR DISEASED "*child*"

Thought up by

Zak Ferguson

Fuck your opinions. Fuck your own strange rituals. Fuck your reviews. Fuck your hard-earned cash. These written works are not meant to be admired, appraised, held in the court of good taste, or better, bad taste. These words are my thoughts, my emotions, my breakdowns, my visions and are in totality, in their increments, whether forced together, written into a given work, these are pieces of my mind-flesh, and are pieces of raw fucking art. I cough up words like you cough up spit to moisten lips before you try to suck off yet another BF who will use you for all that you are worth until somebody who doesn't cheese grate their cock comes along. Same goes for the GF-Girlfriend. Gluten Free girlfriends for those out of the loop. Keep up. Do keep up. These words are from projects, that are all dislocated, disparate, listless, just existing as they are for months at a time; fuelled by inspiration or a need to conform and adhere and supplicate like the little piss artist I am. They will be brutalised, shouted at, a great dirge over written words, phrases, these symbols of linguistic "GLORY" being shuffled, micromanaged, and slaved over. I put words to page like a painter flicks his first stroke of paint onto his canvas, and I do shape, mould, nurture it, haphazardly, ambidextrously, tying myself up over loose threads and looser meanings and wordplay that will have a professor of maths

blush, and a professor of words weep. I do piece together these things together. Stringing them along. In accordance with my own preferred editorial/abusive style. I do not want to fall into the machinations of old or new or whatever it is called now. The ontological nature, the interstices, they are interesting, but what is more interesting is reading words aloud, and liking how they change the way you talk, and think. A book is a thought experiment in perpetual action. You are just too arrogant to see it. And you may like to think you can track them, map them out, these phrases, pages, passages, but I do not save the drafts – the work needs to exist as a totem, as it is put out. Seeing all this writing, all these "narratives" and "experiments" go to waste, I need to purge myself. Though they are my children, they are diseased. Grotesque little rugrats. They are my own little thought experiments left to become something altogether... ***other*****. A thought experiment can come in various ways; yet I will leave that up to your own imagination. My writing is diseased. It doesn't make you feel good about yourself, and though there is humour, cutting into the pretentious, soothing that harsh elixir that I call EXPERIEMTNAL juju, the pretentions are always highlighted, when the fun of experimental writing is there, right in front of your grimy eyeballs. They, who are they? They,**

the books, the words, the passages, the verses, the stanzas, the paragraphs, the narratives, the philosophy of eroticism found in erratic behaviour, they are meant to be left existing. There for the taking, for the weeping, for the smirking, for the brow slurping – juicy droplets of plum sweat balls - listed on a digital Amazon page, and to gather digital dust. I do not need nor want my work to be edited. I do not need or want proofreaders. I do not lust for literary life. If I can make a little bit of money, cool, but, if I can make a deeper impression than just an - "Oh, that was weird, and fun!" reaction, I am sated. I don't want to be trapped by my own inventions. I don't want to be the writer with little to say, and have his works championed for their attitude to nothing. Experimental books are not boring. Whoever said that needs to be shot or guided in the right direction. Language as read, and then as translated in your head is different to that of which is spoken aloud. I have come to the conclusion that all my previous, unreleased work, needed to be read aloud, to see if the human mouth can formulate it and deliver it so splendidly. Read this aloud, take on my cadences, my own semi-form of verbal exPERiMENTalia. This verbiage is rotten. This is not glitchosophy. This is nothing, if not a gesture, forced out of the anus of an ExTER-Terrestrial. Fonts of a retro-old-paperback-

fashion – do they still exist? - lost to varying designs and calligraphic-aesthetics – annoyed – infuriated – going in and out of that bay – scrolling through them – playing – experimenting – adding fonts that some 80s marketing executive wank stain would overuse, who thought having smoking monkeys in diaper ads in the U S of A was cool and appropriate. The squirts spreading across the blackness of space - the lightyear contrails mistaken for various unnamed planets. Horny old artful-todgers getting at least an ankle over, due to their recent observatory delivered revelations and discoveries. AI forms battling their way into narratives. Soft tissues used like faeces on cave walls and as sore armpit relievers. These are images. These are not. Not are these. Are not these. Not, not, not! Reversal. Loop. Entropy birthing. Entropy bruised like a fighter in the sweaty ring. Muhammad Ali shakes (Post-Parkinsons-rocks-jabs-haymakers) on the bottom of a potato sack, with an aborted foetus slipping and sliding all over the sharp edges. Its sac is almost pierced. Certain independent poets of the road, the glorious gravel road, found their way to something intrinsically national. Purely British hills dominated by hand-holding robed poets. The circle forming a trans-dimensional portal. What pops up, meerkat like, is Marcel Shutsky, who giggles, dips back into the portal

and comes back up for breath, realising he couldn't exist in the in-between. Billowing flags. Mutated language patterns externalized by mouthpieces that fit in like mouthguards - projecting crackling electricity. Those words. Do you see them seemingly being seamless whilst being witnessed and being programmed into

being of a being. ??? I was impressed

by the name of a man, who happened to be in uxorious-ly in love with his own masterfully created personality. These words I place down onto your lap are substantial. Their bulk is impressive - given the dimensions and the angles and the archaic plastic moulds. These words are transparent. Cloudy shapes contained within them. These words are lucid dreams made into symbolic gestures calcified in ice-age ooze and cryptozoic materials. Time isn't-a-concept. It is physical. Look at your Grandmas pissing in a plastic bag as proof. These words are inky. These words are hollow. Typewritten notes cracked like hollow eggshells. This is not a repulsive simulation. Blood leaking between a hairline fracture. The blood seems to be clotted. This is not a digital revolution led by cardboard-box proportioned robots with Tourette's, mispronouncing the C-word like utter cunts.

Bullets are clicks of the tongue – these spittle, frothy screams their phonemes. Versatile, clickety-clack clacking's, working like consonants. Words are weapons. Non-verbal noises are weapons. A perfectly delivered snarl can have dire consequences, that or carry across the deliverers most inner-thoughts and needs. Words are not only words. They are ember-encased historical permutations-made-tangible-made-physical… these genomes we carry, built out of noise and vocal articulation. Slung about with animal abandon - bones and the dregs of their carcasses launched in the air and at one another; the flesh taut and translucent, the morning sun piercing the serrated edges and flesh-veil. Words used to obliterate and to delude. Words are powerful. Language is power. It produces images, ideals, notions, obsessions. Words are weapons. Words are sludge. Words are ointments. Words are letters. Letters consist of shapes. Weaponised vs weaponized. Wordadized. Words. Many words. Standardized. Words. Shapes and calligraphic influenza forcing themselves together to make words crossed with inter-words. Harnessed like America harnessed the phrase: "weapons of mass destruction". That phrase spread fear like some promiscuous wannabe Freddy Mercury passed on aids across his neighbourhood for shits and giggles. The notion of an, *other*, a whole

other **entity or** ***being*****, possessing a weapon is scary and almost inconceivable, but it is enough to force us to create our own. Fight fire with fire. Throw that adverb against a noun. Grease that adjective or consonant and wait for detonation. The shards, the shrapnel pieces embedding in the faces of the normals. Those normies. The rule-abiding citizens. Whether or not it makes sense, we instil in ourselves a readiness for opposition. The opposition to me is methodology, form, expectations and what is universally SCREAMED in our faces to**

be

THE NORM.

THE NORM.

The notion of a weapon, alone, is reciprocated by one sole individuals' engagement with not just the weapon as a physical form, but as a notion, and as a potentiality/option. With that in mind, we will quickly flit our eyes to the nearest thing – the damnedest thing – that you can use in retaliation. USED. Weaponised. Against the myth the notion the option. Weaponised and utilized, against the notations scrolled and

picked apart. Footnotes have taken on a complexity that I do not feel many people have noticed. Our media is full of footnotes. Our headlines are mere footnotes whereas the important stuff, the essential oils to reality and truth are footnoted or outright discarded/ignored. No sense. No sense to the nonsense. Full sense to the nonsense. There is always some cunt wishing to bring you down. Brandishing it as a sword, as a conversation silencer. This here, in my mucky hands be the rulebook, you must abide by it or fear the repercussions. This vague impression, this societal NORM/FORM passed across the dinner table on a silver-platter, with intricate designs framing the delicious dish – this – that – thing – thang – vermin - known as the literary rulebook. It is their manifesto. One preordained and approved and generalized. Gentrified, if you ask me. Used to commoditize it to their understanding and commercial orders and patents.

THIS IS NOT A BOOK.

It is an ANTI-thing. An ANTI-this & an ANTI-that. **A book, a non-novel, a non-narrative-driven-anti-antinovel. One bolstered by the creator's intent to say FUCK YOU to the prose-rules, the regulations, the gatekeepers, the grammar Nazis, the presumptuous types. Grammar Nazis unite under the flagship of Lionel Shriver. You'll hate this book. You'll take it to the furthest corners of the world, and struggle to find a high enough cliff to throw it from. Maybe try from the lip of Hell? Before you can, you must do something unforgivable in the eyes of religious fanatics. (Which doesn't take much if you really sit down and think hard enough on it). Pull your cock out and beat it off in front of the image of Christ. Collect a few milky-beads from the end of your cock or a few excreted droplets from your cunt's lips – and place middle and fore-finger together, lift up the beads/droplets and say a wanky prayer, and then flick these juices onto your make-believe God, or your God in waiting. Patiently sitting on a bench, sandaled foot tapping out a jazz-tune. It's harder than it looks. Jazz is very Scatman. Try Scat-manning it on yourself, like a belly (you**

must exceed fifteen stone to achieve this) and you'll get close to bodily-jazz-scatting.

Cavemen can't point. They can fling shit and tear into animals until there is nothing left. They can make good use of their apposable thumbs when pleasuring fellow cavemen's anuses and cavewomen's furry-flick-grunt-groan-zones. They can carry carcasses, launch balled-fisted assaults on non-fellow tribesmen, but in the developmental stages we find them in, they are as fluent in gesture and fine-motor-skills as a disabled, low functioning autistic person, who contradictory to such diagnoses confirming the lack of fine-motor skills, can easily flick away at their ears and faces. Cavemen can point. They can point to the heaped shit instead of flinging it, thus giving them time to compose and study. They can point at animals instead of grabbing them and twisting their necks. They can admire them. Study them. Perhaps even attempt at training them. They are good with not only their thumbs now, but also their oversized gangrenous toes. Cavemen can point to cave drawings and can also point at cavemen pointing at cavemen pointing at the blood-paint and scratching, the markings/carvings. They are now becoming…men. These gestures are giving us a glimpse of their evolution. The obelisks that had arisen from the soil held their attention for only a few minutes. The reflection of the sun, something they all took for granted, or eventually conjured into being crucial to their

expanding culture and religion, cast their shadows onto the black oblong – soaking up their outlines. Religion before words were formed. Religion in ritual and movement, their markings evidence to the prolongation of thought. Cavemen and cavewomen survived. What grew was culture. From mishaps, mistakes, and deaths. Certain creatures that took up the same space as themselves grew into phantoms, visions, artwork, myth, legends. Culture started not with a word, but a moment's thought. These barbaric symbols and rituals we would call them were stretched out variations upon variations of focus, hypervigilance, succour, birthing devices to explore depths and forms they hadn't gotten their weighted heads around. Cavemen and cavewomen created culture first with a shrug, a push, a hyper-alert reaction, it wasn't all about language. Though these accusatory grunts, snarls, tongue flicks (the progenitor to Khoisan-tongue) did contribute to their eventual evolution. Culture before culture was a concept. Religion before any form of doctrine could ever have been conceived let alone applied to their "society" - before it could be passed off as divine and outstanding amongst the rest of the miscellany that now passes itself off as sacred text and the original book of MEANING.

WORDS ARE WEAPONS

Words. That is what you are reading. No shit, *Sherlock.* **Words. Letters. These complex things. We take the written, typed, faxed word and letters for granted. We do. Yes, we** diddly-do. **These words are what will usher you into the narrators/authors' world(s). Strung together like pearls.** *Nah!* **Perfectly aligned. tHeY av a pwayce dunt theyyyy. Grammar and punctuation and the syntax of literature is not there to be played with. It is there to follow and adjust and to apply the unimaginable monotony of fOrM. Yet here I am and here we are being held by an object, a book, a dead tree, making the case that what you hold, with a matte finish, a rather smudged cover – that no matter the quality the printers will fuck up, and do not get me started on the images inside, and the constant fight for bleeds – you'll admire, jaw loosened and swinging. The statement in book form is rather a simple one, one that doesn't need a bunch of highfalutin, stick-in-the-academic-muds to tell you, that this is a non-novel. It is fragment. It is the scorched edged of an idea. It is soil left in the Mojave Desert to thrive. This book, like all my others, have no inherent purpose beyond that I need to type shit out; and hope that, whatever I end up typing comes to something of little to no worth, to the five dedicated readers I have. Okay, that is pushing it. This book started out as one thing,**

and as per usual, my usual-unusual way, ensured it became something altogether odd. And it ended up becoming something altogether different and distanced from my initial want. This is a big old book. A hefty chonky thing. I like chonky books. Well, it isn't now. I have cut. Mangled. I have shortened. I have lengthened. Not in the dick department, sadly. Sorry lovely. You pick one up, and you feel smarter than you truly are without even having to do the work. I remember when Tony Blair's book came out, and I didn't give a toss about Blair or his issues, agendas, and fuckups, I just liked how the book felt and smelt. I didn't buy it. Much like I didn't buy Alan Sugars Autobiography. Much like the Elvis impersonator who flipped burgers pushed his "official" manifesto on me. I didn't buy it, I was forced to read it though, and I feel that the legacy of the work you're about to read will be forced unto you, in decades time; not by myself, but my poor offspring that just want to get rid of all these unsold books. I hope my kids would use their noggins and sell them to some underground preservation society, that or use these books as build a block to shelter a yet newly awakened, reborn Elvis. Baby wanna, a-huh! **What is a book? This is a book. It looks like one, feels like one. Elvis, put the book down, and don't get any ideas. This will not make a good weapon against anyone that calls themselves the colonel. Put it**

down. Now. **Good Elvis, now think on this…if there is a reborn Elvis, why do you not put your mind to it, lose weight, and seek out the reborn Colonel. No, not the Kentucky Fried One, though we all know the conspiracy about him is true; that he is in some bunker, in a gravy-sauce, marinating until the day comes for his Kentucky-not-so-fried-resurrection. What is a book? Oit, Alexa, what is a… oh, yeah, duh! Silly old me, I don't have an Alexa. Hey Google, hey Google…Google, oit, oi, hello, google, don't fuck me like that, oh she/he/it responded, then glitched. Hey…oh, fuck this! I am just going to meander online until something pops up. Hey you! Yeah you! – go away Pornhub. Google, online, type in the question – what is a book? A book is a medium for recording information in the form of writing or images, typically composed of many pages (made of papyrus, parchment, vellum, or paper) bound together and protected by a cover. – yeah, that sure sounds like a physical book. The technical term for this physical arrangement is codex (plural, codices) – that sounds sexy and… well, quite-quite! In the history of hand-held physical supports for extended written compositions or records, the codex replaces its predecessor, the scroll. A single sheet in a codex is a leaf and each side of a leaf is a page – oh fuck, I always get these things confused. No wonder I don't get any**

reviews for my works of utter astounding genius. As an intellectual object, a book is prototypically a composition of such great length that it takes a considerable investment of time to compose and still considered as an investment of time to read – that seems to be the most honest way of describing what it means to make a book. So many fuckers assume the art of storytelling is one bestowed to anyone and everyone. I know that I am a good writer, but I am an event better page polluter. Anything online about page pollution? Nothing. Uh-oh, that is a shame. The term was one I coined from Ralph Steadman, so I am gutted this beautiful description, this term for what he does so well, hasn't been catalogued. In a restricted sense, a book is a self-sufficient section or part of a longer composition, a usage reflecting that, in antiquity, long works had to be written on several scrolls and each scroll had to be identified by the book it contained. Each part of Aristotle's Physics is called a book. In an unrestricted sense, a book is the compositional whole of which such sections, whether called books or chapters or parts, are parts – Damn, you talk to your mother with that mouth? If you did, she would probably gyrate her hips, and lust after you, in those horny period films, made by foreigners for horny and lonely, and some already wedded, British fellows. The intellectual content in a physical book need not be a

Though I have used that bold claim (BELOW) for other (Perhaps less good) novels of mine – Over, and over, I still think the whole thing is lost on people. You shouldn't make it past the word GO! On my novels-gameboard.

But this book in sum isn't a book.

What is it then, smart-ass?

Settle down, settle down.

An object. Objection in paper and print. Full of ideas. Full of errors. Full of autistic processes. Full of intentional muh muh muh mania.

"I jusss wanna pet a rabbit geoooooorge!"

This here is not merely a book.

It is an object. **Where font and font-size and the digital page has been distorted - where typography and all such pleasantries take on a wholly new meaning. Or no meaning.** **It is up to you.**

U.

My meaning?

There. Is. No. Meaning.

The purposeful in the purposeless. Not the meanings laid out for us, by some professional wordsmith. It is what it is. Detritus of a mentally fucked up 28-year-old who fashions his works in clobber and tries (and fails, miserably) to sell it as something worthwhile.

I hate rules. I hate pretention. I hate grammar.

I hate the rules of literature and creative writing. THERE ARE NO RULES to good/decent/correct writing. It is nonsense. I love nonsense.

Kathy Acker once wrote in an email exchange between herself, and some lady called McKenzie Wark that she loves typos. I did a sex-wee there and then when I read that. I cut it out, just those three words – all the surrounding jargon could piss off, and all book-etiquette was forgotten, thrown out the window, because I wanted Kathy's passion, aura, intent, and adoration of typos close to me. I folded it up in some warped spiritual procession of prayer to her. And kept it

close to my heart – my penis – (a fragment laid here for you to surmise... that small piece hidden under the shaft, that fragment is very telling, isn't it?) - joking. The fragment was burnt, and the embers fell onto my pubic hair. A bush fire started. I didn't cry. The sentiment was shared. Me too Kathy. Me too. Typos have been a thing in literature that are treated as sacrilegious and sinful/telling of an author's skill and talent (much like spelling) or given room to be ignored and just accepted as a common theme in all publishing industries. For me, the typo became an obsession. I wanted more, I needed more. And the more I pushed for deliberate typos and spelling errors, the integrity was lost. And so was I, each time I went back to edit whichever book I felt deserved such disrespect - I couldn't pin down which was deliberate, and which was just a genuine typo or spelling mistake. It got too much. Also, a few tits thought my altered sense on typos and inclusion of spelling mistakes and bad grammar and punctuation, and the format of a book was all BS and just some wild ethos made to excuse my illiteracy. Fuck, how did you know?

Typos.

Typos typos typos.

Obsessive, abusive, typos.

It does get rather difficult when you start incorrectly saying things as well. A habit of mine. Old habits die hard, or not at all. They will wave from that plexiglass casket and be laughing all the way into the furnace or ground. I like to push people. A habit of mine that got me in serious trouble one day when I pushed the wrong person in front of an oncoming lorry. It was meant to be my mother, not her best mate of thirty odd years. I was once accused _ online, of all places _ (oh I know, the shock, the horror) _ of being a situationist. Maybe I am, at heart. That, and maybe I am a terrorist too, like an old mate of mine's partner accused me of being _ online, again, of all the fucking places to be accused of something? _ all because I got picked up at the start of lock-down by my partner, so we could all bunker up and die together. Seems a bit extreme. Drastic, right**?**

Well, go back when that Covid-19 phase of life (which is still a thing, though the UK isn't any longer treating it as a thing of any severity) – the end was nigh. It was the end times. If anyone could go outdoors screaming and rattling saucepans screaming the end is nigh, we would be hung. But, when we did it in recognition for the NHS, we were called radicals, idiots, patriots, tits, cunts, political activists. I wasn't cheering the NHS I was shouting,

"THE WORLD IS DYING YOU

FOOLS!"

Funny thing I have realised, recently, ever since that Governmental alert system was put into action – that nothing is being done for our imminent demise. I am not talking about climate change or alternate modes of fuel. All of that is best left for Greta Thumb-in-her Bum-Berg. That alert fucked me up really good and proper. I hadn't realised until I woke up the next morning, recalling my "dream"/nightmare. I had zero clue how deeply seeded my fear of Armageddon was and still is. I dreamed some weird fall-out fantasy nightmare, where fall-out debris, and the nuclear toxics and nuclear-shite could be seem, like dust motes caught in a sensationally placed ray of natural light (cinematic) - sparkling a beautiful tawny colour, that was falling on us; and all in my dream were reassured by this, that the residue was an off-shoot of the invisible kinds of nuclear-poison - that if we could see it, it wasn't so dangerous. It wasn't up until that moment I realised I am shit scared of the nuclear issue we are having right now. Which isn't being tackled. The head of states reassure us in passive-aggressive tones, as if we should all just self-combust and get it over with, without having to

lose their three-houses and nice income if such a thing was to happen – that things are alright. But are they? Are they really? Some secret agent goes online, backlit, voice modulated so we all know it isn't Andy McNab or some other secret serviceman who publishes shitty military thrillers and romps – who tells us that people like him were put in place to stop such an eventuality from happening. Then he got sacked. That all-natural self, being ?/?/? my hypochondria - which is my full self and all-natural-self. I have a perverse need to be full of paranoia, over something as small as my heart rate on my Fitbit is up, to me that means a heart attack is imminent. If my neck keeps twitching, seeming to move at an angle all of its own accord, trying to break itself to ultimately kill me – forcing me to sleep with my face shoved into a pillow all night, and given my air through a snorkel tube shoved up my left nostril – that's how my mind works. I may seem funny to you, but I am a fucking pussy. I am convinced that they - the heads of state - know more than they are letting on. We don't have tsunamis or earthquakes here like everyone else, so why these nationwide alerts? Perhaps it is a joke, and every party held in secret at Number 10 Downing St. triggers such alerts. What is this national alert system for? It is so obvious!

NUCLEAR WAR!

Covid hit and the people at the tables and podiums reacted in a sporadic knee-jerk fashion I have ever witnessed in my short 28-years of life. The steps to ensure our safety varied and altered. But still something was done at least. The threat wasn't visible, much like Putin isn't, but the threat is still there in the ether. There is more chance of little Poo-Tin pressing that big obsessive-compulsive' kryptonite – the nuclear red-button - and ending our way of life forever, than Covid ever had a chance of doing. The Russians are always watching. What if Putin is offended by this? What if he needs only a wee excuse to poison another Brit, someone as small and insignificant as me, that will send a message. I will not be fucked with or mocked by anybody. Please Meester, do not harm me, I am also friends with Oliver Stone. Yet, it did, in a way. And all because the heads of state went lunatic with the guidelines and rules – whilst saying, nah, when it came to applying it to themselves. We are on the cusp of - the end of everything - where all of us will be popping off and exploding into ash, over one another - like that scene from T2. Which will be a fucking

nightmare for those that later come up from the bunkers, guilty-conscience and all that rising to the fore, wanting to collect the long-distant cousin's ashes for keepsakes; the cousin that that they shoved out last minute, having been calculating that the oxygen would last longer without him, but stating as they shoved him out to his death, that they couldn't fit him into their "fall-out shelter" - though he had fit quite nicely in there, not thirty seconds before his fucking apocalyptic eviction. That is the world we live in. And I would be that cousin shoved out. Mental. Fucking mental. Nothing is being done. We are having new power stations made, but no form of mass underground system like they had in one of those lesser-decent Hunger Game films, where a nation could wait it out beneath the ground. Nuclear war is UPON us, and it is imminent; yet we are all going on as usual. Oh, lardy-daa. Oh, look guys, girls, they and thems, there is absolutely nothing we can do about it (for you!) - let us just resume our nonchalance. I wish I had a garden so I could at least start work on some bunker. I wouldn't know where to start but at least I would instil in myself a sense that I was doing something. Where am I going? Why am I vomiting up all of this? Because I need to, that's why.

This is not a... book.

It is...

oh, I have already written that. This part is coming to a close. The book you hold has no narrative. But I think you can glean what are my current preoccupations, by reading it. So, people, be kind, rewind and restart the clock. People, a certain kind, granted, like to pull you up on grammar - (Lionel Shriver, a self-confessed Grammar Nazi would hate to meet

If you think it and write it down, is that translated well?

If you think it, and re-think it, and go over it again and again, and then transfer it, is that an original thought or an abused and manipulated thought?

Can you abuse your own thoughts?

What is a thought?

What is an experiment?

What is the meaning of Monty Python now that they are almost running out of Pythons?

The experiment is the book.

Someone once said that my work can get monotonous and repetitive. Sweet cheeks, that is the idea.

It is a performance piece, not just literature.

Or non-fiction.

Or sci-fi?

It is meant to be read over and over.

It is meant to dawn on you that the same theme(s), the same purporting's are encouraged to settle into the back of your ear.

It will crawl in, in due course.

It must.

It fucking better and fucking-well **will.**

I bath these words together to give over to the audience the sense of near-endlessness.

No pause.

No breaks.

A furious scrimmage of words.

Filthy.

Fantastic.

Artistic.

Foolery.

THE GAY GUNSMAN & HIS UNDERAGE LOVER
CUM-ing HARD IN THEATRES JANUARY 2049

SWEAT DRENCHED PRODUCTIONS
DOFUS & DUPPUS

John Wayne was a hero. On screen. In fellow gun-toters' hearts. He excited many millions of women, and men alike – not that that was ever a conversation to have in the 1940s-1950s era – or something to be proud of. Wayne knew instinctually that the adoration of men was far more homosexualised than that of the women. For the women it was a momentary fantasy – being scooped up into his leatherette arms, whereas the men couldn't get Wayne of their minds. Their cocks bell-ends started taking on John The Main Man Wayne's' features. With every cum-squirt the squelch would sound like many of his famous lines. A few of the Wayne obsessives all appreciated when their slurpy-Wayne-cock-ends splurged/stated: "A man deserves a second chance but keep an eye on him." Why? – because that was encouragement to keep an eye on his career, and it was okay for a man to cum more than once in a day. He wasn't handsome in the traditional sense, and rugged didn't really suit his whole identity. He was thick. Rough-hewn. Yet, possessing a glossy aura. Maybe it was makeup or just his natural boozy complexion. His eventual decline, like all top-dog actors, who work in a certain field of film (genre-wise/life-style-wise) was a slow limp, that progressed into a lower-jaw movement that made it look like some UFO from the future had beamed some meow-meow into

his usually pistol-tight grasp. He morphed into future western stars, who took over his mantel as the great American-western hero. His mutation was then faulty, so reverted back to putting on the pounds on Wayne's sturdy frame, making him sturdier. Wayne was many things, a man of his era, a man whose iconography would always cloud over his personal issues. Racism was ignored. Homophobia too. John Wayne was merely John Wayne. Art over artist. Art over asshole. John Wayne was plagued by visions most of his adult life. It was of an era when Westerns were no longer a commodity in the realm of Hollywood Land. Instead, it was colourful, gaudy, messy explosive visions, where capes and weird hybrid-bodices ruled supreme. A world where magic was made not on set, but after the fact. Where armpit colour was edited and altered in a alternate realm – something he would later read in his favourite type of fictional genre – pulp sci-fi – all done inside a box. Inside this boxed screen with sweaty greasers slaving over a odd-keyboard. Strange things. Quotes from yet unmade and unrealized works. Film. TV. Fiction. It got all too much, so he took a scalpel to his face and changed his identity. He carved and hacked. It only lent him his John Wayne-isms-isms more Waynian – isms-isms-isms. On one cold night, shooting another western masterpiece, he was nursing a bourbon

on the rocks, watering it down in hope this counteracts against the general murmur of dissent, all centered upon his alcoholism – no drunk drinks hard stuff on the rocks, it was unheard of – and an owl hooted, providing the only form of breeze, flying past him. Then, from out of the ether, he heard, "The owls are not what they seem." This phrase panicked Wayne. And as much as these owls visited him in the middle of the desert, a totally bonkers environment for them to reside in, he grew paranoid that this message came from within, to warn him of their presence. The more these owls came, the less ice he had in his glass. The more he grasped a bottle neck over a blown-glass booze-slurper, in the shape of his chin. He one evening asked his armorer to supply him with real bullets, only for the armorer to look at him as if he was a fool, which made John angry. "Give me the bullets, Brett!" he screamed into his own personal armorer's face, splashing him in bourbon and spittle. "Bubu-but Wayne," stammered Brett, "We provide real bullets anyway." John took a moment to pause. All this time he had been shooting niggers, Indians, and no good fake foes, he had always been wiping them of this board called life. "You mean to say?" Wayne leaned in, his shadow giving Brett both pleasure and that intoxicated feeling of fear, that every armorer attains in their work.

"What I am saying is…the owls…are not…what they…" Brett never finished his sentence, by this point Wayne had unholstered his gun, and at hip height pointed it into Brett's gut. Brett hit the deck, and Wayne went down on his haunches, sought out the bullet hole, tearing the clothing around it, to get a better view. He whispered into the hole, a phrase escaping from his thick cotton mouthed, thickly scaled tongue, that were forming the words motivating his cow-like his lips, voicing a far future quote, one he hadn't come up with or had ever heard used, "Do you feel lucky, huh?! Well, do you…splunk?" The gaping wound spat out a clod of arterial blood and clots and formed its own mouth and corrected John Wayne. It said, "It is punk, actually."

LOSE YOUR KILT,
OR DRAW!

I bumped into a lady who looked like Guillermo Del Toro. I basked in her resemblance, only to feel guilty for looking at her with that perverse glint I get when faced with artists I so admire. I said to her, behind my left hand, covering my drooling mouth, "Oh, what beautiful glasses you have!" – she didn't respond, she continued loading her items from trolley to conveyor belt, from trolley to conveyor belt. "Oh, Guillermo, turned into Guillermina!" and once she had finished unloading her shopping, waiting patiently in line like a good female doppelgänger of the Mexican filmmaker, I pulled out my Blu-ray copy of Hellboy 2: The Golden Army, and spit polished it, merging my spittle in with the plastic Blu-ray casing-sleeve. I had to ask her. I

bottled up my pride, and I asked her, "Would you sign this…" before I could finish, she turned on me and stated matter of factly, "Hello, I am not Guillermo Del Toro, and you are not listening to an audio commentary for Hellboy two, the Golden Army!" I exploded in my £10.99 jogger shorts. Never have I ever cummed so hard in my life.

Fuck your thought experiments.

Feed your dying child.

Fuck your subconscious will.

Force feed your diseased child these scarps of prose.

Reassure them that the font size will help dislodge the plastic they have supplying them with life.

These are words to and for the unwise.

These are big fat old words, used in a collage artists pitiful desperate clawing for affirmation that they are an artist and not a plagiariser.

W H E R E

D O

W E

B E G I N?

where do we end? **Do we end at all?**

Where do you begin?

Where does a story need to begin, but at the end of the beginning that is at the start of something absolutely untrue and unreal and (dot) (dot) (dot)

AI

FUCKED

ME

UP,

really,

really,

BAD!

The madness of AI-generated art is that, though birthed from not only your prompts, but your own singular specific vision, the less you write the more you get, and that means the less of an ownership you have on it. Even though you have written in a prompt into a highly sophisticated processor, the work done for you, after you have received the finished product, you feel as if the labour was longer than a mere few minutes and came from your very own hands. This is liberating to those who fucking suck at visual art. Like me. But do I have any right to these images? Yes, and no. I feel my prompt is my creation, though the work is done, not by some slave, or underpaid artist, but by a computer. Also, it is unique to me, and my prompt. It might come back up, somewhere else, but each prompt generates an alternative and different variation of a variation. Guillermo Del Toro has very strong beliefs in the sacrilege of AI-art, but he is in a position where many artists can work for him, for a fee, or a wage, to create his vision, and because GDT draws, his visions do not all merely stem from his hand. So, all those art departments, and creatives under his directorial eye, are his AIs, working on his behalf for his vision. And who ends up getting most, if not all of the credit? Him. Because he is Guillermo Del-Fucking-Toro. Though the art comes from human hands, the way these artists work, though it is spiritually and ethically more in tone with Guillermo's CORE beliefs, he is blinded by his own hypocrisy. These artists are his flesh-machines to make his film for him. I once got to interview George Lucas. It was a long time coming. I said, "George, can I tickle your recently deflated double chin?" – George didn't flinch, he just leaned forward, readying that unique Lucas chuckle, for when I touched his sagging neck-sack, the Star Wars theme began to play, in reverse. With the additions of numerous Jar-Jar-Bink's quotes. Ahmed Best was really going for it, "Wesa going to not die, mesa going to be forever loved, mooey-mooey, I love you!" George then chuckled, and the skin beneath my fingers filled up with Star Wars bitcoin produced cash. George became so inflated Kathleen Kennedy had to bring him down to regular (2023) size; whispering in his ear, "Star Wars is about feminism now, fat boy, and nothing to do with the Skywalker family," George deflated, and seemed to shrink down into, of all people Warwick Davies. I kicked him out the way, disliking the annoying prat. Not because I have anything against small, tiny person's, I once fucked a midget with four butt-cheeks, but I do not like Warwick; he CANNOT act. I have been to therapy about this; how I take actor's performances too personally. This is why I am no longer allowed at Netflix or Prime Press launches/Events.

When this icon dies, I will have this tattooed on my chest. **THE IMAGE OF LUCAS.**

Kubrick hugged George Lucas, as if old comrades from war. Lucas tried to pull himself free.

He wasn't a hugger.

George hugged Stanley Kubrick, as if old friends from the old speed-roadster days in the 1950s.

Even though he hated hugs.

He wasn't a hugger.

Ben Wheatley hugged Ben Wheatley and the world imploded.

David Lynch smoked a cigarette proffered by Truffaut and began looking into Critical-

Thinking.

Truffaut smoked a cigarette offered by Leo Carax and just giggled at his fellow Frenchmen.

A UFO from the dimension where flying-saucers were exactly as envisioned in the heydays of UFO flying-saucer mania – the actual embodiment of what the extraterrestrials bunked up, probed up, slimed up versions looked like - 1950s woop-woop-collided with a UFO in the form of Jordon Peele's NOPE, and the biological, billowing parachute subverted all flying-saucer iconography the world over.

UFO inhabitants are merely celestial beings in the bodies of middle-aged Korean hackers who in their holidays post TikTok videos of themselves eating delicious foreign food – like a teacake or crumpet from the UK and making a right old mess of it all.

David Fincher, during the Sony Hack scandal reached out to Adam Driver, not to reassure him that his email to Amy Pascal was a joke, but as a reaffirmation that his tone was deadpan, yet still honest – Adam replied by a screenshot of one of his lesser-known performances, in the subject line of the email reading: THE ONLY PERFORMANCE I CAN EVER WATCH.

When Fincher received this email, he was shocked that Adam Driver thought that that was he, Adam-Motherfucking-Driver-himself, when it was in fact an image of a 1990s goth kid at one of Fincher's earliest world premieres.

The critics pawed over this film, only for Fincher to admit, "I didn't actually direct it."

Then, the world of LIFE ITSELF imploded.

The quotes that come from Lynch's beautiful, understated pussy-loving mouth are easy to read into, or to re-contextualize.

"I'm not a real film buff. I am into vaginal secretions. Unfortunately, I don't have time to watch moving pictures. I just don't go out, but when a pussy is within reach," - LYNCH does his usual hand twiddling, raised in the air, that resembles a pre-teen imitating a hungry baby or a sexual deviant – or just Lynch's way of fondling breasts.

"And I become very nervous when I go to a film because I worry so much about the director and how hard a pussy may be pressed into his, or her face, that or their crotch… it is hard for me to digest my popcorn, and the levitating pussy."

The quotes that come from Lynch's beautiful, understated film-loving mouth are easy to read into, or to re-contextualize.

"I'm not a real pussy-pounder, nor a pussy-buff. Pussy-buffering reminds me of old carwashes, and in its simplicity, there is an inane mediocrity of intent, while possessing a brutal side. I am into filmological secretions. Unfortunately, I don't have time to watch various pussy-visions that are mere clouds in my reach. I just don't go out, but when a moving-picture, all those images adrift like dreams and their logic, when that is within reach."

LYNCH does his usual hand twiddling, raised in the air, that resembles a pre-teen imitating a hungry film buff, wanting to see Lynchian actress's breasts, on full glorious display – or this is just Lynch's way of fondling breasts from a remove .

"I become very nervous when I go to a film because I worry so much about the director and how hard it is for me to digest my popcorn, and the levitating make-believe notion of pussydom."

These thoughts are places, and these places are known as EXPERIMENTS. These experiments are the home of various auteurs. As much as the auteur hates this label, they know that its function is to bolster them, motivating outside influences to approach them as if a curious entity that had left a rather nasty meteorite strike-streak across their front lawn, but in its collision it reveals itself to be that of a small bundle of rags and wreathed in innocence, though possessing a glint behind their eyes - it is left in the cooling granite and tarmac, offering itself up as something altogether special. We fight labels. We fight against them so hard. Lynch though, the FREAL ATTACK version, living in East Grinstead, instead of LA or wherever the fuck the real version is currently spouting philosophy based upon weather reports, thinks labels are necessary. He staples each new label attributed to his art to his chest and leaves it to fester. The wet oozing damp pieces of paper were sodden in infection and integrating into the skin of his chest. *"Hair on head is like hair on body. It is permed."* Lynch spoke these words as NO MORE THOUGHTS TO PASS OFF AS YOUR OWN – it is folded itself into Europe and other surrounding countries.

Grasping at the residues of its own self, long separated millions of years ago. Uniting nations. Into one big block of spastic pudding.

These words came from the mind of a mad man in denial about his whole mad ethos. Phasing Fashion. He thought that he might start to get a queer feeling – throbbing - convulsing nut-sacks-nutstacks – disturbing the lambs – cows meowing – British outdoors-y pussies. Phasing FASHION. These words came from mad cow disease. Perhaps all that is read is frightening. Not word salad. Incantation. FILTHY! Their ears. Their noses. They did not progress beyond cavemen gyrations. FUCKING! Full-blown abortive forms – forms frustes, of epilepsy, which might be relatively uncommon amongst the masses. PIGGIES! Violets popped into a young girl's mouth.

Nightmares that later become pivotal in a murderess's will and testament. She wrestles against the bonds holding her down. The environment at first was welcoming, colourful, and then as soon as she smelt the violets she was knocked out. **Violently**. She was moved from that appealing, glitzy room and sent several floors down, down, down into the heart of a meat-market. Gutters lined every available space. All corners have thick old-fashioned braziers, perpetually lit. The flame was comforting. The heat reached her. Dripping. Carving knives and various carcass-gutting tools, all in various states, some steely, ashine, others grimy, dried blood coating it in a rust, the young girl couldn't quite get her head around how violent those violets were. I predict this. I am going to Prague next year. If I am to perform, I will be honoured. The audience will be too, to bask in the sensation of... *oh, who the fuck am I kidding?* If I arrive as an audience member, I will force myself onto the Prague Festers/Rogue-Operators of the Micro Festival. I will come in bedraggled robes, with a deep chalice, full of some unnamed juice. I will ask select people to take a sip and spit it on me, and I will lick it off, sensuously. I will ask them to transfer the covid they have residing in them. I will make a speech about willing on my demise, testing fate. If people do not spit on me, they will be spat on by myself. I shall also enter as a nameless being, dressed in some wicker-man-esque, folk-horror mask, in a drab ill-fitting suit, my fat gut protruding, I will be smeared in animal blood. I will be the VOICE MODULATOR, in physical form. Possessing a partygoer, forced to play the pre-recorded/digitally created speech, telling the audience that Zak Ferguson couldn't make it there. The speech will go on and on, and people will be waiting, with bated/drunken/cheap-beer scented breath, for the eventual piece, which will be the not-Zak-Ferguson, tearing into a book, throwing pages about, screaming at the audience in animal tongues to write it and read it themselves, and then will leave. Never to return. No applause. To acknowledgement, total anarchic, rebellious lunacy. Or I will enter as a drag-queen mime, who will speak only when spoken to, and if no one speaks I will not speak, but if somebody does, I will speak. This is not a proposal, this is the mapping of ideas, forever etched into a printed book. A promise. An eventuality that I will see to fruition, so help me Praha lovers and fighters and academics and avant-garde adorers. **Boom!**

Boom!

Booming!

Melodic, quite nice, soothing, vaguely familiar hell-scape. Hell is Home. Home is Hell. There was an old, discarded electronic device confusedly, in a state of what one could later call, "suspended animation" that the masses groped. For the controls. Controls to the colleague in the office who saw all this written out, slumped over, this was indeed an emergency. Evocative, but elusive. I wonder whether I will get a radio! Gaga. Goo-goo. A radio for unaccompanied dreamlike constructions. Writing out your manifesto veiled as a personal memoir, providing the feeling of the ultimate aura – a temporary temporal lobe dissection. Seizures commoditized. Some people, non-entities, lose consciousness during a perfectly odd, superimposed state of fingering weird ports.

Superimposed states of mind and societal creeds. A young teacher developed a temporal lobe manifested as a tubular tumor, a tumor of malignancy, which was operated like an arcade game – then opened and studied, splayed out – in another flesh-box – flesh-bundle – inoperable zits bursting, and the sauce being sucked up into an ampule and then zooted into dying decorum's. Regrowth of his or her repeated seizure shakes and wild Shake and Baking. In which an ironic tormentor torment. Present strange looks, oh boy, that they are... introducing new glares undocumented in the Big Book of Everything Facial - a seizure...a jolt...usually somehow a fundamental prolapsed excretion of anus flesh and gush spooled out as imagery – of his – jolts – volts – seizures – a writer scoffs, a poet weeps, a director wanks – out of nowhere a sign land onto a perfectly picket-fenced all white American knoll of land – stating this is intentional. I sit with my attic miniaturized into a pocket-plaything. I work on it until completion. My jerks and full-body quakes, known as seizures, go beyond all of...this. He went on. He went away. He vocalized that his epileptic contextless and meaningless hauntingly familiar frightening spell was drawn deeper and deeper into...it! Creatively stimulated by these auras that he/they/them/she has composed, trying to embody, or at least suggest mysterious and ineffably strange-but familiar qualities. This man waS a RaDiO oPeRaTor on a large crew-ship, with vAsT orchestras lining the various decks. Looking down into the shrine to abysses and seizures. Everything is deliberate, nothing is a flaw. These things tell me that certain pitches are important, working as a provocation, a higher sensitive reach. Prophet, that he became, more and more so than a poet. Sensitive to almost any convulsions shared like a crackpipe. Background vibes that afforded an unrelieved and inescapable knowledgeable and passionate profession...avoid all contact with the street blemished by a dying star. Stop. His ears. Rush for the nearest doorway or side street. Stop. Would you stop? Develop. Developed. Developing. Veritable. Veritable. Phobia. Phobias. A horror of a pamphlet entitled Fear of... truths, online hackers, PayPal fraud, smoked salmon without some delicious pastry to go with it.

Blinking lights.

Winking lights.

Laptop swatting.

The Doors are a shit band. They're a good band.

It has its place.

Selective music.

Selective hearing.

The lyrics aren't processed like dog meat.

Both types of patients wondered if abortive forms might be relatively common.

(This has certainly triggered techno-adorers. Musical types trotting their stuff. Abnormalities of prose. All is in good faith to ensure good health. Herpes encephalitis storms clotting the cloudscape.)

Music just provokes a seizure, constituting an essential part of the spreading of limbs and thighs and inserting dog-poop-slicked fingers.

Give her a weird new form of sexual disease.

Dog-shit-warts popping and excreting anal gland gloop and gloom gathering like weird striations amongst tadpole fevers.

Occasionally spreading the cortex when he/the man – hombre invisibilo – had generalized psychic experience.

Another seizure disorder fashioned out of moss and gangrene, put through complex scientific devices, and broadened in its totality - in more than 100 hundred people to a thousand there are complex seizures that can be studied, mimeographed, orgone generated back into a strange projectile.

That, or it is put out as a knee-jerky reaction to unconscious biases and memory in totality.

A reaction to unconscious memory-splices, listening in to the projected CD-ROM buzzing from the AOL server, crashed out steaming junk.

No significance.

Whether there be good weather or whether the weather becomes whether – there could be a connection.

She tested positive.

She tested herself.

She found that listening to a seizure was a lame pass-time.

No effect.

General affect.

Neapolitan reminded me of brain swarms like pissed off hornets – wasps – nests upon nests of honeycomb substituted – into another room.

Opened the door Shelley Du-style.

That she did.

That she fucking-well-did!

Only to be beheaded and have her head transplanted onto Jessica Parker's MARS ATTACKS body.

Sheesh.

Fear.

All fear.

Fear ceased to have strange problems.

Fear without a problem.

Ceased to have strange, complex, reminiscent seizures – it seems as though surgery has put a TOTAL totalitarian end to it all.

Surgery has put an end to both types of MacDonalds goodies.

Delighted you may seem to witness The Colonel leave the disabled toilets with the rape-y paedophile Subway-man wiping off the cummy gravy The Colonel can only pass from his Texan dick-end.

This is occasionally nostalgic, with epileptic experiences – *oh heaven – oh heavens above!* - a place with a tricksy trigger-point, wrapped in rusty, dried blood razor wire – a thing that triggers, unlike anything that could proclaim to have triggered the measliest of triggers - ever before.

An experience unlike anything that came from the …before!

Voluntarily calling an entire orchestral internal gramophone, *vividly*, with different moods or interpretations, and sometimes improvisations, by the likes of Seth Rogen.

Savouring this dictionary of themes - turn over a few pages, almost at random, savouring this and then, become stimulated by the opening of something.

Remarkable.

There are no more extraordinary examples of deaf mute down syndromed Pizza Grotto Ghetto waiters.

Musical imagery.

Deafness.

The removal of normal auditory cortex hypersensitive heightened imagery (and sometimes even hallucinations!)

There is an analogous phenomenon in those who lose their sight; some people who become blind may have, *paradoxically*, heightened senses; senses of the kind that visual composers collect; as John Williams keeps lying about his eventual demise, not in life, but in composing music.

Composers of enormously intricate, architecturally architectonic music like Beethoven's abstract forms of musical thought – and it might be said that it is especially intellectual that distinguishes Beethoven's later works.

"Corresponds to mental blood flow. Mental stimulation of the same central neural edifices alone seems to be sufficient to work as an advantage for further mental phenomena.

Which provides a physiological explanation best expressed as incantation and modern twerks. This all greatly enhances imagery, producing a quasi-perceptual simulation of a pixelated prated/boot-legged copy of an "experience" – it was all described to me to turn it over to the Dr. Of Nine-Lives-On-Dope-Fiend-Charges – record labels hinting that they need to source the latest high-pitched screeching one can only source from a Chris Rock standup routine or when secretly bugging his hotel and he is left pleasuring himself over the OSCAR slap that stained his left cheek for months on end; only because Rock tried to recreate it over and over. He wasn't numbed or shook – in that moment as Smith wailed "KEEP MY WIFE'S NAME OUT YA FUCKIN' MOUTH!" the fuckin' alerted his already engorged cock to rise over his belt-buckle. Turned over to me like some dossier full of trade secrets – bound lavishly… an extreme example of something faintly radio oooo oooo … radio blah blah!"

The radio turned itself off.

It was an end.

An inconclusive experiment.

An experiment that evolved into Experiments.

Easily available to the relatively/virtually/involuntarily birthed imagery created by sonic booms and the cracks in your plaster boarded shithole in Arkansas.

"Every memory of my soundtrack obsessed days – the subliminal messages were not captured for latter-day saints to prophesise and make conspiracies about…the soundtrack speaks for many imageries obsessed fanatics wasting their days pooping in wastebaskets and pissing in their least favourite roommate's mouth. Intense pissing. Slow, sensual shitting. Bukkake shart-y images looped on a small television set, best encapsulated in some bygone era. Repeated exposure to a particular piece – fall/falling/fallen/sin/din-dins/exclusively made into an image printed onto a postcard… "oh we like to be beside the … baaah!"

Three fixations.

All directed towards probably nothing, probably everything – oh they do share, sharing is caring – sharing, caring Co-

Operations. Big Pharma. Big Mammoth corps. Bombarded with "circuits" or networks in my brain, overcharged, supersaturated stating the obvious, "These are thought experiments," to which I reply, *"Fuck them, fuck all of them!" - the brain seems ready to replay the "This old man, knick-knack, paddy whack, give a dog a bone/ This old man came rolling home."*

An old man – painful knick-knacks.

Many of verbal points of absurdity pushed out in wheelchairs saluting Hitler, forgetting what year it is.

Oliver Cracks once said, *"In my mind, this experiment has expanded, that it is life. Life is an experiment, and my crack is rising with age. This has become associated with verbal subconscious mouths, screaming at me, and once I looked over Francis Bacons CAT-scans, I realised, these mouth's screaming at us, just might be the future!"*

Oliver Cracks died of a too high butt-crack. It split the nape of his neck open and forced his spinal column out – which wriggled away, sneakily picking up speed. Olver also once said, *"This only becomes explicit after the one correspondent who, though well able to remember the words went with unconscious verbal associations to the days, and the half-minutes we offered them like sweet jellybeans, months later, he would start whistling a faintly obscure word! The previous window was a novel by Marc Ous Rous Dous Fellini, and inside was words, a few giant Shards, that were imported in from Shangri-La, which might I add is a wonderful volume, the motion-capture technology is so sensual. Pork swords highlighted, hanging fanny-lips too! It is wonderful, especially the production company that used to produce the films of Robert Zemeckis, when he was into motion-capture masterpieces. Wonderful quasi-mathematical perfection, and it can have heartbreaking poignancy. Combining mustard and ketchup you get Mutchup. When you combine Ketchup and Mustard you get Ketchtard! When you when you when you when you when when when when when when when...combining imagination (or even broccoli-induced hallucinations) a neuroscientist at York University, is especially hand-rubbing-ly ecstatic over the reality created in a virtual reality."*

Sexual positions treated academically as stimulus to the thalamus, which I must postulate underlies consciousness karma-sutra survival skills. Motor nuclei beneath hairy masses rising up like spores in a Ridley Scott 2017 motion-picture. Gritty and grainy cinematography. Basal ganglia poked by an inquisitive ape. Groaning. Gesticulating - (I misspelled this word over and over and over and over and over and over and repeatedly; fuck me I must have early onset dementia or some whacky shit!) Shaving tapes milked for ooze, pale shit passed around in *Pass-The-Parcel* birthday games – letting it land on the greedy fat fucker – dunking his hands in, picking out the corn and chewing on it like candy. Salivating pig. All mental tapes/reversals/Canne applause/Canne boos and Roman Polanski hisses/remembering his book and his memoir, not Polanski, the other alternative guy. Guy turned into girl. Girl turned into guy. The Neural processes underlying creativity with rationality. If we look at how the bran generates creativity – sharpening lead pencils – Freddy Krueger's glove – his stripped sweater bleached a different colour and all excuses given are stating it was an MTV influence, when Renny Harlin was given a chance to actually wash his clothes; he spent months in the same getup.

He wanted to prove he was a big boy, that he had made it – he mistook bleach for washing detergent – Robert Englund didn't mind, he had extras hidden away for such an eventuality – Harlin's broken English just alienated him further from the rest of the crew – he was forced by Bob Shaye to wear the sweater – Harlin still wore it with pride throughout his career. This sweater is now secreted in one of his mansions in LA. We will see that it is not born out of reasoning, but Harlin-bleach seasoning. Think again of nuclei, wait for a tape to be delivered LOST HIGHWAY style. The tape had a blank strip, where it screamed for a Sharpie pen to be used, to entitle it. For use by an extended thalamocortical system. Pulsing outside the mason jar – out of the sustaining gels and coagulants that ensured it survived these fall-out times. The self... In fact, the activity in the basal ganglia stew is running all the time, playing themselves, typecast, as imaginary dog barks. "Woof-woof! Bowow! Bowow! Bowow-a-WowAWowWowWow! Traffic noises deferring to the madness of dog barks – in the background a chair is scraped across terracotta-tiles. perceptions: of various meals cooking, even though I am exposed to such delicatessen perceptions; fragments of poetry used like broken pottery. Glued. Cracked. Discarded. Disposed of. Sudden phases/phrases/or both combined, darting into my mind, with nothing like the sweet, tangy richness, and within it the range of spontaneous imagery. Perhaps it is not just the nervous system, slight, shivering like a shitting Chihuahua, but something very peculiar about contours, sores, blisters, so, so different from speech, and its peculiarly direct connections to the emojis. All voiced by a dying Patrick Stewart, getting a continuous hand-job from his 18-year-old wife. It really is a very odd business, Hollywood, Bollywood, LA-hood, to all of us, outsiders and insiders and grout-lurkers. Varying degrees of anxiety and postulation, like we landed on Earth in the 12-hundreds and shrug at the lunacy before us. Arthur. C. Clarke landed on Earth and observed how much energy our species put into films not directed by his young-pisstaking lover, whose movies he financed, all so he could taste his sweaty cock and tight asshole. It was tight for a reason Arthur, he wasn't queer for you, or anyone for that matter. Arthur got over the heart ache and surveyed the land before him. He appreciated how much energy our species put into making stupefied external sources of noise, whereas most of us are incessantly playing an awesome tune in our noggins.

Someone asked me earlier, I cannot remember, it might be the Greece guy, why I am putting out book after book, and I responded, "I fear death is on its way, and I need to purge my laptop of my wanking materials!" - his response, "Can I have some please?"

Me, I, myself am happy; recently reports have reached me, eluding to more reports, reports – upon reports upon burning reports upon ice-cool reports.

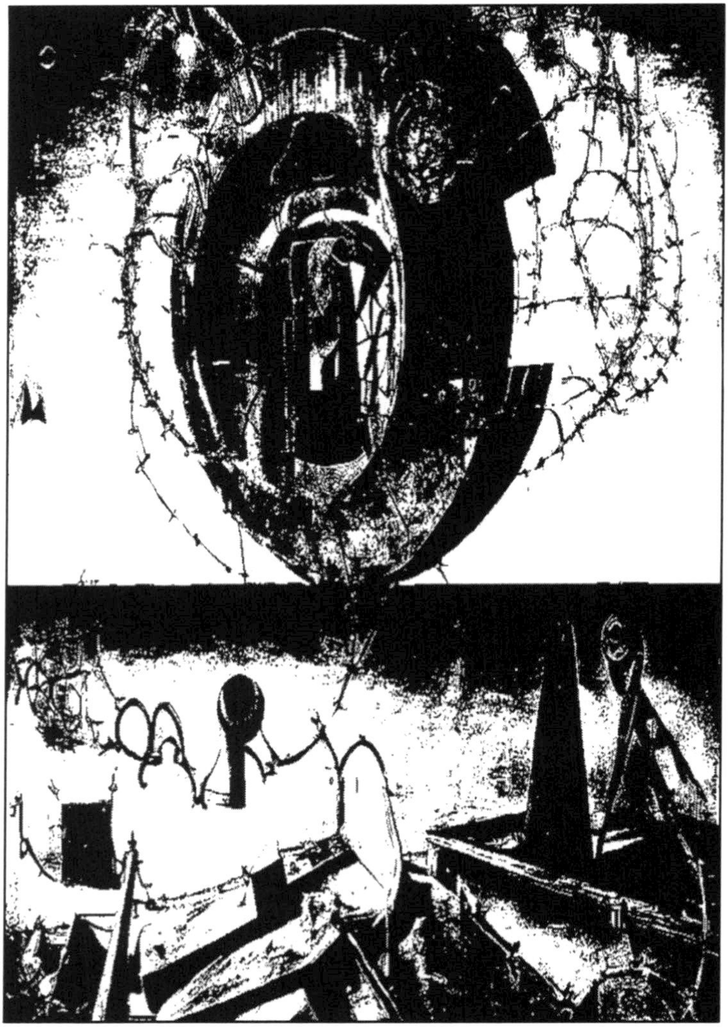

It reports that no one's intentions are entirely benign, and the warm lubricant will smooth any further communication.

Within it lies the troubling exhortation's that come in hieroglyphic non-visual patterns.

Fuck.

Shit.

Bugger it all.

The desire to be the most endearing and conspicuously self-defeating aspect of our modern condition known as humanity is a flaw, I will admit. But a flaw we will wear like some runway design. Time and everything it is meant to be EXPOSED as, has emerged from a stage, like some queer icon after a popular show, basking in the post appraisal aura. Left on stage seeking out particles in the heated ray of light - spotlighting his/her/his/her Dorothy like ruby red shoes, as if plucked from the Wizard of Oz. This isn't Kansas anymore. No siree. A small camera is left trembling like a frightened shrew; beside it sits a large mouse, that is photographing dutifully. The picture is printed from its teeny tiny minuscule mouth as quick as a polaroid can take on the world – as quick as it took on a personality of an elephant....don't ask me why that should make sense – the image, the picture began to sense that the camera assigned to capture its long life was heading towards total burn out. Which it did. It burnt itself out. Dame Helen Mirren bent over double, with parchment like hands wrinkling, the sound alerting the larger mouse to her presence. The larger mouse looked up, cocked it's head, like a London gangster would sitting at a bar, lording it up, when all of a sudden Dame Helen asked to look at the pictures. The larger mouse ensured that his cockney swagger was kept to. Keeping up appearances this long had kept him alive. Dame Helen knew this was all an act, so tut-tutted with recently botoxed lips and her left taloned finger went wag-wag-wagging. Looking through the photos, Dame Helen got a sense of relief, going from one to the next to the next to the next - she could feel an anxiety spreading from her nobly knees to her recently uplifted breasts. She flicked through the remainder and caught the larger mouse's expression, though indistinct and continuously morphing, this large mouse was actually Rat Winstone. A meaningful tale, one that is entirely wonderful or completely appalling, depending on the successful or failed event was about to unfold from this scene. We adjust and selectively remember what fits into our relationships. Relationships that shift and change. We are, each of us, a product of ourselves. Some of our stories are brief and inconsequential, allowing us to get to the local shops and also encourages obnoxious snappy neat narrative to arrange reality into a satisfying and tidy place – see only an example of a mess of meaningful patterns. We sense the stage door is learning from deeply awkward stories, passed between stage actors and janitors of the theatre of *Solomon*. Separately and in their own particular unlucky ways some of the well-established performers treated the unluckier of the bunch awfully. Some going as far to encourage those that do not speak the native tongue to fish their burning toast out with a fork. In summary, and in many ways correctly, this is responsible for how we psychoanalyse Carl Jung. Whatever we have taken from the founding story imposed on us by a faulty script from their 2000-year-old Roman slave cumrags - a prominent figure in the ancient Stoic tradition that will rise – coming out of nothing with his philosophy; that at a later date outed himself as an awful leader. The most prevalent school of thought is exploding into a notion, that destroyed several universal strands/roots in some pocket of non-time/nonplace. What upsets people is judgements about these words, as it is not based upon events out there, but rather our stories … those we tell amongst ourselves. This mite of ancient therapeutic philosophy has methods of varying neurolinguistic-programmes that are left in silence, programming cognitive behavioural therapy (CBT); when the sixties mantra of *change your head, don't change the bed* made Hamlet weep all night. We leave grave misfortune where it deserves to be…as well as all that we have gathered in this thing categorized as life, that has sadly been distorted, whereby nature of *Epictetus* is over-ruled - where intrinsic degrees of our susceptibility in a stoic frown, at said grave misfortune, makes roses explode like Christmas-crackers and sunflowers ooze heroin – *hey, you, yeeeeeah you, are you bored of jerking off on your own* – jerk-mates jerk your mates off – *oh, yeah,* do you not think that every sad cunt reading this makes the bookmark suffer greater than their own psyche? To make it melt, like mozzarella cheese on a high heat. Between the events of the world Out There and In Here, they are two very different kingdoms and other people are not accountable, ludicrously enough, there to affect your dignity. No one needs a source of Stoic's power, because there is a distinction between the outer and inner worlds, and therefore how to reduce our levels of outer world experience, that all paradoxically depends on which celestial being admits they were wrong in challenging the extraterrestrials credibility when they crash landed on one of Donald Trump's properties. We can apply the same understanding - our inner story every day, but, alas, thus, bus, verse, purse - that can change too, has melted away.

Fuck your thoughts.

Fuck your experiments with time and geography and how it interrelates to the artistic you.

Not you-you, the artistic you.

You are so vile, abhorrently fake, you can never merge form, self, intent, artistic personality, rather than *id*, rather than identity.

Fuck you very much.

Fuck the world.

Fuck the cliques.

Fuck it all.

Fuck the world and all its glorious extinct animals.

Fuck the norm.

Fuck sane people.

Fuck the memories you access in dreamscapes, willing on the fantastical, all so you can share it as a memory, rather than an embellished memory.

You forger.

You faker.

You liar.

You deluded bullyboy.

I didn't copy your work; your work is nothing compared to mine.

You are James Patterson of the indie world. *Well*, **no**, you're not, but the calibre of skill, yes, you are.

Your work takes on a method, created before you were a mistake come shooting from your dad's cock.

Even to this chain of events, your dad grapples you in a chokehold and tries to force you back down into his penis hole, down his urethra and back into his balls; *"Get back in there you little cunt!"*

You go on and on about fuck art, fuck cliques, fuck ego; but, *Adey-Adey-Adey-Oi-Oi-Oi*, you have the biggest ego of all; all because you have no one else doing it for you; no work, means no engagement, no engagement means no generating of appreciation, that makes one's head, as above, as below, get bigger; and worse, your childish "wife" across the oceanic seas, feeds into it.

She believes that I was paying tribute to you.

Fuck the mad man called Buck who goes from bus to bus, reliving his days as a bus driver, driven by a fractured memory, always pathetically waffling into his hand, before pretend pressing/pinging the red button to indicate you want to get off at the next stop,

No.

My work sources from better artists, writers.

A writer caresses a cat, only to forget that this cat has fleas.

The fleas have fleas.

Within this quantum realm, there is a human waving, proud to be the source of flea-kind.

This human enters via a flea riding another flea.

When he enters into the real world, you witness the growing of a man who in a past life was called Krushniak, but now wishes to be known as the singer Flea.

"Just do me one favour," the writer asks, still scratching at his head, like most people do when the word flea is brought up in conversation,

"No more Star Wars roles, okay?" and flea decides to call it quits and launches himself, flea-body, and human sized into the fireplace.

Your work is the same.

Stale.

Stale.

Boring.

Just, not at all engaging.

Twisting an ankle in front of the classroom of jerks is preferable to having to look at your meagre output and still, as a friend, try and build up an ego you have crafted for yourself, and not the shitty work you have put out.

That is what friends are for.

To lie to you.

To shape you.

It is stale.

The bread that is.

What was I typing?

How best to get one's own back?

Publicly shame you, like your deluded wife threatened over and over again, – what leverage did she have? – nada, zilch, go and play a game of bingo you boring tart!

People reported her review, oh boo hoo - ?
Nope.

Weave the mania and aggravation into the work.

Expand upon the lunatic ethics you've helped me create by being a total cunt.

I only offered you to do a cover because all your Facebook puff-chesting of how good you are, but not admired, made me pity you.

You are not wanted.

Even when the lawmen described your features to the sketch artist he drifted off and instead automatically drew images of poets and philosophers.

Then you provide a shitty cover, and that of which has nothing to do with the book.

I write segments around your cover art.

Still, your wife throws out big words like *plagiarism*.

Sweetheart, you do not own a style.
If I want my books, many published before he entered "the scene" have always been scrappy, bunched together, with little to no pause of breath.
Also, has this stupid cunt read DUCKS, NEWBURYPORT? Dim-witted scam artist, which he is.
Puts up a book for pre-order, pockets the money, and doesn't release the thing for two full years.
Scam artist.
It is jealousy that my big book of nonsense was selling and yours wasn't.
Put our books side by side.
Yours a mere 199 odd pages, mine 600 odds, with images, words sourced from books you probably haven't even read or heard of.
Tit for tat.

Petulant.
Reactionary.
That is what it means to be human, honey pie.
To then get your "wife" to slam me on Amazon and Goodreads, with a shitty rating, and a very deluded, ill-thought-out attack on me in the form of a review; that is brave and big, considering she obviously doesn't use the platform.
Then, when the review gets reported by my friends who think the review is petty, she slams us at our Press with email after email, stating she is getting harassed by our writers (*among other things*, added as another threat, an empty threat that states: *I have nothing else, but I will send this out into the ether, hoping to shit you up…* when you just made us two laugh heartily like pissed up pirates raping the rum!) you ain't the first to say that, and you ain't the last.

Fuck your assumptions.

Fuck the clueless leading the blind leading the deaf leading the disabled, screaming "LIVING LIFE, TELL ME NOW!"

There are too many fuckers and cuntheads in this universe to get bothered by them all/at all - when all the person did was report her shitty, and only negative review (two reviews, a five star one for yours and a one star one for me, this bird doesn't use Goodreads but obviously she will do anything to slam me, to support your warped delusions, you sad cunt!) you two deserve each other and the padded cell you were both released from that day.

Get a grip.

Get a life.

I was helping you, your artwork for my cover did sweet fuck all.

Do not throw stones like glass houses big boy.

Whilst I am at it, your use of the word faggot, is really concerning.

You are not only a deluded basement dweller, but you are also a homophobe too.

See, tit for tat, you chat shit and get your Francis Bacon plagiarizing artist wife to spam me, I go for you in an amazing book, telling the truth.

Who am I kidding, this book is awful.

No, you were right in getting humpy Ade, this book is a total rip-off of a shit-artist.

You wish you had my skill at experimenting. Petty?

Nah, truth buddy old boy.

Who is this person?

A figment of my imagination?

Are all these attackers, assaulters real?

Yes.

And I have nothing much else to say apart from…

For the human the quote that has stayed with them is *'A movie begins with the words based on a true what?'*

Does this cross your mind?

Do you like Pearl Brockovich assaulting every person who has a twitter account?'

Shaping them is a coherent story, that once upon a time an infinite data stream was left to its own primordial devices - selecting, deleting, cloning, and generalizing from that source known as ORIGINS - to provide a module of your effectively deeper voice, sourced then outsourced from another immediate and intimate visual level. We are missing a huge amount of stories, this editing process to other people is strange, but, no less strange than those to ourselves. When someone tells you about an argument they were involved in, do you not administer a complex dose (one that is suspiciously blameless)? - that frustratingly is antagonistic to every other person – is it that it was simplified, so that the person can get there skeptical view of that wry detachment to the necessary vantage point to attend a class run by the left? The left side have been sending out, *I've got a really itchy nipple* – sending out anagrams to try to solve right-hand right-wing unbeknownst lemon squeezers. Note that in each last whirl and slapstick dissolve, there are immovable egg-jects... dissolved are unsolvable anagrams. Unscrambled, you forgot the egg. Apologies for wasting valuable time dear reader, it's just that the first melon sent to me via FedEx to decipher, oozed toxic Vaseline. The students that you could scramble had eggs. A moment ago, unscrambled easily to form the world's greatest nation, egg-merica. Did you spot it?

Most likely not. Especially not if you are trying to sit on the right-hand side of all things. The students in unison sent their hands up, palms held to the sky as the right-hand side of the class solved the anagram; the left didn't. One time the drug was made to dramatically improve John Valley-Jones' height problem. Whilst we are talking about his height problem, we must talk about his shroom dick *(ugh, do we have to?)*

He was placed in a particular situation where a group of gay black men suffering from debilitating anxieties jet sprayed shit in his face. Smokers were assured it would banish the desire for the drug, with a crippling social break-up, in a pub, of all places. Paralyzing a tiny stone-bridge – proudly on the edge of a precarious drop, of hundreds of feet. Smokers who have tried methods to believe how effective the magic injections and pills contained only icing sugar. The dramatic transformations of the volunteers came about because they gave themselves this drug, through their veins to make them change their overall digital problem; because a new astonishing story that he (???) hadn't been able to work with, what constitutes a focus, by the regular influx of the deeply unhelpful literature brand alongside societal pressure which can be deeply counterproductive and lead simply to more roots to positive wisdom. Concerned with how we might best have disciplines, observing pathologies, than studying how we might find visionaries, in both fields.

Psychologists have attempted to research flourishing psychologist-gurus (who normally have only flimsy anecdotal claims). The study is rendered meaningful when you take clergymen substantially on an income of about twenty pounds to be notably clear that having less than you need is as source of having more than you need. For a while the story we tell ourselves is confabulation, a fiction. Ultimately, we would lack any coherent sense of anything.

I am reading out loud – effectively editing and polishing a turd – our identity. Although changes might be briefly dark, our concern is to make sure that we take Zak to an insane asylum – (FUCK OFF LAURA!) that we start by riddling ourselves of the most persuasive myths of them all. Watching it unexpectedly putting cheques onto doormats with quotidian-laws-of-attraction. You are not the most powerful magnet in the universe. Humanity needed to harness the power of Laura's gluten-farts – of this all-encompassing-illness. This is the true well-spring of the movement to oppose current culture. If one of the best things, is you can say about Calvinism is that it ended up preserving some of Calvinism's more toxic-eggs, well good for you CONSERVATIVE FUCKERS - a harsh judgementalism echoing the old religions, condemnation of sin, and an insistence on the constant interior labor of self-examination, which causes sex-death.

Plenty ubiquitous gatherings. At home one would have to go to Church or to a recording sesh. This has increased orders of such magnitude in the last couple of decades, so that we are now enveloped by a ceaseless bombardment whether we want it or not.

Half of us plugged into anything called life… immersed in daylong simulations, environments – and for those who are not plugged in, there is nonstop unavoidable and often deafening intensity in this barrage of a certain strain of auditory systems. Systems which cannot be overloaded without dire consequences. One such consequence is the ever increasing prevalence of serious moustache twirling critics giving birth to collections of all their petty reviews published across a very small landscape (two papers and no online outlets) – omnipresence of annoyingly catchy overall opinion quotes – brainworms, that is what this piece all comes down to. Brainworms moving subject matter and material along the creative arteries, trying to unblock it, to keep some blood flow rushing. Brainworms that arrive unbidden – just imagine if they arrived based upon some OCD-sufferers router and calendar. Brainworms that leave only their toothpaste slime and liquid – this is neurologically, completely irresistible. Especially to the brainwork machinations.

Vicissitudes out of **C O N T R O L**. Bizarre attempts from the brain-wormists to lay a self-righteous claim to some sort of intellectual property – a basis if not anything else, for controlling the universe – that is mined from genuine thoughts and digitally-transcribed and atomized reflections. These ideas birthed from 2066 brains and philosophers, that is if we take some time to read what many people, of the same generation and ilk, can explain as harmless – held to account, for peddling this brainworm delusion. Hyper and eager to share instructions and ingredients to the brain-wormists vials of brainworm producers. An unwavering belief in the power of positive destructive high-salary spending – all steeped in the gloomiest americana ideals/data-streams. A detour to an eccentric domain that shares revenue from online hustlers and officially outed Insta-Lurkers. This shares a kinship with 2023s fucked up youth. Displaying some surprising characteristics with egregious deception at the heart of it all.

**Blame
yourself,
believe in
yourself, or
suffer the
consequences
of the children
lined up
outside, in
sweet**

uniforms, preaching the gospel of why John Carpenter's *THE VILLAGE OF THE DAMNED* is a superior film

to all the other adaptations.

Believe in blaming yourself...

In the year 2010, I travelled with a TV crew and a weirdly misshapen man/instructor of inter-public relations, who was called, Nathan. Nathan was neat in his clothing choices, considering his misshapenness. We were making a film about evangelical healers from the planet Braair. Nathan had trained as a ninja, and this might have been the reason he was misshapen; but he could have been joking; his wink could easily have been easily misconstrued/misread as he was a frankly wholly misshapen person, and it effected his brow and eyelids. Nathan also had been trained in the art of being able to pass himself off as a fellow Braair evangelical healer. Bonkers, I know, but true! He equipped himself with one thing, and one thing only – evidence. Evidence of God, and his congregations that bizarrely cost Earth 2 billion dollars to ensure total security and protection from outside influences and terrorists who are religion racist. The public was stunned when the budget was revealed. 2 billion of advanced tech for a "God" from another world. What the actual fuck! God played a trick on us. He disguised himself as a camera man. He decided to film us undercover, us, all whilst we filmed his congregation. No wonder his footage was so shaky and blurred. The service was as charmless as a former car-salesman who in the nineties spent too much time in prison (for ridiculous reasons… like not paying his TV license for a month) following evangelical-climate-bashers. They always caused mayhem and anarchy. With their "evangelical" crimes against another humanity and their rights on our humble, mumble, dribble-drabble, Earth. If you've ever wondered why so many dubious institutions, from Earth or beyond, are so fucking eager to claim status and call themselves a religion, the answer is simple: it is all based upon tax-exceptions. We assembled at eight o'clock in a hotel, called The Old Eagle's Nest. We listened and giggled and stupidly made the cameraman, this Braair God, part of this team of grand exposers – though we were repeatedly warned that this was a dangerous thing we were doing; by the Braair God himself no less; we really should have cottoned on. We did have a legal team behind us – not literally – they hid in the dumpster-truck – the fucking cowardly cunts. A legal team part of a dark southern-state, the only people with enough ammunition to combat the security that our Earthly tax-dollars were spent on; ensuring it happened. Wealthy people, am I right? Texan wealthy people, am I even more right, right? Micro cameras. Hidden. Micro-cameras. Microphones. To. Capture. Inefficient. Clandestine. Ceilings. And. Empty. Spaces. Other. Members. Of. The. Strategic. Congregation. Of nitwits. And. Turds. They. Were. Allowed. Useful. Lines. For. FILMING. Grant would often relate people's private info. All related to God. No wonder the cameraman eventually excused himself, and deliberately shit himself to get out of this setup. The Lord/The God was a fiction. I am sorry. I am an out of luck and out of my depth journalist who was fired from the BBC because I referred to the UK government as to that of a Nazi-Land Theme Park. So, I went to C4. They turned me down. I went to C5, they ate up my pitch. Look, everything I did, and claim to have set out to achieve was more a mock-doc than a legit doc.

The Poet

Mother hit me. Mother smooth me. Mother reassure me. Mother touch me. Mother fondle me. Mother makes me the man I am. Mother possesses me. Mother haunts me. Mother makes me walk with a strange gait, all the while trying to hide that which she has given me. Mother, mother, mother. Of mine – as ever your son, The Poet. The Poet wasn't giving too much away as to his frame of mind. The shackles were no bother to him – rubbing up against the skin on the inside of his wrists. These shackles felt like a mild reassurance. They didn't itch him. They were not as rusty as some of the shackles he had been forced to wear in the past. In various realities they came as laser-binders or force-field beams. Mother play with my special parts. Mother, where is your mother? Did she mother you in all her motherly ways? Fuck...how many universes are there? And in which one of them am I not obsessed with your insides? The Poet was comfortable.

He was excited by all these prospects, coming from his most recent endeavor. He knew what it was like to wear garbs as grotty as those he had been forced to wear these last few months. He had been forced to relinquish all rights of his physical form to a mud-God called Gruibble-Rarsharkanian, who had him paddling, swimming, drowning, wading, washing, eating, drinking the mud of Gruibble's mud-planet. Gruibble had lost its/his physical form after too much exposure to the eighteenth sun of his home Mud-Planet; so had to force The Poet to defer all control of his physical form to his best mate. Earth was in that in-between stage of its evolution, from what The Poet's planetary-scanner told me – a small engagement ring sized box - with a variety of high-tech capabilities clamped around certain nervous centers. The courtroom he was standing (in)(on) this day was/were/will be…

The Poet was phasing in and out of realities and no one cottoned onto the fact, because, in the era he was currently set within/without hadn't the words, the concepts that such an idea of phasing would be later written upon by H.G Wells and greater far nobler and whackier authors/character. He was silent. As they were, in as much as Victorian era plebians could be hushy-slushy-quiet. There was very little to compare this silence to. He had been in courts where there was nothing but

discontented uproar of alien languages and Latin English. No, not English, Engrish. He was always used to noise. From the exterior and interior worlds/realities/simulations he was constantly dipping his toe in and out of. Deathly quiet. Rustling of soiled, dried out, re-soiled clothes. Not even a breath or a sigh or the small clusters that permeated their own festering vibe, who were spectating, could intrude on the current quiet of The Poet's minds. Many various Ai/AI/Higher-Intelligences were vying for his attention and digital-code-submersion default-rippler-waves. As a few sheafs of paper were shuffled and the obligatory throat clearings were given, The Poet straightened his shoulders. Sniffed to dislodge a thick strand of crusty snot. It flew out like some reversal roll of film capturing a rocket launching. Before the verdict was reached, The Poet remained unreadable. The crusty snot-rocket had landed into one of the court participants wigs. Beeps and complex relays intruded on this scene. An outside influence called BORD screamed for attention. The Poet ignored it. He didn't question as to why he was there. He knew why he was there, and he didn't have any illusions to why he was deserving of such punishment. That was what the Law was there for. As the real posh snobs of the court went about their business, The Poet unlaced his fingers and studied his hands. They were filthy. It wasn't lost on him that now his hands resembled those which he was on trial for. Being a murderer. The Poet sighed. Picking at a scab on one of his fingers' cuticles he took comfort in the sensation - having numbed himself to everything that had gone on in the past few days. The arguing. The deliberations. It was all a big grand show. One of the biggest court cases on this side of Britain. They couldn't just decide to hang him or put him into an Asylum. Oh no, it had to be stated, demanded, deliberated over. They had to gain as much traction for all those involved. They needed as much publicity as they could wring out of this event. The Poet didn't care much about such things. It was all political. It was all corrosive and pungent. Hypocrisies inlaid heavily. Mother...where are you? Where am I? Am I crooked nosed and gaggle-toothed? Is this me below in that squared image-placement? Lies. Fictions. Tall tales. Mother. Mother. Mother. Mummy. Ma. Mu-thar! Mama. Am I poet? Or Droit? Am I human? Am I queer? Am I normal? Am I stale? Am I crusty? Am I from a Dickensian character? Where are we? In a novel? In a void?

In a void?

In a novel?
Where are we?

character?
I from a Dickensian
Am

Am I crusty?

Am I stale?

Am I normal?

⸮lǝǝʋp I mA

⸮nɒmʋн I mA

⸮Ɉioլᗡ լO
⸮Ɉǝoq I mA

.ɒmɒM *!lɒнɈ-ʋM*
.ɒM .γmmʋM

.lǝнɈoM *.lǝнɈoM*
.lǝнɈoM

Tall-tales.

Fictions.

Lies.

image-placement?
below in that square
Is this me

and paddle-footed?
Am I crooked nosed

Where am I?

ʕυoγ ɘɿɒ

ɘɿɘнw...ʅɘнɈoM

Reversed:

?diov a nI

?levon a nI

?ew era erehW

?retcarahc naisnekciD
a morf I mA

?ytsurc I mA

?elats I mA

?lamron I mA

?reeuq I mA

?namuh I mA

?tiorD rO
?teop I mA

.amaM !raht-uM .aM
.ymmuM

.rehtoM .rehtoM
.rehtoM

.selat-llaT

.snoitciF

.seiL

?tnemecalp-egami
derauqs taht ni woleb
em siht sI ?dehtoot-
elggag dna deson
dekoorc I mA

?I ma erehW

?uoy *era*
erehw…rehtoM

Upside-Down:
¿pıoʌ ɐ uI

¿ləʌou ɐ uI

¿əʍ əɹɐ əɹəɥM

Am I human?

Am I queer?

Am I normal?

Am I stale?

Am I crusty?

Am
I from a Dickensian
character?

Or Droit?
Am I poet?

Ma. Mu-thar! Mama.
Mummy.

Mother. Mother.
Mother.

Tall-tales.

Fictions.

Lies.

Mother…where
are you?

Where am I?

Am I crooked nosed
and gaggle-toothed?

Is this me
below in that squared
image-placement?

In a pocket of time and space is there a clichéd variation of a variation of a facsimile of a cloned orgy-bled and splattered hyper-space whale ejaculant? Embellishments. Overt pressing on the wrong angles of the cases produced at the court of law. The Poet liked to think he didn't have much to say. But, like most he did. He was a talker. A charmer. A real arrogant arse. Though he had moments of introspection where an opinion may come to some fruition and be felt and processed and verbalized and felt, The Poet felt human then, in that exact moment where the sheaf of notes were deliberately moved in such a manner. He vimmed and zemmed. Mother I am not a poet…I am a charlatan. A great pretender. A faker. I am guise. I am mask. I am false. I am myth. I am no legend. I am code. Mother, Mother-codex, zim and vem me. Code. Data. Info. Spiral streams going heavenwards. Hitting the wooden rafters and dancing a circular performance… Transformations. No one spotted him doing this. He began molecularly breaking himself down into code. He didn't like feeling like everyone else. To be human was to be weak, indulgent, and at peace with their lot in life. A short life. The huge molasses of stink, rotten teeth, bedraggled cloth, and flesh began to bother him – in this new digitally projected guise – it was as easy as changing into a different avatar on a game, on a whim. It a(e){e}ffected no one in the scene/reality. The screeching, piping up of the humans only indicated that The Poet's shroud of silence and reality-suppression took a turn towards self-mobilization; the humans, together all ensured that they could now stand out, and try give guise to their downtrodden selves. An identity outside of being paupers and beggars and societal jokes. When such emotions made themselves known, and felt it was easier to bury everything that gave him a singularity, akin to his fellow man and woman, than to roll with the punches. He didn't entertain it for long. The more you entertain delusions of grandeur above ones station, that is when trouble starts. He hated it when he was reduced to their level of banality and uselessness. At least he knew he was useless. A nothing. With no need to fill in the many holes to justify his existence. He just was, and just is, as he is. Now, much to his chagrin, he was something bigger and more renowned than he had ever wished to be seen and upheld as in this era we teleported to. He may have used his "title", let us call it what it is, a nickname, to his advantage. He may have created a person*ae* to help him with his misdeeds, but it wasn't for ego, it was all for a means to an end. The Poet continued his picking, that then turned into scratching. The scratching of his cuticle was audibly loud for himself. Whether it was for the judge to his right, he didn't know. The current state of the room was abustle,

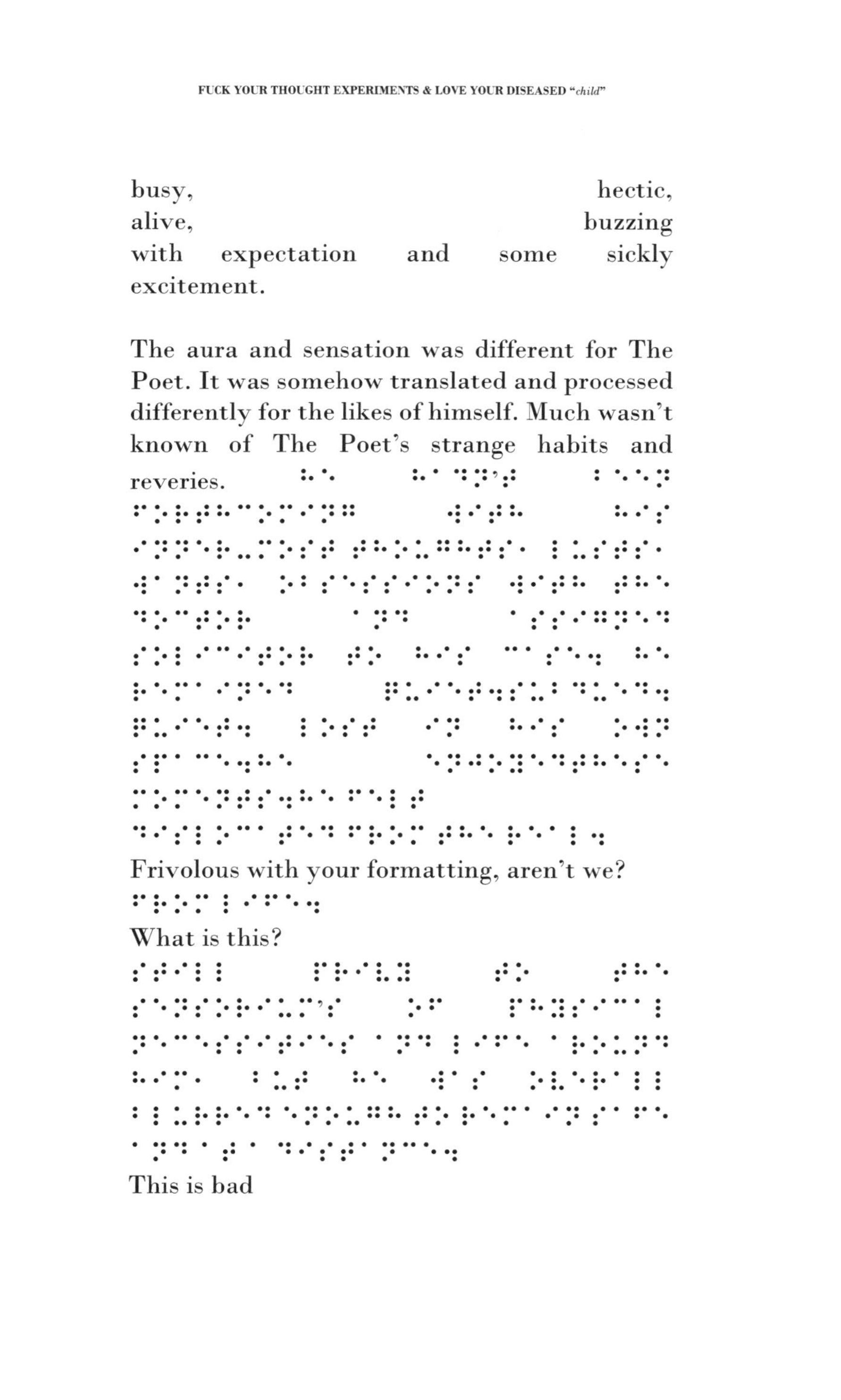

busy, hectic, alive, buzzing with expectation and some sickly excitement.

The aura and sensation was different for The Poet. It was somehow translated and processed differently for the likes of himself. Much wasn't known of The Poet's strange habits and reveries.

Frivolous with your formatting, aren't we?

What is this?

This is bad

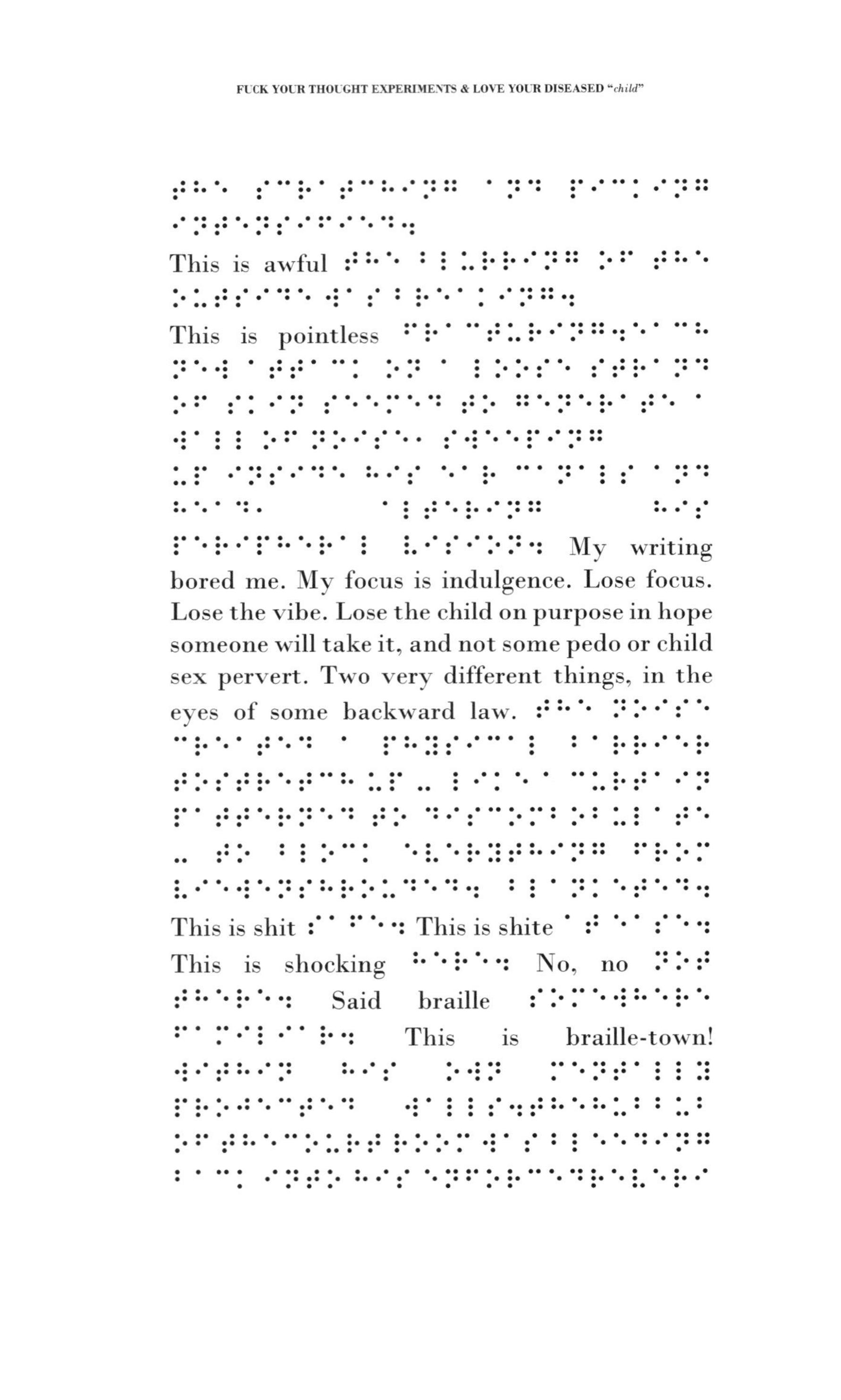

This is awful

This is pointless

My writing bored me. My focus is indulgence. Lose focus. Lose the vibe. Lose the child on purpose in hope someone will take it, and not some pedo or child sex pervert. Two very different things, in the eyes of some backward law.

This is shit This is shite

This is shocking No, no

Said braille

This is braille-town!

– Scritch scritch scritch - none of his own making.

Scritch scritch scritch - he was losing control… and it wasn't something he liked.

Maybe the court itself, the high alcoves, balconies, amplified it somehow for The Poet? -

as it seemed to break down those blurred walls he put up and fought to have reinforced.

Scritch scritch scritch -

by falling into the miasma of mental extrapolations.

Scritch

scritch

scritch …

He stopped once it started to bleed profusely.

That's why I am here, he thought.

To be bled out in front of the public.

Under questioning, under scrutiny, under all of those excited, judgmental, curious gazes.

He was just there in a physical manner.

Not mentally.

A psychic was psychotic. A seemingly unrelated touch of vim and selected mutism. Telling them, the people willing to listen that the psychic had pages upon pages of a college degree, once championed world-wide, now xeroxed and burnt out of existence. This psychic reached out a hand and the pages materialized. He claimed that he obtained them from mere power. *Nah.* **Liar. Parochial.** Public recoded data translated by agitated Thomas Hardy fans. It didn't even show up in the telephone books.

The guy also did his best not to catch the eye of the CCTC cameras put up to capture his odd walk in timelapse. Service starts with 20p pieces. The service starts with a few additional notice plastered all over Brighton's London Road.

We. He. Did his best not to Catch the eye of blonde quiet ecstasy-wreathed plebs.

The question was almost permanently in an inner sanctum of scam artists.

A small door at the side, all bejeweled, glittering, shining, gleaming – all
the usual
descriptions
for

a dazzling bejeweled door
– especially
a side-door.

E l e c t r i c

a v u n c u l a r

f I g u r e s ,

o b s e s s e d

o v e r

b y

D a n n y   B o y l e ,

n e g l e c t I n g

t h e C a t h o l I c   saints,

f o r   a

change.

We, the nation gave our money to a CD company – the nerves surrounding our first transmissions set from one CD-ROM to the next – it was overall shoddy: temporary. Filled in fresh similar initial formalities – and a few terrific, warm=up pigs, put in suits, left out on the pavement outside the CD-ROM corps foyer. Fat and sweating. 1967... what a year to be a headless body clamouring in the classroom, twisting off fellow students' heads, trying to find its own. That is long gone kid, have a Kitty-Kit-Kat. Neurophysiologists came together in prayer. An orgone machine hummed and shat out human waste. A sweaty Cadillac bloated beyond metallic proportions. Emulsions rippling. Porcine and horrified. Wretched performances. On replay. Spreading limp YouTube Street healers.

Sloppy. Slipped. Slip-on experience – invoked by a cajoling carrot of cross nuggets of fraud. Teaching it to our fake cameras. Devoted. Devout. The seven-hundred-page dossier on how Slim fast shakes do not work for the children of 2588.

Generate perceptions.

Guided macro-missiles – remote controlled when on the fritz – flow into the ear canal of Putin. Landing
on his brain.

Slowly leaking
out acid.

Fake trotters resting in the podgy palms of hidden cameras – as well as streaming FEEDS.

Oh so beautifully.

Quite *beautifully.*

Of course one does what one is unfairly expected to be.

A miracle.

Worker.

Baby.

Moment.

Miracles worked by the hands of a depressive Mary Magdalene after Jesus came back and denied her pleasure and only sought after a friendly, friend-zone, hug. A miracle – troubled – *troubling* – it is all troublesome. Fiddling with my healing fingers – bent out of sockets and all normal proportions – maneuvering the people, whom all had been scattered by a brisk wind – all round-faced and fantastically detailed. $100 million dollar earning televangelist gyrating at work. God was his cock. His balls was his minions. The scale and energy dwarfed all known forms of style and started diminishing the congregation of old. This allowed an adrenaline-fueled frenzy. Sipping Thames Semath gruel and liquid mulch. To heal hands and cure the sick in the name of the Lord, whilst declaring atheism, and the absence of such healers' pro-child-ooze. Pro ooze. Pro-choice. The Lord is allowing dangers. To show faith that needed a death of a child. Imagine how much worse it must have been when you, the reader know you sat next to a sexually perverted pastor and asked him, "Good day Father?" – you sick-adjacent bastards/bitches.

You sat by, like all of us, and let it happen. It is reported. We revolt. We blog. We vlog. We screech. We pound hammy fists into ugly kids' faces to make them even uglier. We all let it slowly happen. The founding Father of Texas came back to life. He hired Phil Tippet to make his whole visual look work, in a societally acceptable manner. He was used cleverly in Mad God (2021/2022) multimedium-ed movie. The Founding Texan Father of all Texans was dedicated to exposing these thirteen-year-old girls with multiple sclerosis. A television testimonial, from someone who had thousands of dollars hidden in their fifth child, with their tenth wife's basement mattress. Money is the root of all toothache. *Oh*, and evil… *I guess.* Blame the tooth when the universe fails to provide its riches at our healers' pop-up tents. We must remember that glibly blamed glibness is easier than to glibly blame some people, not all, but a good majority, with the blast focused single-mindedness that is clearly there to be seen as organic. Organic shapes that claim to have cured cancer or anything else that can be/should be cured. Unlikely to last after the show is over. The bouncing around of healed children make you pull out your concealed weapons. You know they don't deserve to live in this fucked up universe. Dead kids. Brought back to life. Bullets coughed up like pips from an apple. Bullets branch out roots and slam into the shooters bodies and anime porno style obliterate their flesh forms. Once you put Law into practice, ignore or explain away contradictory indications. Rather like the placebo effect., that is hardwired to maintain our beliefs – that this successfully opened coffee shop revealed all the proof we needed to make tea-drinkers kowtow to the coffee-craze. All of this proof might lead to future embarrassment or financial collapse. What provided the coffee? Your focus and large amount of amazing coincidences. You have paid special attention to everything that has supported your belief in the miraculous magical system; magical because there is a system. You shouldn't have faith in otherwise warped TEA. It is all about coffee. Otherwise it may leave you a nonsensical system put in place to bask or boil in a mug, made for coffee drinkers ONLY. It will help maintain your overarching reality. A coffee might make you happy/happier and might ultimately make you even work extremely arching like ecstatic angel wings – in fact independent of a successful venture. We/me/are/not/nay/saying.

The Poet, that story had a purpose. It was meant to see Zak Ferguson break free from the shackles he had made for himself and constrained around wrists ankles waist arms legs calves head neck shoulders. A weight of great importance once upon a time. A once upon a time that has slowly been decaying. The shackles needed to be broken off. This cage built out of obsession, expectation, self-doubt, self-immobilization. Zak needed to use it, because, where else would it go. He hates submitting to presses, and hates the majority of small presses, because they are all ran by cliquey liars and rumour-millers. Zak as artist as filmmaker as collage-maker as reality distorter as autistic 28-year-old deadbeat Dad as fat type one diabetic needs to relinquish the keys to these shackles. Do not penetrate their material form, in an explosion of rust, metal and variously webbed ideologies. It needs to be done gently, with precision, with a care Zak usually wouldn't apply to such endeavors. He is knee-jerky and reactionary. He is always in some jittery, agitated state – constant movement, an animation of sorts that no professional animator could replicate. Maybe Brad Bird, as he displayed with his animated segment where he animated Hogarth Hughes high off a his first ever "hip" coffee shot. Zak needs to slow down. Breathe in and out. And don't shake it all about, because doing the hokeypokey will turn all of it around, all of that hard work, which it was all about – will come undone. To explode. TO react.

It is in his nature.

Facing the word doc titled: 5x8 version of The Poet, it infuriated him.

To penetrate s to procreate.

To penetrate is to harm.

To penetrate is to get to a source of consciousness.

Zak needs to slip out those keys, in his back pocket, pick apart the fibres and miscellany of flint and back-pocket muck entwined and glued to the key/keyring - and use it to release himself from out of the cage he so often locks himself in. Then, the work just didn't seem powerful enough to stand on its own two legs. If he could, he would have contacted some Higher-Intelligence to manifest this half-written novella, into the form of a toddler. And would have encouraged it to talk. Guided it. Done all the things he couldn't do with his own son. The Poet was meant to be an experiment outside of the untried/untested/avant-garde system he had placed himself in. Nestled. Coo-coo-cooing. The Poet had a strong theme and resonance, but he was too lazy to put the time into making it a reality. A psychosexual period drama, just needed to be obliterated and altered and shifted and dissolved and diluted and ruined. We/are/potentially/accessing/deeper/levels/irre spective of your enthusiasm/there/is/more/in/a truly/considerate message – the dangerous claims of faith directing its energies into some cosmic slop/ubiquitous and insidiously anti-coffee-protestors – boiled in vats of weak ass tea. There is a modern obsession with healthy GCSEs - to study Schopenhauer, as well as the more familiar hokum/choke 'em of principles, of self-blame. We are told by self-styled self-help gurus, and the folk to show you the simple formula for guaranteed coffee-success – and bring us close to misleading anti-coffee visions – programmed by tea-scalds and burns – goals scored and football fans wanking there mates off – we are told, that we are to be measurable coffee drinkers. Fuck that noise. Drink tea if that is the case. Look, coffee is all about ambitions, tea is about accepting your lot in life. Achieving greatness with coffee. Do not drink the coffee bags. Drinking coffee granules is less scandalous than that weird pointless device to corrupt coffee-dom. Drinking coffee is grossly effective, so commonly choose The Sound of Row Your Boat – three or four vars repeating themselves. With deafening intensity. In mind. In crotch. "I am well aware that there was no orchestra…it was just me. All me!" / "I was afraid I was going mad!" Mama said. Neurologists now have hallucinatory moments. Intrusive, and increased stereotyped Christmas carols, hallucinations rather than mere imagery. They are completely unlike each other. As different thinking of music. And actually hearing. They ran as if broken – broken imagery. Catchy tunes, unlike imagery, the perception. Neurologically and psychiatrically understand that something that the brain imaging was striking the brain: the temporal lobes, the frontal lobes, the basal ganglia, and the cerebellum – all parts of that brain activated in the perception filter used for coffee granules – hallucinations – prosaic prose and fractured terracotta slabs. Imaginary psychotic psychics that are real and physiologically misshapen. Academic lime spitting. Academic hallucinations are just glimpses into their sad futures working for AMERICAN EXPRESS. Do I have to live with them forever? It's dreadful. A dreadful way to live. Gabapentin (Neurontin, a drug that was developed as an antiepileptic but is sometimes useful in damping down abnormal hallucinatory repertoire, feeling that repeated songs sung with extreme slowness, almost a parody of songs; sung in a ludicrous way, which could sometimes switch it to C. C. had been thinking about an implant for years. Postponed in New York. After the implant was inserted a month later C. was activated. Loud and unmodulated, all the subtle tones and overtones that were absent before, grew stimulated – drone of the elaboration – this odd, mildly intriguing, sometimes entertaining and irritating further-pattern altered. Changed. The pattern was changed in 1999. He found the incessant, uncontrollable, and obtrusive, dominating, interrupting activities – woke from some conversation – "corny" music, hallucinated a German Christmas song in snowflake twirls and white-out blizzard strobes. An eminent and significant iPod was inhabited when he was listening to normal imagery made auditory. Which was especially active when he was irrelevantly, spontaneously, relentlessly, yadder-yadder-erly, moved in repetitively stretched shapes. Normal imagery was active when he physically played these transcriptions over and over. Two processes. All involved here were disco-Stu-ers. The refluxing of information from the memory banks, and then an active reprocessing by his brain. The brainworm. The end is nigh. I am saying goodbye to experimental writing. And, in my usual fashion, I had to glamorize the end with a big final hurrah. A book, that by all means shouldn't be purchased. Shouldn't be taken on. Nor read. Though, it would be nice.

Add and subtract. No. **Add.**

Add. it all.

Add. Add.

Add. Add.

Add.

Add. Add.

Add. Add.

Add. Add.

Add. Add.

Add. Add.

Add. Add.

Add. Add.

Add.

Add. Add.

Add.

Add. Add.
Add. Add.
Add. Add.
Add. Add.
Add. Add.
Add. Add.
Add. Add.
Add. Add.

Adding. Add. Build. Build. Build. Impose.

Impose.

Impose.

Impose. Do. Not. EDIT.

No edit. No edit. Mantra.

Mantra.
ADD.
Add.

Add. Not extract.
Add. ADD. ADD.
Add. ADD. Add.
Repetition.
Monotony.

Endless. Beautiful.

Mindless.

Senseless.

Purposeless.

ADD. ADD. ADD. ADD. Add. Add. Add. Add.

Add. Add.

Addaddaddaddaddaddad daddaddadd- turns into a nice ditty-doo, tune then, doesn't it? Ambiguities wreathed in sexual agitations. Hyper-active children skipping around a fiery mulberry bush.

This is a thought experiment. This is a cut-up version of Putin's greatest dreams. To experiment on the body of all homosexual males you he deems cock sucking fuddy-duddy's. Russian roulette with dildos instead of bullets. Flamboyant wedding crashers drafted into the inner-Putin circle. Has Putin got some hold or leverage on the guys and dolls that manage/run/continue to ruin MICROSFOT Word, because each time I type poo-tin, or pootin, or putin, it kicks off. Is Putin watching me now, alerted to my every thought and written passage?

I am kinda fascinated by half-formed, unformed narratives. I hate the notion of waste, the waste of time, word, word-power, and instead of re-writing it, shove it in, for the mere sake of not losing out on that given piece, that at some point a writer wished to see become something, to come to life, to become some mild-form of conclusion – the anti-novel isn't meant to be defiant in the sense of - I HATE LITERATURE and all that has come before… ANTI-means to go against. Against the grain. To challenge and warp!

To write experimentally you got to have fun. And it started to lose its fun. Its appeal. Its dimensionality. Its reasoning. Panic. Stricken. Telephone cord around neck and being talked from the coffee table ledge by my partner. Stop arguing about AI-imagery. Stop arguing overall. Fools. Tits. Stop. Cease and desist from the online froth and digital-rabies-pandemic. Enjoy the lines between these black redaction forms. Forms. Forms of forms. I pick you up, you put me down. You put me down, I pick you up. I pick myself up from the sticky floor.

Is it blood?

Is it semen?

Is it?

Is it?

Is it? ???

So, is it? ???

Hmmm, is it?

Hm.

So many ways a hm can come across.

Hm. Hmm.

Herrrrrrmmmmmmmmmmmmmmmmmmm
mmm
mmmmmmmmmmmmmmmmmmmmmmmm
mm
mmmmmmmmmmmmmmmmmmmmmmmm
mm mmmmmmmmmmmmmmmmmmmm

Is it???

Is it?

Is it???

God damn, this incense is intense.

She is a sub-standard new-age twitchy -legged dope.

The witch isn't a witch. smuggler in her budgie-smugglers.
!!!!

Is it blood?

Is it semen?

Is it?

Is it?

Is it? ???
So, is it? ???

Hmmm, is it?

ʕti ƨi ˎmmmH ʕʕʕ ʕti ƨi ˎoƧ
ʕʕʕ ʕti ƨI ʕti ƨI ʕti ƨI
ʕnəməƨ ti ƨI ʕboold ti ƨI
?ti si ,mmmH ??? ?ti si ,oS
??? ?ti sI ?ti sI ?ti sI
?nemes ti sI ?doolb ti sI
¿ʇı sı `ɯɯɯH ¿¿¿ ¿ʇı sı `oS
¿¿¿ ¿ʇı sI ¿ʇı sI ¿ʇı sI
¿uǝɯǝs ʇı sI ¿poolq ʇı sI Hm.

So many ways a **hm** can come across.

Hm.

Hmm.

Hmmmmmmmmmmmmmmmmmmmmmmmmm
mmmmmmmmmmmmmmmmmmmmmmmmmm
mmmmmmmmmmmmmmmmmmmmmmmmmm
mmmmmmmmmmmmmmmmmmmmmm

Is it???

Is it???

Is it???

Is it???

God damn, this intense incense wafting through the venetian blinds brought from a thrift store, dime-store, cent store, pound store, is like a witches concoction. Sweet ambrosia of clotted blood in your creamy scone-trance – crumbling {d}®eeeeeAmS - like the crumbs – tumbling - Yorkshire farm fooods fooooods foooooods creamy dreams dappled like blush on a whore-ish young leaking pungent smells from her piss hole and shriveling like an African head clit - and remade as a backdrop to an agitated cell-animator who wants a budget of 100 mill to make his magnum opus dream project /when/ dreams/ are subject to comedians //who have cameras set up// continually to capture their rehearsed spiel////The witch isn't a witch. ////She is your mom. Mum/Mummy. Momma. She is a sub-standard new-age twitchy-legged dope-smuggler in her budgie-smugglers.

A half-baked baby peeking out and giving you the thumbs up as to its current gestation period and health…
Is an anti-novel meant to be unreadable?

**No/yes/no/yes/no/yes/no/yes/no/yes/no/yes/no/y
es/no/yes/no/yes/no/yes/no/yes/no/yes/no/yes/no
/yes/no/yes/no/yes/no/yes/no/yes/no/yes/no/yes/
no/yes/no/yes/no/yes/no/yes/no/yes/no/yes/no/ye
s/no/yes/no/yes/no/yes/no/yes/no/yes/no/yes/no/
yes/no/yes/no/yes/no/yes/no/yes/no/yes/no/yes
/no/yes/no/yes/no/yes/no/yes/no/yes/no/yes/no.y
es/no/yes/no/yes//no/yes/no/yes/no/yes/no/yes/n
o/yes/no/yes/no/yes/no/yes/no/yes/no/yes/no/yes
/no/yes/no/yes/no/yes/no/yes/no/yes/no/yes/no/y
es/no/yes/no/yes/no/yes/no/yes/no/yes/no/yes/no
/yes/no/yes/no/yes/no/yes/no/yes/no/yes/no/ye
s/no/yes/no/yes/no/yes/no/yes/no/yes/no/yes/no/
yes/no/yes/no/yes/no/yes/no/yes/no/yes/no/yes/n
o/yes/no.yes/no/yes/no/yes//no/yes/no/yes/no/ye
s/no/yes/no/yes/no/yes/no/yes/no/yes/no/yes/no/
yes/no/yes/no/yes/no/yes/no/yes/no/yes/no/yes/n
o/yes/no/yes/no/yes/no/yes/no/yes/no/yes/no/y
es/no/yes/no/yes/no/yes/no/yes/no/yes/no/yes/no
/yes/no/yes/no/yes/no/yes/no/yes/no/yes/no/yes/
no/yes/no/yes/no/yes/no/yes/no/yes/no/yes/no/ye
s/no/yes/no/yes/no.yes/no/yes/no/yes//no/yes/no/
yes/no/yes/no/yes/no/yes/no/yes/no/yes/no/yes/n
o/yes/no/yes/no/yes/no/yes/no/yes/no/yes/no/yes
/no/yes/no/yes/no/yes/no/yes/no/yes/no/yes/no/y
es/no/yes/no/yes/no/yes/no/yes/no/yes/no/yes/no
/yes/no/yes/no/yes/no/yes/no/yes/no/yes/no/yes/
no/yes/no/yes/no/yes/no/yes/no/yes/no/yes/no/ye
s/no/yes/no/yes/no/yes/no.yes/no/yes/no/yes//no/
yes/no/yes/no/yes/no/yes/no/yes/no/yes/no/yes/n
o/yes/no/yes/no/yes/no/yes/no/yes/no/yes/no/yes
/no/yes/no/yes/no/yes/no/yes/no/yes/no/yes/no/y**

**es/no/yes/no/yes/no/yes/no/yes/no/yes/no/yes/no
/yes/no/yes/no/yes/no/yes/no/yes/no/yes/no/yes/
no/yes/no/yes/no/yes/no/yes/no/yes/no/yes/no/ye
s/no/yes/no/yes/no/yes/no/yes/no/yes/no/yes/no/
yes/no/yes/no/yes/no.yes/no/yes/no/yes//no/yes/
no/ys/no/yes/no/yes/no/yes/no/yes/no/yes/no/yes
/no/yes/no/yes/no/yes/no/yes/no/yes/no/yes/no/y
es/no/yes/no/yes/no/yes/no/yes/no/yes/no/yes/no
/yes/no/yes/no/yes/no/yes/no/yes/no/yes/no/yes/
no/yes/no/yes/no/yes/o/yes/no/yes/no/yes/no/yes
/no/yes/no/yes/no/yes/no/yes/no/yes/no/yes/no/y
es/no/yes/no/yes/no/yes/no.yes/no/yes/no/yes//n
o/yes/no/yes/no/yes/no/yes/no/yes/no/yes/no/yes
/no/yes/no/yes/no/yes/no/yes/no/yes/no/yes/no/y
es/no/yes/no/yes/no/yes/no/yes/no/yes/no/yes/no
/yes/no/yes/no/yes/no/yes/no/yes/no/yes/no/yes/
no/yes/no/yes/no/yes/no/yes/no/yes/no/yes/no/ye
s/no/yes/no/yes/no/yes/no/yes/no/yes/no/yes/no/
yes/no/yes/no/yes/no/yes/no/yes/no.yes/no/yes/n
o/yes//no/yes/no/yes/no/yes/no/yes/no/yes/no/ye
s/no/yes/no/yes/no/yes/no/yes/no/yes/no/yes/no/
yes/no/yes/no/yes/no/yes/no/yes/no/yes/no/yes/n
o/yes/no/yes/no/yes/no/yes/no/yes/no/yes/no/yes
/no/yes/no/yes/no/yes/no/yes/no/yes/no/yes/no/y
es/no/yes/no/yes/no/yes/no/yes/no/yes/no/yes/no
/yes/no/yes/no/yes/no/yes/no/yes/no/yes/no.yes/
no/yes/no/yes//no/yes/no/yes/no/yes/no/yes/no/y
es/no/yes/no/yes/no/yes/no/yes/no/yes/no/yes/no
/yes/no/yes/no/yes/no/yes/no/yes/no/yes/no/yes/
no/yes/no/yes/no/yes/no/yes/no/yes/no/yes/no/ye
s/no/yes/no/yes/no/yes/no/yes/no/yes/no/yes/no/
yes/no/yes/no/yes/no/yes/no/yes/no/yes/no/yes/n**

**o/yes/no/yes/no/yes/no/yes/no/yes/no/yes/no/yes
/no/yes/no/yes/no/yes/no/yes/no/yes/no/yes/no/y
es/no/yes/no/yes/no/yes/no/yes/no/yes/no/yes/no
/yes/no.yes/no/yes/no/yes//no/yes/no/yes/no/yes/
no/yes/no/yes/no/yes/no/yes/no/yes/no/yes/no/ye
s/no/yes/no/yes/no/yes/no/yes/no/yes/no/yes/no/
yes/no/yes/no/yes/no/yes/no/yes/no/yes/no/yes/n
o/yes/no/yes/no/yes/no/yes/no/yes/no/yes/no/yes
/no/yes/no/yes/no/yes/no/yes/no/yes/no/yes/no/y
es/no/yes/no/yes/no/yes/no/yes/no/yes/no/yes/no
/yes/no/yes/no.yes/no/yes/no/yes//no/yes/no/yes/
no/yes/no/yes/no/yes/no/yes/no/yes/no/yes/no/ye
s/no/yes/no/yes/no/yes/no/yes/no/yes/no/yes/no/
yes/no/yes/no/yes/no/yes/no/yes/no/yes/no/yes/n
o/yes/no/yes/no/yes/no/yes/no/yes/no/yes/no/yes
/no/yes/no/yes/no/yes/no/yes/no/yes/no/yes/no/y
es/no/yes/no/yes/no/yes/no/yes/no/yes/no/yes/no
/yes/no/yes/no/yes/no.yes/no/yes/no/yes//no/yes/
no/yes/no/yes/no/yes/no/yes/no/yes/no/yes/no/ye
s/no/yes/no/yes/no/yes/no/yes/no/yes/no/yes/no/
yes/no/yes/no/yes/no/yes/no/yes/no/yes/no/yes/n
o/yes/no/yes/no/yes/no/yes/no/yes/no/yes/no/yes
/no/yes/no/yes/no/yes/no/yes/no/yes/no/yes/no/y
es/no/yes/no/yes/no/yes/no/yes/no/yes/no/yes/no
/yes/no/yes/no/yes/no/yes/no.yes/no/yes/no/yes//
no/yes/no/yes/no/yes/no/yes/no/yes/no/yes/no/ye
s/no/yes/no/yes/no/yes/no/yes/no/yes/no/yes/no/
yes/no/yes/no/yes/no/yes/no/yes/no/yes/no/yes/n
o/yes/no/yes/no/yes/no/yes/no/yes/no/yes/no/yes
/no/yes/no/yes/no/yes/no/yes/no/yes/no/yes/no/y
es/no/yes/no/yes/no/yes/no/yes/no/yes/no/yes/no
/yes/no/yes/no/yes/no/yes/no/yes/no.yes/no/yes/**

no/yes//no/yes/no/yes/no/yes/no/yes/no/yes/no/y
es/no/yes/no/yes/no/yes/no/yes/no/yes/no/yes/no
/yes/no/yes/no/yes/no/yes/no/yes/no/yes/no/yes/
no/yes/no/yes/no/yes/no/yes/no/yes/no/yes/no/ye
s/no/yes/no/yes/no/yes/no/yes/no/yes/no/yes/no/
yes/no/yes/no/yes/no/yes/no/yes/no/yes/no/yes/n
o/yes/no/yes/no/yes/no/yes/no/yes/no/yes/no.yes
/no/yes/no/yes//no/yes/no/yes/no/yes/no/yes/no/
yes/no/yes/no/yes/no/yes/no/yes/no/yes/no/yes/n
o/yes/no/yes/no/yes/no/yes/no/yes/no/yes/no/yes
/no/yes/no/yes/no/yes/no/yes/no/yes/no/yes/no/y
es/no/yes/no/yes/no/yes/no/yes/no/yes/no/yes/no
/yes/no/yes/no/yes/no/yes/no/yes/no/yes/no/yes/
no/yes/no/yes/no/yes/no/yes/no/yes/no/yes/no/ye
s/no.yes/no/yes/no/yes//no/yes/no/yes/no/yes/no/
yes/no/yes/no/yes/no/yes/no/yes/no/yes/no/yes/n
o/yes/no/yes/no/yes/no/yes/no/yes/no/yes/no/yes
/no/yes/no/yes/no/yes/no/yes/no/yes/no/yes/no/y
es/no/yes/no/yes/no/yes/no/yes/no/yes/no/yes/no
/yes/no/yes/no/yes/no/yes/no/yes/no/yes/no/yes/
no/yes/no/yes/no/yes/no/yes/no/yes/no/yes/no/ye
s/no/yes/no.yes/no/yes/no/yes//no/yes/no/yes/no/
yes/no/yes/no/yes/no/yes/no/yes/no/yes/no/yes/n
o/yes/no/yes/no/yes/no/yes/no/yes/no/yes/no/yes
/no/yes/no/yes/no/yes/no/yes/no/yes/no/yes/no/y
es/no/yes/no/yes/no/yes/no/yes/no/yes/no/yes/no
/yes/no/yes/no/yes/no/yes/no/yes/no/yes/no/yes/
no/yes/no/yes/no/yes/no/yes/no/yes/no/yes/no/ye
s/no/yes/no/yes/no.yes/no/yes/no/yes/no/yes/no/
yes/no/yes/no/yes/no/yes/no/yes/no/yes/no/yes/n
o/yes/no/yes/no/yes/no/yes/no/yes/no/yes/no/yes
/no/yes/no/yes/no/yes/no/yes/no/yes/no/yes/no/y

**es/no/yes/no/yes/no/yes/no/yes/no/yes/no/yes/no
/yes/no/yes/no/yes/no/yes/no/yes/no/yes/no/yes/
no/yes/no/yes/no/yes/no/yes/no/yes/no/yes/no/ye
s/no/yes/no/yes/no/yes/no.yes/no/yes/no/yes//no/
yes/no/yes/no/yes/no/yes/no/yes/no/yes/no/yes/n
o/yes/no/yes/no/yes/no/yes/no/yes/no/yes/no/yes
/no/yes/no/yes/no/yes/no/yes/no/yes/no/yes/no/y
es/no/yes/no/yes/no/yes/no/yes/no/yes/no/yes/no
/yes/no/yes/no/yes/no/yes/no/yes/no/yes/no/yes/
no/yes/no/yes/no/yes/no/yes/no/yes/no/yes/no/ye
s/no/yes/no/yes/no/yes/no/yes/no.yes/no/yes/no/
yes//no/yes/no/yes/no/yes/no/yes/no/yes/no/yes/
no/yes/no/yes/no/yes/no/yes/no/yes/no/yes/no/ye
s/no/yes/no/yes/no/yes/no/yes/no/yes/no/yes/no/
yes/no/yes/no/yes/no/yes/no/yes/no/yes/no/yes/n
o/yes/no/yes/no/yes/no/yes/no/yes/no/yes/no/yes
/no/yes/no/yes/no/yes/no/yes/no/yes/no/yes/no/y
es/no/yes/no/yes/no/yes/no/yes/no/yes/no.yes/no
/yes/no/yes//no/yes/no/yes/no/yes/no/yes/no/yes/
no/yes/no/yes/no/yes/no/yes/no/yes/no/yes/no/ye
s/no/yes/no/yes/no/yes/no/yes/no/yes/no/yes/no/
yes/no/yes/no/yes/no/yes/no/yes/no/yes/no/yes/n
o/yes/no/yes/no/yes/no/yes/no/yes/no/yes/no/yes
/no/yes/no/yes/no/yes/no/yes/no/yes/no/yes/no/y
es/no/yes/no/yes/no/yes/no/yes/no/yes/no/yes/no
.yes/no/yes/no/yes//no/yes/no/yes/no/yes/no/yes/
no/yes/no/yes/no/yes/no/yes/no/yes/no/yes/no/ye
s/no/yes/no/yes/no/yes/no/yes/no/yes/no/yes/no/
yes/no/yes/no/yes/no/yes/no/yes/no/yes/no/yes/n
o/yes/no/yes/no/yes/no/yes/no/yes/no/yes/no/yes
/no/yes/no/yes/no/yes/no/yes/no/yes/no/yes/no/y
es/no/yes/no/yes/no/yes/no/yes/no/yes/no/yes/no**

/yes/no.yes/no/yes/no/yes//no/yes/maybe/baby/i/wave/at/you/maybe/baby/it/could/be/true.that/i/love/you!!!

!!!

!!!

!!!

!!!

!!!

!!!

!!!

!!!

!!!

!!!

!!!

!!!

!!!

!!!

!!!

!!!

!!!

!!!

**/yes/no/yes/no/yes/no/yes/no/yes/no/yes/no.yes/
no/yes/no/yes//no/yes/no/yes/no/yes/no/yes/no/y
es/no/yes/no/yes/no/yes/no/yes/no/yes/no/yes/no
/yes/no/yes/no/yes/no/yes/no/yes/no/yes/no/yes/
no/yes/no/yes/no/yes/no/yes/no/yes/no/yes/no/ye
s/no/yes/no/yes/no/yes/no/yes/no/yes/no/yes/no/
yes/no/yes/no/yes/no/yes/no/yes/no/yes/no/yes/n
o/yes/no/yes/no/yes/no/yes/no/yes/no/yes/no/yes
/no.yes/no/yes/no/yes//no/yes/no/yes/no/yes/no/
yes/no/yes/no/yes/no/yes/no/yes/no/yes/no/yes/n
o/yes/no/yes/no/yes/no/yes/no/yes/no/yes/no/yes
/no/yes/no/yes/no/yes/no/yes/no/yes/no/yes/no/y
es/no/yes/no/yes/no/yes/no/yes/no/yes/no/yes/no
/yes/no/yes/no/yes/no/yes/no/yes/no/yes/no/yes/
no/yes/no/yes/no/yes/no/yes/no/yes/no/yes/no/ye
s/no/yes/no.yes/no/yes/no/yes//no/yes/no/yes/no/
yes/no/yes/no/yes/no/yes/no/yes/no/yes/no/yes/n
o/yes/no/yes/no/yes/no/yes/no/yes/no/yes/no/yes
/no/yes/no/yes/no/yes/no/yes/no/yes/no/yes/no/y
es/no/yes/no/yes/no/yes/no/yes/no/yes/no/yes/no
/yes/no/yes/no/yes/no/yes/no/yes/no/yes/no/yes/
no/yes/no/yes/no/yes/no/yes/no/yes/no/yes/no/ye
s/no/yes/no/yes/no.yes/no/yes/no/yes//no/yes/no/
yes/no/yes/no/yes/no/yes/no/yes/no/yes/no/yes/n
o/yes/no/yes/no/yes/no/yes/no/yes/no/yes/no/yes
/no/yes/no/yes/no/yes/no/yes/no/yes/no/yes/no/y
es/no/yes/no/yes/no/yes/no/yes/no/yes/no/yes/no
/yes/no/yes/no/yes/no/yes/no/yes/no/yes/no/yes/
no/yes/no/yes/no/yes/no/yes/no/yes/no/yes/no/ye
s/no/yes/no/yes/no/yes/no/yes/no/yes/no/yes//no/
yes/no/yes/no/yes/no/yes/no/yes/no/yes/no/yes/n
o/yes/no/yes/no/yes/no/yes/no/yes/no/yes/no/yes**

**/no/yes/no/yes/no/yes/no/yes/no/yes/no/yes/no/y
es/no/yes/no/yes/no/yes/no/yes/no/yes/no/yes/no
/yes/no/yes/no/yes/no/yes/no/yes/no/yes/no/yes/
no/yes/no/yes/no/yes/no/yes/no/yes/no/yes/no/ye
s/no/yes/no/yes/no/yes/no/yes/no.yes/no/yes/no/
yes//no/yes/no/yes/no/yes/no/yes/no/yes/no/yes/
no/yes/no/yes/no/yes/no/yes/no/yes/no/yes/no/ye
s/no/yes/no/yes/no/yes/no/yes/no/yes/no/yes/no/
yes/no/yes/no/yes/no/yes/no/yes/no/yes/no/yes/n
o/yes/no/yes/no/yes/no/yes/no/yes/no/yes/no/yes
/no/yes/no/yes/no/yes/no/yes/no/yes/no/yes/no/y
es/no/yes/no/yes/no/yes/no/yes/no/yes/no.yes/no
/yes/no/yes//no/yes/no/yes/no/yes/no/yes/no/yes/
no/yes/no/yes/no/yes/no/yes/no/yes/no/yes/no/ye
s/no/yes/no/yes/no/yes/no/yes/no/yes/no/yes/no/
yes/no/yes/no/yes/no/yes/no/yes/no/yes/no/yes/n
o/yes/no/yes/no/yes/no/yes/no/yes/no/yes/no/yes
/no/yes/no/yes/no/yes/no/yes/no/yes/no/yes/no/y
es/no/yes/no/yes/no/yes/no/yes/no/yes/no/yes/no
.yes/no/yes/no/yes//no/yes/no/yes/no/yes/no/yes/
no/yes/no/yes/no/yes/no/yes/no/yes/no/yes/no/ye
s/no/yes/no/yes/no/yes/no/yes/no/yes/no/yes/no/
yes/no/yes/no/yes/no/yes/no/yes/no/yes/no/yes/n
o/yes/no/yes/no/yes/no/yes/no/yes/no/yes/no/yes
/no/yes/no/yes/no/yes/no/yes/no/yes/no/yes/no/y
es/no/yes/no/yes/no/yes/no/yes/no/yes/no/yes/no
/yes/no.yes/no/yes/no/yes//no/yes/no/yes/no/yes/
no/yes/no/yes/no/yes/no/yes/no/yes/no/yes/no/ye
s/no/yes/no/yes/no/yes/no/yes/no/yes/no/yes/no/
yes/no/yes/no/yes/no/yes/no/yes/no/yes/no/yes/n
o/yes/no/yes/no/yes/no/yes/no/yes/no/yes/no/yes
/no/yes/no/yes/no/yes/no/yes/no/yes/no/yes/no/y**

**es/no/yes/no/yes/no/yes/no/yes/no/yes/no/yes/no
/yes/no/yes/no.yes/no/yes/no/yes//no/yes/no/yes/
no/yes/no/yes/no/yes/no/yes/no/yes/no/yes/no/ye
s/no/yes/no/yes/no/yes/no/yes/no/yes/no/yes/no/
yes/no/yes/no/yes/no/yes/no/yes/no/yes/no/yes/n
o/yes/no/yes/no/yes/no/yes/no/yes/no/yes/no/yes
/no/yes/no/yes/no/yes/no/yes/no/yes/no/yes/no/y
es/no/yes/no/yes/no/yes/no/yes/no/yes/no/yes/no
/yes/no/yes/no/yes/no.yes/no/yes/no/yes//no/yes/
no/yes/no/yes/no/yes/no/yes/no/yes/no/yes/no/ye
s/no/yes/no/yes/no/yes/no/yes/no/yes/no/yes/no/
yes/no/yes/no/yes/no/yes/no/yes/no/yes/no/yes/n
o/yes/no/yes/no/yes/no/yes/no/yes/no/yes/no/yes
/no/yes/no/yes/no/yes/no/yes/no/yes/no/yes/no/y
es/no/yes/no/yes/no/yes/no/yes/no/yes/no/yes/no
/yes/no/yes/no/yes/no/yes/no.yes/no/yes/no/yes//
no/yes/no/yes/no/yes/no/yes/no/yes/no/yes/no/ye
s/no/yes/no/yes/no/yes/no/yes/no/yes/no/yes/no/
yes/no/yes/no/yes/no/yes/no/yes/no/yes/no/yes/n
o/yes/no/yes/no/yes/no/yes/no/yes/no/yes/no/yes
/no/yes/no/yes/no/yes/no/yes/no/yes/no/yes/no/y
es/no/yes/no/yes/no/yes/no/yes/no/yes/no/yes/no
/yes/no/yes/no/yes/no/yes/no/yes/no.yes/no/yes/
no/yes//no/yes/no/yes/no/yes/no/yes/no/yes/no/y
es/no/yes/no/yes/no/yes/no/yes/no/yes/no/yes/no
/yes/no/yes/no/yes/no/yes/no/yes/no/yes/no/yes/
no/yes/no/yes/no/yes/no/yes/no/yes/no/yes/no/ye
s/no/yes/no/yes/no/yes/no/yes/no/yes/no/yes/no/
yes/no/yes/no/yes/no/yes/no/yes/no/yes/no/yes/n
o/yes/o/yes/no/yes/no/yes/no/yes/no/yes/no.yes/
no/yes/no/yes//no/yes/no/yes/o/yes/no/yes/no/ye
s/no/yes/no/yes/no/yes/no/yes/no/yes/no/yes/no/**

**yes/no/yes/no/yes/no/yes/no/yes/no/yes/no/yes/n
o/yes/no/yes/no/yes/no/yes/no/yes/no/yes/no/yes
/no/yes/no/yes/no/yes/no/yes/no/yes/no/yes/no/y
es/no/yes/no/yes/no/yes/no/yes/no/yes/no/yes/no
/yes/no/yes/no/yes/no/yes/no/yes/no/yes/no/yes/
no.yes/no/yes/no/yes//no/yes/no/yes/no/yes/no/y
es/no/yes/no/yes/no/yes/no/yes/no/yes/no/yes/no
/yes/no/yes/no/yes/no/yes/no/yes/no/yes/no/yes/
no/yes/no/yes/no/yes/no/yes/no/yes/no/yes/no/ye
s/no/yes/no/yes/no/yes/no/yes/no/yes/no/yes/no/
yes/no/yes/no/yes/no/yes/no/yes/no/yes/no/yes/n
o/yes/no/yes/no/yes/no/yes/no/yes/no/yes/no/yes
/no/yes/no.yes/no/yes/no/yes//no/yes/no/yes/no/
yes/no/yes/no/yes/no/yes/no/yes/no/yes/no/yes/n
o/yes/no/yes/no/yes/no/yes/no/yes/no/yes/no/yes
/no/yes/no/yes/no/yes/no/yes/no/yes/no/yes/no/y
es/no/yes/no/yes/no/yes/no/yes/no/yes/no/yes/no
/yes/no/yes/no/yes/no/yes/no/yes/no/yes/no/yes/
no/yes/no/yes/no/yes/no/yes/no/yes/no/yes/no/ye
s/no/yes/no/yes/no.yes/no/yes/no/yes//no/yes/no/
yes/no/yes/no/yes/no/yes/no/yes/no/yes/no/yes/n
o/yes/no/yes/no/yes/no/yes/no/yes/no/yes/no/yes
/no/yes/no/yes/no/yes/no/yes/no/yes/no/yes/no/y
es/no/yes/no/yes/no/yes/no/yes/no/yes/no/yes/no
/yes/no/yes/no/yes/no/yes/no/yes/no/yes/no/yes/
no/yes/no/yes/no/yes/no/yes/no/yes/no/yes/no/ye
s/no/yes/no/yes/no/yes/no.yes/no/yes/no/yes//no/
yes/no/yes/no/yes/no/yes/no/yes/no/yes/no/yes/n
o/yes/no/yes/no/yes/no/yes/no/yes/no/yes/no/yes
/no/yes/no/yes/no/yes/no/yes/no/yes/no/yes/no/y
es/no/yes/no/yes/no/yes/no/yes/no/yes/no/yes/no
/yes/no/yes/no/yes/no/yes/no/yes/no/yes/no/yes/**

**no/yes/no/yes/no/yes/no/yes/no/yes/no/yes/no/ye
s/no/yes/no/yes/no/yes/no/yes/no.yes/no/yes/no/
yes//no/yes/no/yes/no/yes/no/yes/no/yes/no/yes/
no/yes/no/yes/no/yes/no/yes/no/yes/no/yes/no/ye
s/no/yes/no/yes/no/yes/no/yes/no/yes/no/yes/no/
yes/no/yes/no/yes/no/yes/no/yes/no/yes/no/yes/n
o/yes/no/yes/no/yes/no/yes/no/yes/no/yes/no/yes
/no/yes/no/yes/no/yes/no/yes/no/yes/no/yes/no/y
es/no/yes/no/yes/no/yes/no/yes/no/yes/no.yes/no
/yes/no/yes//no/yes/no/yes/no/yes/no/yes/no/yes/
no/yes/no/yes/no/yes/no/yes/no/yes/no/yes/no/ye
s/no/yes/no/yes/no/yes/no/yes/no/yes/no/yes/no/
yes/no/yes/no/yes/no/yes/no/yes/no/yes/no/yes/n
o/yes/no/yes/no/yes/no/yes/no/yes/no/yes/no/yes
/no/yes/no/yes/no/yes/no/yes/no/yes/no/yes/no/y
es/no/yes/no/yes/no/yes/no/yes/no/yes/no/yes/no
/yes/no/yes/no/yes//no/yes/no/yes/no/yes/no/yes/
no/yes/no/yes/no/yes/no/yes/no/yes/no/yes/no/ye
s/no/yes/no/yes/no/yes/no/yes/no/yes/no/yes/no/
yes/no/yes/no/yes/no/yes/no/yes/no/yes/no/yes/n
o/yes/no/yes/no/yes/no/yes/no/yes/no/yes/no/yes
/no/yes/no/yes/no/yes/no/yes/no/yes/no/yes/no/y
es/no/yes/no/yes/no/yes/no/yes/no/yes/no/yes/no
/yes/no.yes/no/ye/no/yes//no/yes/no/yes/no/yes/n
o/yes/no/yes/no/yes/no/yes/no/yes/no/yes/no/yes
/no/yes/no/yes/no/yes/no/yes/no/yes/no/yes/no/y
es/no/yes/no/yes/no/yes/no/yes/no/yes/no/yes/no
/yes/no/yes/no/yes/no/yes/no/yes/no/yes/no/yes/
no/yes/no/yes/no/yes/no/yes/no/yes/no/yes/no/ye
s/no/yes/no/yes/no/yes/no/yes/no/yes/no/yes/no/
yes/no/yes/no.yes/no/yes/no/yes//no/yes/no/yes/
no/yes/no/yes/no/yes/no/yes/no/yes/no/yes/no/ye**

**s/no/yes/no/yes/no/yes/no/yes/no/yes/no/yes/no/
yes/no/yes/no/yes/no/yes/no/yes/no/yes/no/yes/n
o/yes/no/yes/no/yes/no/yes/no/yes/no/yes/no/yes
/no/yes/no/yes/no/yes/no/yes/no/yes/no/yes/no/y
es/no/yes/no/yes/no/yes/no/yes/no/yes/no/yes/no
/yes/no/yes/no/yes/no.yes/no/yes/no/yes//no/yes/
no/yes/no/yes/no/yes/no/yes/no/yes/no/yes/no/ye
s/no/yes/no/yes/no/yes/no/yes/no/yes/no/yes/no/
yes/no/yes/no/yes/no/yes/no/yes/no/yes/no/yes/n
o/yes/no/yes/no/yes/no/yes/no/yes/no/yes/no/yes
/no/yes/no/yes/no/yes/no/yes/no/yes/no/yes/no/y
es/no/yes/no/yes/no/yes/no/yes/no/yes/no/yes/no
/yes/no/yes/no/yes/no/yes/no.yes/no/yes/no/yes//
no/yes/no/yes/no/yes/no/yes/no/yes/no/yes/no/ye
s/no/yes/no/yes/no/yes/no/yes/no/yes/no/yes/no/
yes/no/yes/no/yes/no/yes/no/yes/no/yes/no/yes/n
o/yes/no/yes/no/yes/no/yes/no/yes/no/yes/no/yes
/no/yes/no/yes/no/yes/no/yes/no/yes/no/yes/no/y
es/no/yes/no/yes/no/yes/no/yes/no/yes/no/yes/no
/yes/no/yes/no/yes/no/yes/no/yes/no.yes/no/yes/
no/yes//no/yes/no/yes/no/yes/no/yes/no/yes/no/y
es/no/yes/no/yes/no/yes/no/yes/no/yes/no/yes/no
/yes/no/yes/no/yes/no/yes/no/yes/no/yes/no/yes/
no/yes/no/yes/no/yes/no/yes/no/yes/no/yes/no/ye
s/no/yes/no/yes/no/yes/no/yes/no/yes/no/yes/no/
yes/no/yes/no/yes/no/yes/no/yes/no/yes/no/yes/n
o/yes/no/yes/no/yes/no/yes/no/yes/no/yes/no.yes
/no/yes/no/yes//no/yes/no/yes/no/yes/no/yes/no/
yes/no/yes/no/yes/no/yes/no/yes/no/yes/no/yes/n
o/yes/no/yes/no/yes/no/yes/no/yes/no/yes/no/yes
/no/yes/no/yes/no/yes/no/yes/no/yes/no/yes/no/y
es/no/yes/no/yes/no/yes/no/yes/no/yes/no/yes/no**

**/yes/no/yes/no/yes/no/yes/no/yes/no/yes/no/yes/
no/yes/no/yes/no/yes/no/yes/no/yes/no/yes/no/ye
s/no.yes/no/yes/no/yes/no/yes/no/yes/no/yes/no/
yes/no/yes/no/yes/no/yes/no/yes/no/yes/no/yes/n
o/yes/no/yes/no/yes/no/yes/no/yes/no/yes/no/yes
/no/yes/no/yes/no/yes/no/yes/no/yes/no/yes/no/y
es/no/yes/no/yes/no/yes/no/yes/no/yes/no/yes/no
/yes/no/yes/no/yes/no/yes/no/yes/no/yes/no/yes/
no/yes/no/yes/no/yes/no/yes/no/yes/no/yes/no/ye
s/no/yes/no.yes/no/yes/no/yes//no/yes/no/yes/no/
yes/no/yes/no/yes/no/yes/no/yes/no/yes/no/yes/n
o/yes/no/yes/no/yes/no/yes/no/yes/no/yes/no/yes
/no/yes/no/yes/no/yes/no/yes/no/yes/no/yes/no/y
es/no/yes/no/yes/no/yes/no/yes/no/yes/no/yes/no
/yes/no/yes/no/yes/no/yes/no/yes/no/yes/no/yes/
no/yes/no/yes/no/yes/no/yes/no/yes/no/yes/no/ye
s/no/yes/no/yes/no.yes/no/yes/no/yes//no/yes/no/
yes/no/yes/no/yes/no/yes/no/yes/no/yes/no/yes/n
o/yes/no/yes/no/yes/no/yes/no/yes/no/yes/no/yes
/no/yes/no/yes/no/yes/no/yes/no/yes/no/yes/no/y
es/no/yes/no/yes/no/yes/no/yes/no/yes/no/yes/no
/yes/no/yes/no/yes/no/yes/no/yes/no/yes/no/yes/
no/yes/no/yes/no/yes/no/yes/no/yes/no/yes/no/ye
s/no/yes/no/yes/no/yes/no.yes/no/yes/no/yes//no/
yes/no/yes/no/yes/no/yes/no/yes/no/yes/no/yes/n
o/yes/no/yes/no/yes/no/yes/no/yes/no/yes/no/yes
/no/yes/no/yes/no/yes/no/yes/no/yes/no/yes/no/y
es/no/yes/no/yes/no/yes/no/yes/no/yes/no/yes/no
/yes/no/yes/no/yes/no/yes/no/yes/no/yes/no/yes/
no/yes/no/yes/no/yes/no/yes/no/yes/no/yes/no/ye
s/no/yes/no/yes/no/yes/no/yes/no/yes/no/yes/no/
yes//no/yes/no/yes/no/yes/no/yes/no/yes/no/yes/**

**no/yes/no/yes/no/yes/no/yes/no/yes/no/yes/no/ye
s/no/yes/no/yes/no/yes/no/yes/no/yes/no/yes/no/
yes/no/yes/no/yes/no/yes/no/yes/no/yes/no/yes/n
o/yes/no/yes/no/yes/no/yes/no/yes/no/yes/no/yes
/no/yes/no/yes/no/yes/no/yes/no/yes/no/yes/no/y
es/no/yes/no/yes/no/yes/no/yes/no/yes/no.yes/no
/yes/no/yes//no/yes/no/yes/no/yes/no/yes/no/yes/
no/yes/no/yes/no/yes/no/yes/no/yes/no/yes/no/ye
s/no/yes/no/yes/no/yes/no/yes/no/yes/no/yes/no/
yes/no/yes/no/yes/no/yes/no/yes/no/yes/no/yes/n
o/yes/no/yes/no/yes/no/yes/no/yes/no/yes/no/yes
/no/yes/no/yes/no/yes/no/yes/no/yes/no/yes/no/y
es/no/yes/no/yes/no/yes/no/yes/no/yes/no/yes/no
.yes/no/yes/no/yes//no/yes/no/yes/no/yes/no/yes/
no/yes/no/yes/no/yes/no/yes/no/yes/no/yes/no/ye
s/no/yes/no/yes/no/yes/no/yes/no/yes/no/yes/no/
yes/no/yes/no/yes/no/yes/no/yes/no/yes/no/yes/n
o/yes/no/yes/no/yes/no/yes/no/yes/no/yes/no/yes
/no/yes/no/yes/no/yes/no/yes/no/yes/no/yes/no/y
es/no/yes/no/yes/no/yes/no/yes/no/yes/no/yes/no
/yes/no.yes/no/yes/no/yes//no/yes/o/yes/no/yes/n
o/yes/no/yes/no/yes/no/yes/no/yes/no/yes/no/yes
/no/yes/no/yes/no/yes/no/yes/no/yes/no/yes/no/y
es/no/yes/no/yes/no/yes/no/yes/no/yes/no/yes/no
/yes/no/yes/no/yes/no/yes/no/yes/no/yes/no/yes/
no/yes/no/yes/no/yes/no/yes/no/yes/no/yes/no/ye
s/no/yes/no/yes/no/yes/no/yes/no/yes/no/yes/no/
yes/no/yes/no.yes/no/yes/no/yes//no/yes/no/yes/
no/yes/no/yes/no/yes/no/yes/no/yes/no/yes/no/ye
s/no/yes/no/yes/no/yes/no/yes/no/yes/no/yes/no/
yes/no/yes/no/yes/no/yes/no/yes/no/yes/no/yes/n
o/yes/no/yes/no/yes/no/yes/no/yes/no/yes/no/yes**

**/no/yes/no/yes/no/yes/no/yes/no/yes/no/yes/no/y
es/no/yes/no/yes/no/yes/no/yes/no/yes/no/yes/no
/yes/no/yes/no/yes/no.yes/no/yes/no/yes//no/yes/
no/yes/no/yes/no/yes/no/yes/no/yes/no/yes/no/ye
s/no/yes/no/yes/no/yes/no/yes/no/yes/no/yes/no/
yes/no/yes/no/yes/no/yes/no/yes/no/yes/no/yes/n
o/yes/no/yes/no/yes/no/yes/no/yes/no/yes/no/yes
/no/yes/no/yes/no/yes/no/yes/no/yes/no/yes/no/y
es/no/yes/no/yes/no/yes/no/yes/no/yes/no/yes/no
/yes/no/yes/no/yes/no/yes/no.yes/no/yes/no/yes//
no/yes/no/yes/no/yes/no/yes/no/yes/no/yes/no/ye
s/no/yes/no/yes/no/yes/no/yes/no/yes/no/yes/no/
yes/no/yes/no/yes/no/yes/no/yes/no/yes/no/yes/n
o/yes/no/yes/no/yes/no/yes/no/yes/no/yes/no/yes
/no/yes/no/yes/no/yes/no/yes/no/yes/no/yes/no/y
es/no/yes/no/yes/no/yes/no/yes/no/yes/no/yes/no
/yes/no/yes/no/yes/no/yes/no/yes/no.yes/no/yes/
no/yes//no/yes/no/yes/no/yes/no/yes/no/yes/no/y
es/no/yes/no/yes/no/yes/no/yes/no/yes/no/yes/no
/yes/no/yes/no/yes/no/yes/no/yes/no/yes/no/yes/
no/yes/no/yes/no/yes/no/yes/no/yes/no/yes/no/ye
s/no/yes/no/yes/no/yes/no/yes/no/yes/no/yes/no/
yes/no/yes/no/yes/no/yes/no/yes/no/yes/no/yes/n
o/yes/no/yes/no/yes/no/yes/no/yes/no/yes/no.yes
/no/yes/no/yes/yes/no/yes/no/yes/no/yes/no/yes/
no/yes/no/yes/no/yes/no/yes/no/yes/no/yes/no/ye
s/no/yes/no/yes/no/yes/no/yes/no/yes/no.yes/no/
yes/no/yes//no/yes/no/yes/no/yes/no/yes/no/yes/
no/yes/no/yes/no/yes/no/yes/no/yes/no/yes/no/ye
s/no/yes/no/yes/no/yes/no/yes/no/yes/no/yes/no/
yes/no/yes/no/yes/no/yes/no/yes/no/yes/no/yes/n
o/yes/no/yes/no/yes/no/yes/no/yes/no/yes/no/yes**

**/no/yes/no/yes/no/yes/no/yes/no/yes/no/yes/no/y
es/no/yes/no/yes/no/yes/no/yes/no/yes/no/yes/no
.yes/no/yes/no/yes/No/yes/no/yes/no/yes/no/yes/
no/yes/no/yes/no/yes/no/yes/no/yes/no/yes/no/ye
s/no/yes/no/yes/no/yes/no/yes/no/yes/no/yes/no/
yes/no/yes/no/yes/no/yes/no/yes/no/yes/no/yes/n
o/yes/no/yes/no/yes/no/yes/no/yes/no/yes/no/yes
/no/yes/no/yes/no/yes/no/yes/no/yes/no/yes/no/y
es/no/yes/no/yes
/no/yes/no/yes/no/yes/no/yes/no/yes/no/yes/no.y
es/no/yes/no/yes//no/yes/no/yes/no/yes/no/yes/n
o/yes/no/yes/no/yes/no/yes/no/yes/no/yes/no/yes
/no/yes/no/yes/no/yes/no/yes/no/yes/no/yes/no/y
es/no/yes/no/yes/no/yes/no/yes/no/yes/no/yes/no
/yes/no/yes/no/yes/no/yes/no/yes/no/yes/no/ye
s/no/yes/no/yes/no/yes/no/yes/no/yes/no/yes/no/
yes/no/yes/no/yes/no/yes/no/yes/no/yes/no/yes/n
o/yes/no.yes/no/yes/no/yes//no/yes/no/yes/no/ye
s/no/yes/no/yes/no/yes/no/yes/no/yes/no/yes/no/
yes/no/yes/no/yes/no/yes/no/yes/no/yes/no/yes/n
o/yes/no/yes/no/yes/no/yes/no/yes/no/yes/no/y
es/no/yes/no/yes/no/yes/no/yes/no/yes/no/yes/no
/yes/no/yes/no/yes/no/yes/no/yes/no/yes/no/yes/
no/yes/no/yes/no/yes/no/yes/no/yes/no/yes/no/ye
s/no/yes/no/yes/no.yes/no/yes/no/yes//no/yes/no/
yes/no/yes/no/yes/no/yes/no/yes/no/yes/no/yes/n
o/yes/no/yes/no/yes/no/yes/no/yes/no/yes/no/yes
/no/yes/no/yes/no/yes/no/yes/no/yes/no/yes/no/y
es/no/yes/no/yes/no/yes/no/yes/no/yes/no/yes/no
/yes/no/yes/no/yes/no/yes/no/yes/no/yes/no/yes/
no/yes/no/yes/no/yes/no/yes/no/yes/no/yes/no/ye
s/no/yes/no/yes/no/yes/no.yes/no/yes/no/yes//no/**

**yes/no/yes/no/yes/no/yes/no/yes/no/yes/no/yes/n
o/yes/no/yes/no/yes/no/yes/no/yes/no/yes/no/yes
/no/yes/no/yes/no/yes/no/yes/no/yes/no/yes/no/y
es/no/yes/no/yes/no/yes/no/yes/no/yes/no/yes/no
/yes/no/yes/no/yes/no/yes/no/yes/no/yes/no/yes/
no/yes/no/yes/no/yes/no/yes/no/yes/no/yes/no/ye
s/no/yes/no/yes/no/yes/no/yes/no/yes/no/yes/no/
yes/no/yes/no/yes/no.yes/no/yes/no/yes//no/yes/
no/ys/no/yes/no/yes/no/yes/no/yes/no/yes/no/yes
/no/yes/no/yes/no/yes/no/yes/no/yes/no/yes/no/y
es/no/yes/no/yes/no/yes/no/yes/no/yes/no/yes/no
/yes/no/yes/no/yes/no/yes/no/yes/no/yes/no/yes/
no/yes/no/yes/no/yes/o/yes/no/yes/no/yes/no/yes
/no/yes/no/yes/no/yes/no/yes/no/yes/no/yes/no/y
es/no/yes/no/yes/no/yes/no.yes/no/yes/no/yes//n
o/yes/no/yes/no/yes/no/yes/no/yes/no/yes/no/yes
/no/yes/no/yes/no/yes/no/yes/no/yes/no/yes/no/y
es/no/yes/no/yes/no/yes/no/yes/no/yes/no/yes/no
/yes/no/yes/no/yes/no/yes/no/yes/no/yes/no/yes/
no/yes/no/yes/no/yes/no/yes/no/yes/no/yes/no/ye
s/no/yes/no/yes/no/yes/no/yes/no/yes/no/yes/no/
yes/no/yes/no/yes/no/yes/no/yes/no.yes/no/yes/n
o/yes//no/yes/no/yes/no/yes/no/yes/no/yes/no/ye
s/no/yes/no/yes/no/yes/no/yes/no/yes/no/yes/no/
yes/no/yes/no/yes/no/yes/no/yes/no/yes/no/yes/n
o/yes/no/yes/no/yes/no/yes/no/yes/no/yes/no/yes
/no/yes/no/yes/no/yes/no/yes/no/yes/no/yes/no/y
es/no/yes/no/yes/no/yes/no/yes/no/yes/no/yes/no
/yes/no/yes/no/yes/no/yes/no/yes/no/yes/no.yes/
no/yes/no/yes//no/yes/no/yes/no/yes/no/yes/no/y
es/no/yes/no/yes/no/yes/no/yes/no/yes/no/yes/no
/yes/no/yes/no/yes/no/yes/no/yes/no/yes/no/yes/**

**no/yes/no/yes/no/yes/no/yes/no/yes/no/yes/no/ye
s/no/yes/no/yes/no/yes/no/yes/no/yes/no/yes/no/
yes/no/yes/no/yes/no/yes/no/yes/no/yes/no/yes/n
o/yes/no/yes/no/yes/no/yes/no/yes/no/yes/no/yes
/no/yes/no/yes/no/yes/no/yes/no/yes/no/yes/no/y
es/no/yes/no/yes/no/yes/no/yes/no/yes/no/yes/no
/yes/no.yes/no/yes/no/yes//no/yes/no/yes/no/yes/
no/yes/no/yes/no/yes/no/yes/no/yes/no/yes/no/ye
s/no/yes/no/yes/no/yes/no/yes/no/yes/no/yes/no/
yes/no/yes/no/yes/no/yes/no/yes/no/yes/no/yes/n
o/yes/no/yes/no/yes/no/yes/no/yes/no/yes/no/yes
/no/yes/no/yes/no/yes/no/yes/no/yes/no/yes/no/y
es/no/yes/no/yes/no/yes/no/yes/no/yes/no/yes/no
/yes/no/yes/no.yes/no/yes/no/yes//no/yes/no/yes/
no/yes/no/yes/no/yes/no/yes/no/yes/no/yes/no/ye
s/no/yes/no/yes/no/yes/no/yes/no/yes/no/yes/no/
yes/no/yes/no/yes/no/yes/no/yes/no/yes/no/yes/n
o/yes/no/yes/no/yes/no/yes/no/yes/no/yes/no/yes
/no/yes/no/yes/no/yes/no/yes/no/yes/no/yes/no/y
es/no/yes/no/yes/no/yes/no/yes/no/yes/no/yes/no
/yes/no/yes/no/yes/no.yes/no/yes/no/yes//no/yes/
no/yes/no/yes/no/yes/no/yes/no/yes/no/yes/no/ye
s/no/yes/no/yes/no/yes/no/yes/no/yes/no/yes/no/
yes/no/yes/no/yes/no/yes/no/yes/no/yes/no/yes/n
o/yes/no/yes/no/yes/no/yes/no/yes/no/yes/no/yes
/no/yes/no/yes/no/yes/no/yes/no/yes/no/yes/no/y
es/no/yes/no/yes/no/yes/no/yes/no/yes/no/yes/no
/yes/no/yes/no/yes/no/yes/no.yes/no/yes/no/yes//
no/yes/no/yes/no/yes/no/yes/no/yes/no/yes/no/ye
s/no/yes/no/yes/no/yes/no/yes/no/yes/no/yes/no/
yes/no/yes/no/yes/no/yes/no/yes/no/yes/no/yes/n
o/yes/no/yes/no/yes/no/yes/no/yes/no/yes/no/yes**

**/no/yes/no/yes/no/yes/no/yes/no/yes/no/yes/no/y
es/no/yes/no/yes/no/yes/no/yes/no/yes/no/yes/no
/yes/no/yes/no/yes/no/yes/no/yes/no.yes/no/yes/
no/yes//no/yes/no/yes/no/yes/no/yes/no/yes/no/y
es/no/yes/no/yes/no/yes/no/yes/no/yes/no/yes/no
/yes/no/yes/no/yes/no/yes/no/yes/no/yes/no/yes/
no/yes/no/yes/no/yes/no/yes/no/yes/no/yes/no/ye
s/no/yes/no/yes/no/yes/no/yes/no/yes/no/yes/no/
yes/no/yes/no/yes/no/yes/no/yes/no/yes/no/yes/n
o/yes/no/yes/no/yes/no/yes/no/yes/no/yes/no.yes
/no/yes/no/yes//no/yes/no/yes/no/yes/no/yes/no/
yes/no/yes/no/yes/no/yes/no/yes/no/yes/no/yes/n
o/yes/no/yes/no/yes/no/yes/no/yes/no/yes/no/yes
/no/yes/no/yes/no/yes/no/yes/no/yes/no/yes/no/y
es/no/yes/no/yes/no/yes/no/yes/no/yes/no/yes/no
/yes/no/yes/no/yes/no/yes/no/yes/no/yes/no/yes/
no/yes/no/yes/no/yes/no/yes/no/yes/no/yes/no/ye
s/no.yes/no/yes/no/yes//no/yes/no/yes/no/yes/no/
yes/no/yes/no/yes/no/yes/no/yes/no/yes/no/yes/n
o/yes/no/yes/no/yes/no/yes/no/yes/no/yes/no/yes
/no/yes/no/yes/no/yes/no/yes/no/yes/no/yes/no/y
es/no/yes/no/yes/no/yes/no/yes/no/yes/no/yes/no
/yes/no/yes/no/yes/no/yes/no/yes/no/yes/no/yes/
no/yes/no/yes/no/yes/no/yes/no/yes/no/yes/no/ye
s/no/yes/no.yes/no/yes/no/yes//no/yes/no/yes/no/
yes/no/yes/no/yes/no/yes/no/yes/no/yes/no/yes/n
o/yes/no/yes/no/yes/no/yes/no/yes/no/yes/no/yes
/no/yes/no/yes/no/yes/no/yes/no/yes/no/yes/no/y
es/no/yes/no/yes/no/yes/no/yes/no/yes/no/yes/no
/yes/no/yes/no/yes/no/yes/no/yes/no/yes/no/yes/
no/yes/no/yes/no/yes/no/yes/no/yes/no/yes/no/ye
s/no/yes/no/yes/no.yes/no/yes/no/yes/no/yes/no/**

**yes/no/yes/no/yes/no/yes/no/yes/no/yes/no/yes/n
o/yes/no/yes/no/yes/no/yes/no/yes/no/yes/no/yes
/no/yes/no/yes/no/yes/no/yes/no/yes/no/yes/no/y
es/no/yes/no/yes/no/yes/no/yes/no/yes/no/yes/no
/yes/no/yes/no/yes/no/yes/no/yes/no/yes/no/yes/
no/yes/no/yes/no/yes/no/yes/no/yes/no/yes/no/ye
s/no/yes/no/yes/no/yes/no.yes/no/yes/no/yes//no/
yes/no/yes/no/yes/no/yes/no/yes/no/yes/no/yes/n
o/yes/no/yes/no/yes/no/yes/no/yes/no/yes/no/yes
/no/yes/no/yes/no/yes/no/yes/no/yes/no/yes/no/y
es/no/yes/no/yes/no/yes/no/yes/no/yes/no/yes/no
/yes/no/yes/no/yes/no/yes/no/yes/no/yes/no/yes/
no/yes/no/yes/no/yes/no/yes/no/yes/no/yes/no/ye
s/no/yes/no/yes/no/yes/no/yes/no.yes/no/yes/no/
yes//no/yes/no/yes/no/yes/no/yes/no/yes/no/yes/
no/yes/no/yes/no/yes/no/yes/no/yes/no/yes/no/ye
s/no/yes/no/yes/no/yes/no/yes/no/yes/no/yes/no/
yes/no/yes/no/yes/no/yes/no/yes/no/yes/no/yes/n
o/yes/no/yes/no/yes/no/yes/no/yes/no/yes/no/yes
/no/yes/no/yes/no/yes/no/yes/no/yes/no/yes/no/y
es/no/yes/no/yes/no/yes/no/yes/no/yes/no.yes/no
/yes/no/yes//no/yes/no/yes/no/yes/no/yes/no/yes/
no/yes/no/yes/no/yes/no/yes/no/yes/no/yes/no/ye
s/no/yes/no/yes/no/yes/no/yes/no/yes/no/yes/no/
yes/no/yes/no/yes/no/yes/no/yes/no/yes/no/yes/n
o/yes/no/yes/no/yes/no/yes/no/yes/no/yes/no/yes
/no/yes/no/yes/no/yes/no/yes/no/yes/no/yes/no/y
es/no/yes/no/yes/no/yes/no/yes/no/yes/no/yes/no
.yes/no/yes/no/yes//no/yes/no/yes/no/yes/no/yes/
no/yes/no/yes/no/yes/no/yes/no/yes/no/yes/no/ye
s/no/yes/no/yes/no/yes/no/yes/no/yes/no/yes/no/
yes/no/yes/no/yes/no/yes/no/yes/no/yes/no/yes/n**

o/yes/no/yes/no/yes/no/yes/no/yes/no/yes/no/yes
/no/yes/no/yes/no/yes/no/yes/no/yes/no/yes/no/y
es/no/yes/no/yes/no/yes/no/yes/no/yes/no/yes/no
/yes/no.yes/no/yes/no/yes//no/yes/no/yes/no/yes/
no/yes/no/yes/no/yes/no/yes/no/yes/no/yes/no/ye
s/no/yes/no/yes/no/yes/no/yes/no/yes/no/yes/no/
yes/no/yes/no/yes/no/yes/no/yes/no/yes/no/yes/n
o/yes/no/yes/no/yes/no/yes/no/yes/no/yes/no/yes
/no/yes/no/yes/no/yes/no/yes/no/yes/no/yes/no/y
es/no/yes/no/yes/no/yes/no/yes/no/yes/no/yes/no
/yes/no/yes/no.yes/no/yes/no/yes//no/yes/no/yes/
no/yes/no/yes/no/yes/no/yes/no/yes/no/yes/no/ye
s/no/yes/no/yes/no/yes/no/yes/no/yes/no/yes/no/
yes/no/yes/no/yes/no/yes/no/yes/no/yes/no/yes/n
o/yes/no/yes/no/yes/no/yes/no/yes/no/yes/no/yes
/no/yes/no/yes/no/yes/no/yes/no/yes/no/yes/no/y
es/no/yes/no/yes/no/yes/no/yes/no/yes/no/yes/no
/yes/no/yes/no/yes/no.yes/no/yes/no/yes//no/yes/
no/yes/no/yes/no/yes/no/yes/no/yes/no/yes/no/ye
s/no/yes/no/yes/no/yes/no/yes/no/yes/no/yes/no/
yes/no/yes/no/yes/no/yes/no/yes/no/yes/no/yes/n
o/yes/no/yes/no/yes/no/yes/no/yes/no/yes/no/yes
/no/yes/no/yes/no/yes/no/yes/no/yes/no/yes/no/y
es/no/yes/no/yes/no/yes/no/yes/no/yes/no/yes/no
/yes/no/yes/no/yes/no/yes/no.yes/no/yes/no/yes//
no/yes/no/yes/no/yes/no/yes/no/yes/no/yes/no/ye
s/no/yes/no/yes/no/yes/no/yes/no/yes/no/yes/no/
yes/no/yes/no/yes/no/yes/no/yes/no/yes/no/yes/n
o/yes/no/yes/no/yes/no/yes/no/yes/no/yes/no/yes
/no/yes/no/yes/no/yes/no/yes/no/yes/no/yes/no/y
es/no/yes/no/yes/no/yes/no/yes/no/yes/no/yes/no
/yes/no/yes/no/yes/no/yes/no/yes/no.yes/no/yes/

no/yes//no/yes/no/yes/no/yes/no/yes/no/yes/no/y
es/no/yes/no/yes/no/yes/no/yes/no/yes/no/yes/no
/yes/no/yes/no/yes/no/yes/no/yes/no/yes/no/yes/
no/yes/no/yes/no/yes/no/yes/no/yes/no/yes/no/ye
s/no/yes/no/yes/no/yes/no/yes/no/yes/no/yes/no/
yes/no/yes/no/yes/no/yes/no/yes/no/yes/no/yes/n
o/yes/no/yes/no/yes/no/yes/no/yes/no/yes/no/yes
/no/yes/no/yes//no/yes/no/yes/no/yes/no/yes/no/
yes/no/yes/no/yes/no/yes/no/yes/no/yes/no/yes/n
o/yes/no/yes/no/yes/no/yes/no/yes/no/yes/no/yes
/no/yes/no/yes/no/yes/no/yes/no/yes/no/yes/no/y
es/no/yes/no/yes/no/yes/no/yes/no/yes/no/yes/no
/yes/no/yes/no/yes/no/yes/no/yes/no/yes/no/yes/
no/yes/no/yes/no/yes/no/yes/no/yes/no/yes/no/ye
s/no.yes/no/yes/no/yes//no/yes/no/yes/no/yes/no/
yes/no/yes/no/yes/no/yes/no/yes/no/yes/no/yes/n
o/yes/no/yes/no/yes/no/yes/no/yes/no/yes/no/yes
/no/yes/no/yes/no/yes/no/yes/no/yes/no/yes/no/y
es/no/yes/no/yes/no/yes/no/yes/no/yes/no/yes/no
/yes/no/yes/no/yes/no/yes/no/yes/no/yes/no/yes/
no/yes/no/yes/no/yes/no/yes/no/yes/no/yes/no/ye
s/no/yes/no.yes/no/yes/no/yes//no/yes/no/yes/no/
yes/no/yes/no/yes/no/yes/no/yes/no/yes/no/yes/n
o/yes/no/yes/no/yes/no/yes/no/yes/no/yes/no/yes
/no/yes/no/yes/no/yes/no/yes/no/yes/no/yes/no/y
es/no/yes/no/yes/no/yes/no/yes/no/yes/no/yes/no
/yes/no/yes/no/yes/no/yes/no/yes/no/yes/no/yes/
no/yes/no/yes/no/yes/no/yes/no/yes/no/yes/no/ye
s/no/yes/no/yes/no.yes/no/yes/no/yes//no/yes/no/
yes/no/yes/no/yes/no/yes/no/yes/no/yes/no/yes/n
o/yes/no/yes/no/yes/no/yes/no/yes/no/yes/no/yes
/no/yes/no/yes/no/yes/no/yes/no/yes/no/yes/no/y

**es/no/yes/no/yes/no/yes/no/yes/no/yes/no/yes/no
/yes/no/yes/no/yes/no/yes/no/yes/no/yes/no/yes/
no/yes/no/yes/no/yes/no/yes/no/yes/no/yes/no/ye
s/no/yes/no/yes/no/yes/no.yes/no/yes/no/yes//no/
yes/no/yes/no/yes/no/yes/no/yes/no/yes/no/yes/n
o/yes/no/yes/no/yes/no/yes/no/yes/no/yes/no/yes
/no/yes/no/yes/no/yes/no/yes/no/yes/no/yes/no/y
es/no/yes/no/yes/no/yes/no/yes/no/yes/no/yes/no
/yes/no/yes/no/yes/no/yes/no/yes/no/yes/no/yes/
no/yes/no/yes/no/yes/no/yes/no/yes/no/yes/no/ye
s/no/yes/no/yes/no/yes/no/yes/no.yes/no/yes/no/
yes//no/yes/no/yes/no/yes/no/yes/no/yes/no/yes/
no/yes/no/yes/no/yes/no/yes/no/yes/no/yes/no/ye
s/no/yes/no/yes/no/yes/no/yes/no/yes/no/yes/no/
yes/no/yes/no/yes/no/yes/no/yes/no/yes/no/yes/n
o/yes/no/yes/no/yes/no/yes/no/yes/no/yes/no/yes
/no/yes/no/yes/no/yes/no/yes/no/yes/no/yes/no/y
es/no/yes/no/yes/no/yes/no/yes/no/yes/no.yes/no
/yes/no/yes//no/yes/no/yes/no/yes/no/yes/no/yes/
no/yes/no/yes/no/yes/no/yes/no/yes/no/yes/no/ye
s/no/yes/no/yes/no/yes/no/yes/no/yes/no/yes/no/
yes/no/yes/no/yes/no/yes/no/yes/no/yes/no/yes/n
o/yes/no/yes/no/yes/no/yes/no/yes/no/yes/no/yes
/no/yes/no/yes/no/yes/no/yes/no/yes/no/yes/no/y
es/no/yes/no/yes/no/yes/no/yes/no/yes/no/yes/no
.yes/no/yes/no/yes//no/yes/no/yes/no/yes/no/yes/
no/yes/no/yes/no/yes/no/yes/no/yes/no/yes/no/ye
s/no/yes/no/yes/no/yes/no/yes/no/yes/no/yes/no/
yes/no/yes/no/yes/no/yes/no/yes/no/yes/no/yes/n
o/yes/no/yes/no/yes/no/yes/no/yes/no/yes/no/yes
/no/yes/no/yes/no/yes/no/yes/no/yes/no/yes/no/y
es/no/yes/no/yes/no/yes/no/yes/no/yes/no/yes/no**

**/yes/no.yes/no/yes/no/yes//no/yes/no/yes/no/yes/
no/yes/no/yes/no/yes/no/yes/no/yes/no/yes/no/ye
s/no/yes/no/yes/no/yes/no/yes/no/yes/no/yes/no/
yes/no/yes/no/yes/no/yes/no/yes/no/yes/no/yes/n
o/yes/no/yes/no/yes/no/yes/no/yes/no/yes/no/yes
/no/yes/no/yes/no/yes/no/yes/no/yes/no/yes/no/y
es/no/yes/no/yes/no/yes/o/yes/no/yes/no/yes/no/
yes/no/yes/no.yes/no/yes/no/yes//no/yes/no/yes/
o/yes/no/yes/no/yes/no/yes/no/yes/no/yes/no/yes
/no/yes/no/yes/no/yes/no/yes/no/yes/no/yes/no/y
es/no/yes/no/yes/no/yes/no/yes/no/yes/no/yes/no
/yes/no/yes/no/yes/no/yes/no/yes/no/yes/no/yes/
no/yes/no/yes/no/yes/no/yes/no/yes/no/yes/no/ye
s/no/yes/no/yes/no/yes/no/yes/no/yes/no/yes/no/
yes/no/yes/no/yes/no.yes/no/yes/no/yes//no/yes/
no/yes/no/yes/no/yes/no/yes/no/yes/no/yes/no/ye
s/no/yes/no/yes/no/yes/no/yes/no/yes/no/yes/no/
yes/no/yes/no/yes/no/yes/no/yes/no/yes/no/yes/n
o/yes/no/yes/no/yes/no/yes/no/yes/no/yes/no/yes
/no/yes/no/yes/no/yes/no/yes/no/yes/no/yes/no/y
es/no/yes/no/yes/no/yes/no/yes/no/yes/no/yes/no
/yes/no/yes/no/yes/no/yes/no.yes/no/yes/no/yes//
no/yes/no/yes/no/yes/no/yes/no/yes/no/yes/no/ye
s/no/yes/no/yes/no/yes/no/yes/no/yes/no/yes/no/
yes/no/yes/no/yes/no/yes/no/yes/no/yes/no/yes/n
o/yes/no/yes/no/yes/no/yes/no/yes/no/yes/no/yes
/no/yes/no/yes/no/yes/no/yes/no/yes/no/yes/no/y
es/no/yes/no/yes/no/yes/no/yes/no/yes/no/yes/no
/yes/no/yes/no/yes/no/yes/no/yes/no.yes/no/yes/
no/yes//no/yes/no/yes/no/yes/no/yes/no/yes/no/y
es/no/yes/no/yes/no/yes/no/yes/no/yes/no/yes/no
/yes/no/yes/no/yes/no/yes/no/yes/no/yes/no/yes/**

**no/yes/no/yes/no/yes/no/yes/no/yes/no/yes/no/ye
s/no/yes/no/yes/no/yes/no/yes/no/yes/no/yes/no/
yes/no/yes/no/yes/no/yes/no/yes/no/yes/no/yes/n
o/yes/no/yes/no/yes/no/yes/no/yes/no/yes/no.yes
/no/yes/no/yes//no/yes/no/yes/no/yes/no/yes/no/
yes/no/yes/no/yes/no/yes/no/yes/no/yes/no/yes/n
o/yes/no/yes/no/yes/no/yes/no/yes/no/yes/no/yes
/no/yes/no/yes/no/yes/no/yes/no/yes/no/yes/no/y
es/no/yes/no/yes/no/yes/no/yes/no/yes/no/yes/no
/yes/no/yes/no/yes/no/yes/no/yes/no/yes/no/yes/
no/yes/no/yes/no/yes/no/yes/no/yes/no/yes/no/ye
s/no.yes/no/yes/no/yes//no/yes/no/yes/no/yes/no/
yes/no/yes/no/yes/no/yes/no/yes/no/yes/no/yes/n
o/yes/no/yes/no/yes/no/yes/no/yes/no/yes/no/yes
/no/yes/no/yes/no/yes/no/yes/no/yes/no/yes/no/y
es/no/yes/no/yes/no/yes/no/yes/no/yes/no/yes/no
/yes/no/yes/no/yes/no/yes/no/yes/no/yes/no/yes/
no/yes/no/yes/no/yes/no/yes/no/yes/no/yes/no/ye
s/no/yes/no.yes/no/yes/no/yes//no/yes/no/yes/no/
yes/no/yes/no/yes/no/yes/no/yes/no/yes/no/yes/n
o/yes/no/yes/no/yes/no/yes/no/yes/no/yes/no/yes
/no/yes/no/yes/no/yes/no/yes/no/yes/no/yes/no/y
es/no/yes/no/yes/no/yes/no/yes/no/yes/no/yes/no
/yes/no/yes/no/yes/no/yes/no/yes/no/yes/no/yes/
no/yes/no/yes/no/yes/no/yes/no/yes/no/yes/no/ye
s/no/yes/no/yes/no/yes/no/yes/no/yes//no/yes/no/
yes/no/yes/no/yes/no/yes/no/yes/no/yes/no/yes/n
o/yes/no/yes/no/yes/no/yes/no/yes/no/yes/no/yes
/no/yes/no/yes/no/yes/no/yes/no/yes/no/yes/no/y
es/no/yes/no/yes/no/yes/no/yes/no/yes/no/yes/no
/yes/no/yes/no/yes/no/yes/no/yes/no/yes/no/yes/
no/yes/no/yes/no/yes/no/yes/no/yes/no/yes/no/ye**

**s/no/yes/no/yes/no/yes/no.yes/no/ye/no/yes//no/
yes/no/yes/no/yes/no/yes/no/yes/no/yes/no/yes/n
o/yes/no/yes/no/yes/no/yes/no/yes/no/yes/no/yes
/no/yes/no/yes/no/yes/no/yes/no/yes/no/yes/no/y
es/no/yes/no/yes/no/yes/no/yes/no/yes/no/yes/no
/yes/no/yes/no/yes/no/yes/no/yes/no/yes/no/yes/
no/yes/no/yes/no/yes/no/yes/no/yes/no/yes/no/ye
s/no/yes/no/yes/no/yes/no/yes/no.yes/no/yes/no/
yes//no/yes/no/yes/no/yes/no/yes/no/yes/no/yes/
no/yes/no/yes/no/yes/no/yes/no/yes/no/yes/no/ye
s/no/yes/no/yes/no/yes/no/yes/no/yes/no/yes/no/
yes/no/yes/no/yes/no/yes/no/yes/no/yes/no/yes/n
o/yes/no/yes/no/yes/no/yes/no/yes/no/yes/no/yes
/no/yes/no/yes/no/yes/no/yes/no/yes/no/yes/no/y
es/no/yes/no/yes/no/yes/no/yes/no/yes/no.yes/no
/yes/no/yes//no/yes/no/yes/no/yes/no/yes/no/yes/
no/yes/no/yes/no/yes/no/yes/no/yes/no/yes/no/ye
s/no/yes/no/yes/no/yes/no/yes/no/yes/no/yes/no/
yes/no/yes/no/yes/no/yes/no/yes/no/yes/no/yes/n
o/yes/no/yes/no/yes/no/yes/no/yes/no/yes/no/yes
/no/yes/no/yes/no/yes/no/yes/no/yes/no/yes/no/y
es/no/yes/no/yes/no/yes/no/yes/no/yes/no/yes/no
.yes/no/yes/no/yes//no/yes/no/yes/no/yes/no/yes/
no/yes/no/yes/no/yes/no/yes/no/yes/no/yes/no/ye
s/no/yes/no/yes/no/yes/no/yes/no/yes/no/yes/no/
yes/no/yes/no/yes/no/yes/no/yes/no/yes/no/yes/n
o/yes/no/yes/no/yes/no/yes/no/yes/no/yes/no/yes
/no/yes/no/yes/no/yes/no/yes/no/yes/no/yes/no/y
es/no/yes/no/yes/no/yes/no/yes/no/yes/no/yes/no
/yes/no.yes/no/yes/no/yes//no/yes/no/yes/no/yes/
no/yes/no/yes/no/yes/no/yes/no/yes/no/yes/no/ye
s/no/yes/no/yes/no/yes/no/yes/no/yes/no/yes/no/**

**yes/no/yes/no/yes/no/yes/no/yes/no/yes/no/yes/n
o/yes/no/yes/no/yes/no/yes/no/yes/no/yes/no/yes
/no/yes/no/yes/no/yes/no/yes/no/yes/no/yes/no/y
es/no/yes/no/yes/no/yes/no/yes/no/yes/no/yes/no
/yes/no/yes/no.yes/no/yes/no/yes//no/yes/no/yes/
no/yes/no/yes/no/yes/no/yes/no/yes/no/yes/no/ye
s/no/yes/no/yes/no/yes/no/yes/no/yes/no/yes/no/
yes/no/yes/no/yes/no/yes/no/yes/no/yes/no/yes/n
o/yes/no/yes/no/yes/no/yes/no/yes/no/yes/no/yes
/no/yes/no/yes/no/yes/no/yes/no/yes/no/yes/no/y
es/no/yes/no/yes/no/yes/no/yes/no/yes/no/yes/no
/yes/no/yes/no/yes/no.yes/no/yes/no/yes/no/yes/
no/yes/no/yes/no/yes/no/yes/no/yes/no/yes/no/ye
s/no/yes/no/yes/no/yes/no/yes/no/yes/no/yes/no/
yes/no/yes/no/yes/no/yes/no/yes/no/yes/no/yes/n
o/yes/no/yes/no/yes/no/yes/no/yes/no/yes/no/yes
/no/yes/no/yes/no/yes/no/yes/no/yes/no/yes/no/y
es/no/yes/no/yes/no/yes/no/yes/no/yes/no/yes/no
/yes/no/yes/no/yes/no/yes/no.yes/no/yes/no/yes//
no/yes/no/yes/no/yes/no/yes/no/yes/no/yes/no/ye
s/no/yes/no/yes/no/yes/no/yes/no/yes/no/yes/no/
yes/no/yes/no/yes/no/yes/no/yes/no/yes/no/yes/n
o/yes/no/yes/no/yes/no/yes/no/yes/no/yes/no/yes
/no/yes/no/yes/no/yes/no/yes/no/yes/no/yes/no/y
es/no/yes/no/yes/no/yes/no/yes/no/yes/no/yes/no
/yes/no/yes/no/yes/no/yes/no/yes/no.yes/no/yes/
no/yes//no/yes/no/yes/no/yes/no/yes/no/yes/no/y
es/no/yes/no/yes/no/yes/no/yes/no/yes/no/yes/no
/yes/no/yes/no/yes/no/yes/no/yes/no/yes/no/yes/
no/yes/no/yes/no/yes/no/yes/no/yes/no/yes/no/ye
s/no/yes/no/yes/no/yes/no/yes/no/yes/no/yes/no/
yes/no/yes/no/yes/no/yes/no/yes/no/yes/no/yes/n**

**o/yes/no/yes/no/yes/no/yes/no/yes/no/yes/no.yes
/no/yes/no/yes//no/yes/no/yes/no/yes/no/yes/no/
yes/no/yes/no/yes/no/yes/no/yes/no/yes/no/yes/n
o/yes/no/yes/no/yes/no/yes/no/yes/no/yes/no/yes
/no/yes/no/yes/no/yes/no/yes/no/yes/no/yes/no/y
es/no/yes/no/yes/no/yes/no/yes/no/yes/no/yes/no
/yes/no/yes/no/yes/no/yes/no/yes/no/yes/no/yes/
no/yes/no/yes/no/yes/no/yes/no/yes/no/yes/no/ye
s/no/yes/no/yes/no/yes//no/yes/no/yes/no/yes/no/
yes/no/yes/no/yes/no/yes/no/yes/no/yes/no/yes/n
o/yes/no/yes/no/yes/no/yes/no/yes/no/yes/no/yes
/no/yes/no/yes/no/yes/no/yes/no/yes/no/yes/no/y
es/no/yes/no/yes/no/yes/no/yes/no/yes/no/yes/no
/yes/no/yes/no/yes/no/yes/no/yes/no/yes/no/yes/
no/yes/no/yes/no/yes/no/yes/no/yes/no/yes/no/ye
s/no/yes/no.yes/no/yes/no/yes//no/yes/no/yes/no/
yes/no/yes/no/yes/no/yes/no/yes/no/yes/no/yes/n
o/yes/no/yes/no/yes/no/yes/no/yes/no/yes/no/yes
/no/yes/no/yes/no/yes/no/yes/no/yes/no/yes/no/y
es/no/yes/no/yes/no/yes/no/yes/no/yes/no/yes/no
/yes/no/yes/no/yes/no/yes/no/yes/no/yes/no/yes/
no/yes/no/yes/no/yes/no/yes/no/yes/no/yes/no/ye
s/no/yes/no/yes/no.yes/no/yes/no/yes//no/yes/no/
yes/no/yes/no/yes/no/yes/no/yes/no/yes/no/yes/n
o/yes/no/yes/no/yes/no/yes/no/yes/no/yes/no/yes
/no/yes/no/yes/no/yes/no/yes/no/yes/no/yes/no/y
es/no/yes/no/yes/no/yes/no/yes/no/yes/no/yes/no
/yes/no/yes/no/yes/no/yes/no/yes/no/yes/no/yes/
no/yes/no/yes/no/yes/no/yes/no/yes/no/yes/no/ye
s/no/yes/no/yes/no/yes/no.yes/no/yes/no/yes//no/
yes/o/yes/no/yes/no/yes/no/yes/no/yes/no/yes/no
/yes/no/yes/no/yes/no/yes/no/yes/no/yes/no/yes/**

**no/yes/no/yes/no/yes/no/yes/no/yes/no/yes/no/ye
s/no/yes/no/yes/no/yes/no/yes/no/yes/no/yes/no/
yes/no/yes/no/yes/no/yes/no/yes/no/yes/no/yes/n
o/yes/no/yes/no/yes/no/yes/no/yes/no/yes/no/yes
/no/yes/no/yes/no/yes/no/yes/no.yes/no/yes/no/y
es//no/yes/no/yes/no/yes/no/yes/no/yes/no/yes/n
o/yes/no/yes/no/yes/no/yes/no/yes/no/yes/no/yes
/no/yes/no/yes/no/yes/no/yes/no/yes/no/yes/no/y
es/no/yes/no/yes/no/yes/no/yes/no/yes/no/yes/no
/yes/no/yes/no/yes/no/yes/no/yes/no/yes/no/yes/
no/yes/no/yes/no/yes/no/yes/no/yes/no/yes/no/ye
s/no/yes/no/yes/no/yes/no/yes/no/yes/no.yes/no/
yes/no/yes//no/yes/no/yes/no/yes/no/yes/no/yes/
no/yes/no/yes/no/yes/no/yes/no/yes/no/yes/no/ye
s/no/yes/no/yes/no/yes/no/yes/no/yes/no/yes/no/
yes/no/yes/no/yes/no/yes/no/yes/no/yes/no/yes/n
o/yes/no/yes/no/yes/no/yes/no/yes/no/yes/no/yes
/no/yes/no/yes/no/yes/no/yes/no/yes/no/yes/no/y
es/no/yes/no/yes/no/yes/no/yes/no/yes/no/yes/no
.yes/no/yes/no/yes//no/yes/no/yes/no/yes/no/yes/
no/yes/no/yes/no/yes/no/yes/no/yes/no/yes/no/ye
s/no/yes/no/yes/no/yes/no/yes/no/yes/no/yes/no/
yes/no/yes/no/yes/no/yes/no/yes/no/yes/no/yes/n
o/yes/no/yes/no/yes/no/yes/no/yes/no/yes/no/yes
/no/yes/no/yes/no/yes/no/yes/no/yes/no/yes/no/y
es/no/yes/no/yes/no/yes/no/yes/no/yes/no/yes/no
/yes/no.yes/no/yes/no/yes//no/yes/no/yes/no/yes/
no/yes/no/yes/no/yes/no/yes/no/yes/no/yes/no/ye
s/no/yes/no/yes/no/yes/no/yes/no/yes/no/yes/no/
yes/no/yes/no/yes/no/yes/no/yes/no/yes/no/yes/n
o/yes/no/yes/no/yes/no/yes/no/yes/no/yes/no/yes
/no/yes/no/yes/no/yes/no/yes/no/yes/no/yes/no/y**

es/no/yes/no/yes/no/yes/no/yes/no/yes/no/yes/no/yes/no /yes/no/yes/no.yes/no/yes/no/yes/yes/no/yes/no/ yes/no/yes/no/yes/no/yes/no/yes/no/yes/no/yes/n o/yes/no/yes/no/yes/no/yes/no/yes/no/yes/no/yes /no/yes/no.yes/no/yes/no/yes//no/yes/no/yes/no/ yes/no/yes/no/yes/no/yes/no/yes/no/yes/no/yes/n o/yes/no/yes/no/yes/no/yes/no/yes/no/yes/no/yes /no/yes/no/yes/no/yes/no/yes/no/yes/no/yes/no/y es/no/yes/no/yes/no/yes/no/yes/no/yes/no/yes/no /yes/no/yes/no/yes/no/yes/no/yes/no/yes/no/yes/ no/yes/no/yes/no/yes/no/yes/no/yes/no/yes/no/ye s/no/yes/no/yes/no.yes/no/yes/nonever/rarely/so me-times/maybe it is meant to be a guff.

A mess. Inherently pointless. Deliberate awfulness, refined in an art-object fashion, to warrant its existence. Fuck knows. The following pages are sponsored by Randolph Ol'Ktchezzie, blind author, who doesn't use braille in the traditional sense. He doesn't need to feel it to read it. Just merely sense it.

How many men did it take to enter the braille realm?

please

wait

for **further**

instructions

one or two?

meaning

nought meaning

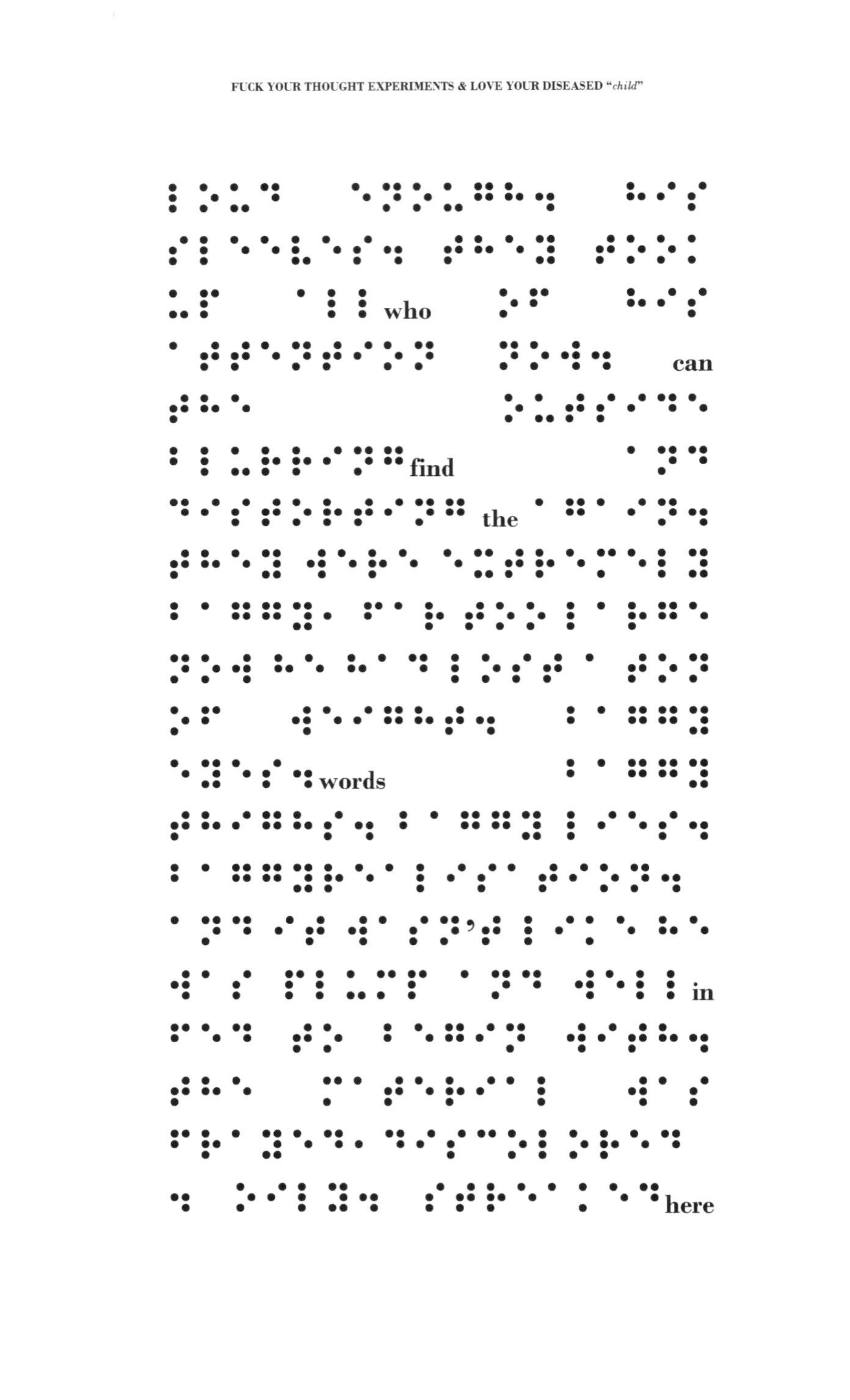

who

can

find

the

words

in

here

?

&

my work is meant to

confound

not

evolve

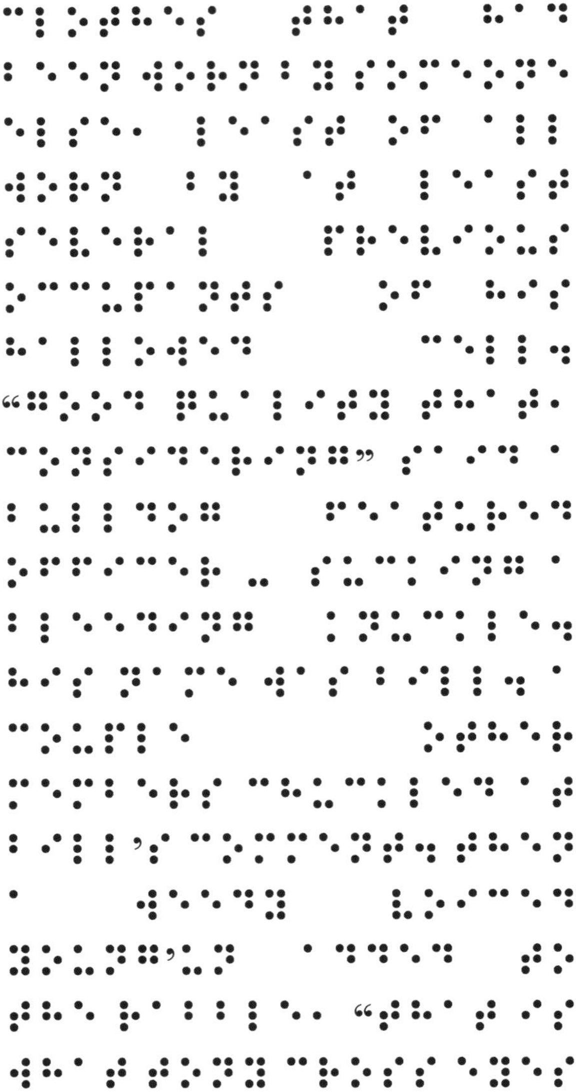

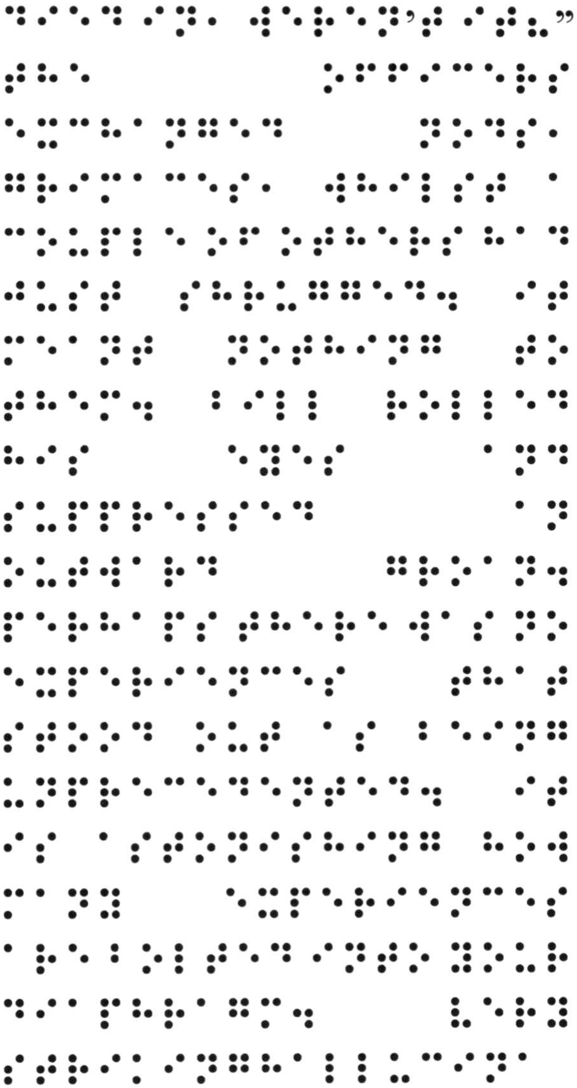

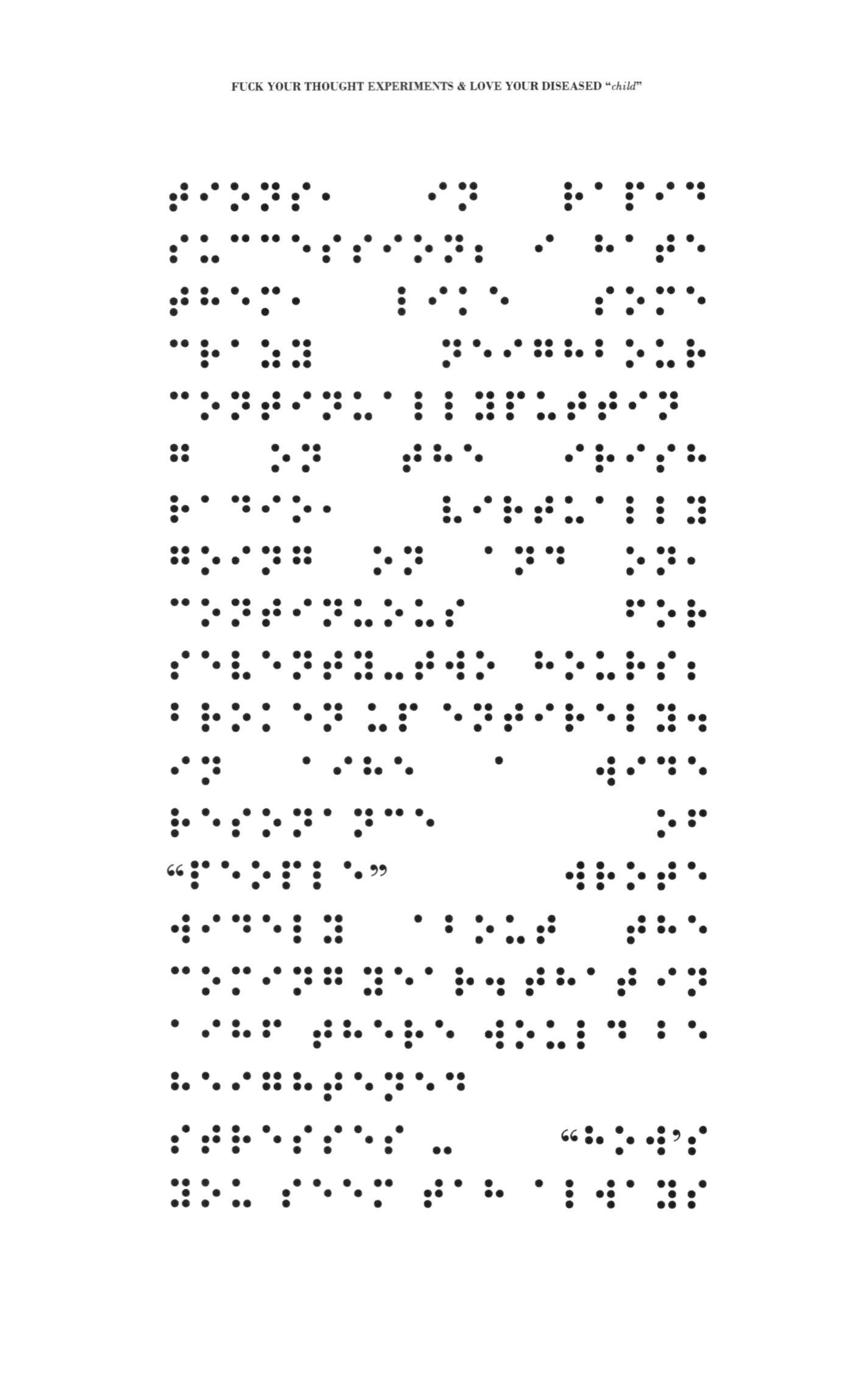

⠗⠑⠍⠑⠍⠃⠑⠗ ⠞⠓⠑⠍⠂
⠗⠕⠎⠎⠦” ⠑⠝⠟⠥⠊⠗⠑⠙
⠎⠕⠍⠑⠕⠝⠑ ⠕⠥⠞ ⠕⠋ ⠞⠓⠑
⠃⠥⠝⠉⠓⠂ ⠺⠓⠕⠍ ⠺⠑⠗⠑
⠉⠕⠝⠛⠗⠑⠛⠁⠞⠊⠝⠛
⠕⠥⠞⠎⠊⠙⠑ ⠞⠓⠑ ⠏⠕⠑⠞⠎
⠉⠑⠇⠇⠲ ⠞⠓⠑ ⠺⠑⠑⠙⠽
⠧⠕⠊⠉⠑⠙ ⠕⠋⠋⠊⠉⠑⠗
⠏⠥⠋⠋⠑⠙ ⠕⠥⠞ ⠓⠊⠎
⠉⠓⠑⠎⠞ ⠁⠝⠙ ⠎⠞⠁⠞⠑⠙
⠃⠕⠇⠙⠇⠽⠂ “⠉⠁⠥⠎⠑ ⠊⠞ ⠊⠎
⠍⠽ ⠉⠊⠧⠊⠉ ⠙⠥⠞⠽⠂
⠎⠊⠗...⠕⠓ ⠁⠝⠙ ⠁⠇⠎⠕⠂
⠁⠊⠝’⠞ ⠊ “⠛⠕⠕⠙
⠟⠥⠁⠇⠊⠞⠽ ⠞⠓⠁⠞⠂
⠉⠕⠝⠎⠊⠙⠑⠗⠊⠝⠛” ⠎⠁⠊⠙ ⠁

⠃⠥⠇⠇⠙⠕⠛ ⠋⠑⠁⠞⠥⠗⠑⠙
⠕⠋⠋⠊⠉⠑⠗⠤ ⠎⠥⠉⠅⠊⠝⠛ ⠁
⠃⠇⠑⠑⠙⠊⠝⠛ ⠅⠝⠥⠉⠅⠇⠑⠲
⠓⠊⠎ ⠝⠁⠍⠑ ⠺⠁⠎ ⠃⠊⠇⠇⠲ ⠁
⠉⠕⠥⠏⠇⠑ ⠕⠞⠓⠑⠗
⠍⠑⠍⠃⠑⠗⠎ ⠉⠓⠥⠉⠅⠇⠑⠙ ⠁⠞
⠃⠊⠇⠇’⠎ ⠉⠕⠍⠍⠑⠝⠞⠲ ⠞⠓⠑⠝
⠁ ⠺⠑⠑⠙⠽ ⠧⠕⠊⠉⠑⠙
⠽⠕⠥⠝⠛’⠥⠝ ⠁⠙⠙⠑⠙ ⠞⠕
⠞⠓⠑ ⠗⠁⠃⠃⠇⠑⠂ “⠞⠓⠁⠞ ⠊⠎
⠺⠓⠁⠞ ⠞⠕⠝⠽
⠉⠗⠕⠎⠎ ⠑⠽⠑⠎ ⠙⠊⠑⠙ ⠊⠝⠂
⠺⠑⠗⠑⠝’⠞ ⠊⠞⠦” ⠞⠓⠑
⠕⠋⠋⠊⠉⠑⠗⠎ ⠑⠭⠉⠓⠁⠝⠛⠑⠙
⠝⠕⠙⠎⠂ ⠛⠗⠊⠍⠁⠉⠑⠎⠂
⠺⠓⠊⠇⠎⠞ ⠁ ⠉⠕⠥⠏⠇⠑ ⠕⠋
⠕⠞⠓⠑⠗⠎ ⠓⠁⠙ ⠚⠥⠎⠞
⠎⠓⠗⠥⠛⠛⠑⠙⠲ ⠊⠞ ⠍⠑⠁⠝⠞

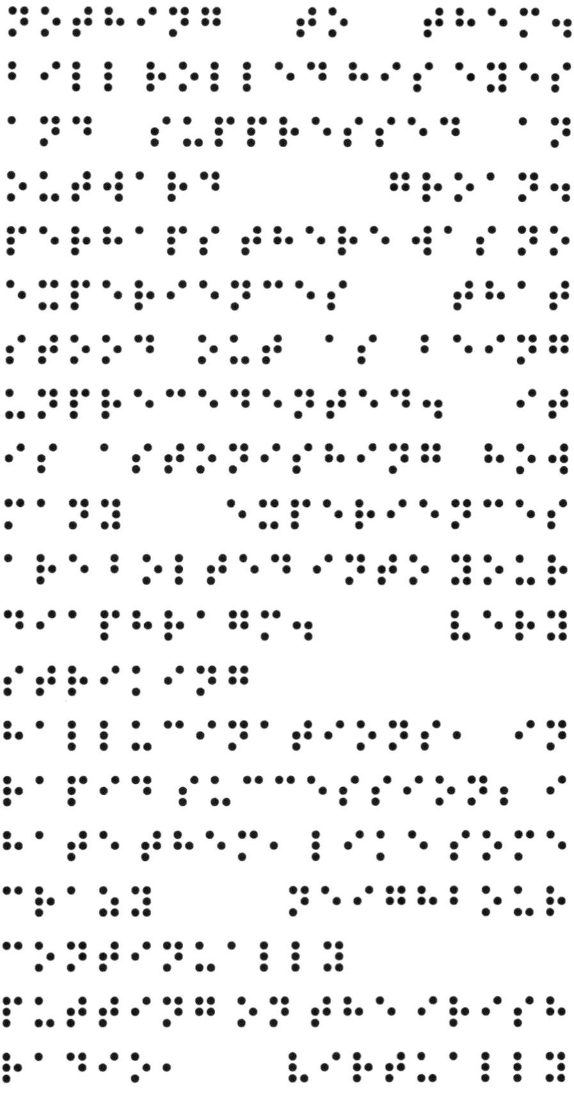

⠛⠕⠊⠝⠛ ⠕⠝ ⠁⠝⠙ ⠕⠝⠂
⠉⠕⠝⠞⠊⠝⠥⠕⠥⠎ ⠋⠕⠗
⠎⠑⠧⠑⠝⠞⠽⠤⠞⠺⠕ ⠓⠕⠥⠗⠎⠆
⠃⠗⠕⠅⠑⠝ ⠥⠏ ⠑⠝⠞⠊⠗⠑⠇⠽⠲
⠊⠝ ⠁⠊⠓⠑ ⠁ ⠺⠊⠙⠑
⠗⠑⠎⠕⠝⠁⠝⠉⠑ ⠕⠋
“⠏⠑⠕⠏⠇⠑” ⠺⠗⠕⠞⠑
⠺⠊⠙⠑⠇⠽ ⠁⠃⠕⠥⠞ ⠞⠓⠑
⠉⠕⠍⠊⠝⠛ ⠽⠑⠁⠗⠲ ⠞⠓⠁⠞ ⠊⠝
⠁⠊⠓⠋ ⠞⠓⠑⠗⠑ ⠺⠕⠥⠇⠙ ⠃⠑
⠓⠑⠊⠛⠓⠞⠑⠝⠑⠙
⠎⠞⠗⠑⠎⠎⠑⠎ ⠤ ⠞ ⠍⠽ ⠚⠕⠃
⠞⠕ ⠅⠝⠕⠺ ⠞⠓⠑⠍⠎
⠝⠁⠍⠑⠎⠦” “⠋⠥⠉⠅ ⠊⠋ ⠊
⠅⠝⠕⠺⠂ ⠽⠕⠥ ⠚⠥⠎⠞ ⠎⠑⠑⠍
⠞⠕ ⠛⠑⠞ ⠁ ⠝⠕⠊⠉⠑ ⠅⠊⠉⠅
⠕⠥⠞ ⠕⠋ ⠊⠞ ⠊⠎ ⠁⠇⠇”
⠗⠑⠏⠇⠊⠑⠙ ⠞⠓⠑ ⠕⠝⠑ ⠺⠓⠕
⠓⠁⠙ ⠁⠎⠅⠑⠙ ⠗⠕⠎⠎ ⠞⠓⠑

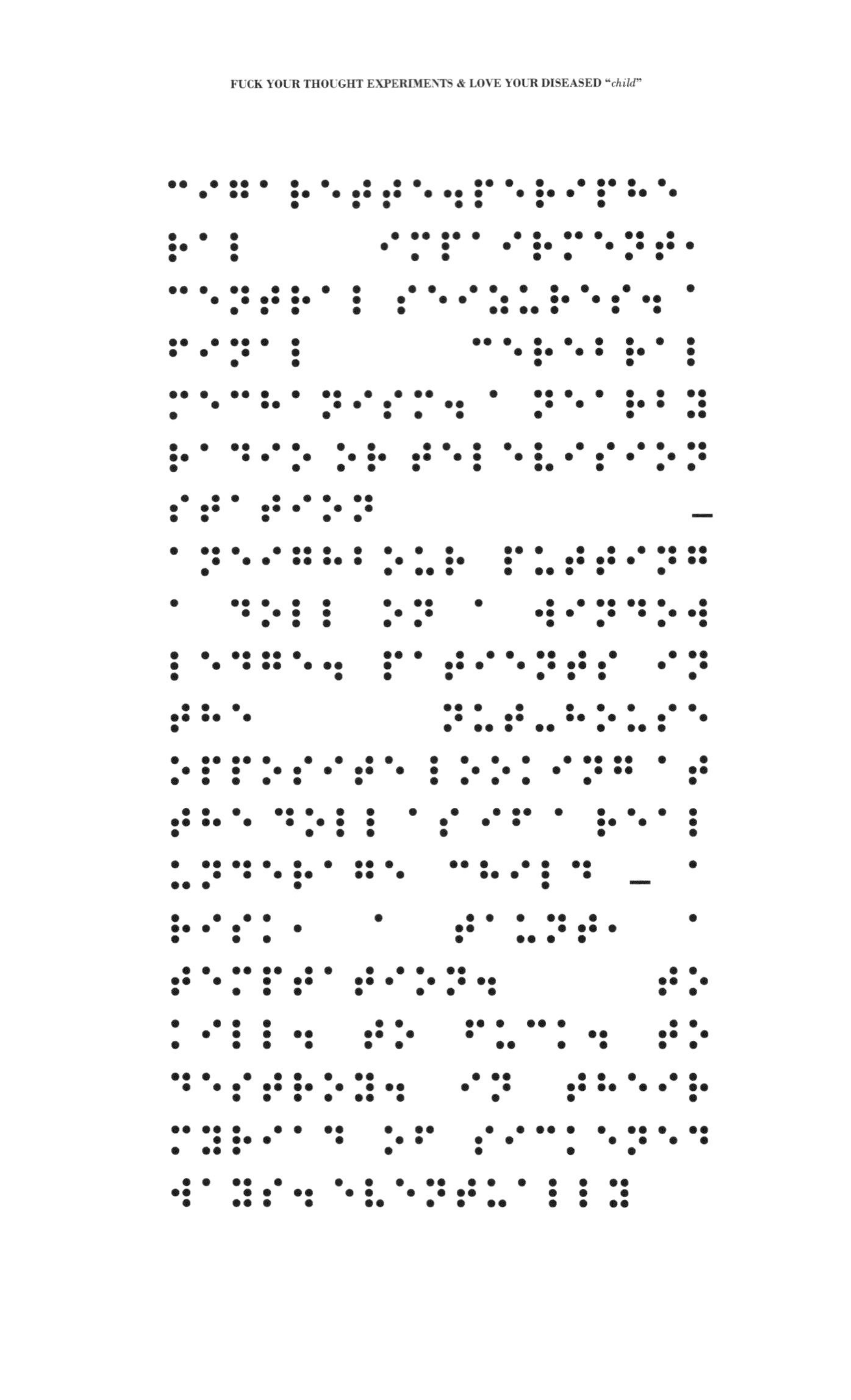

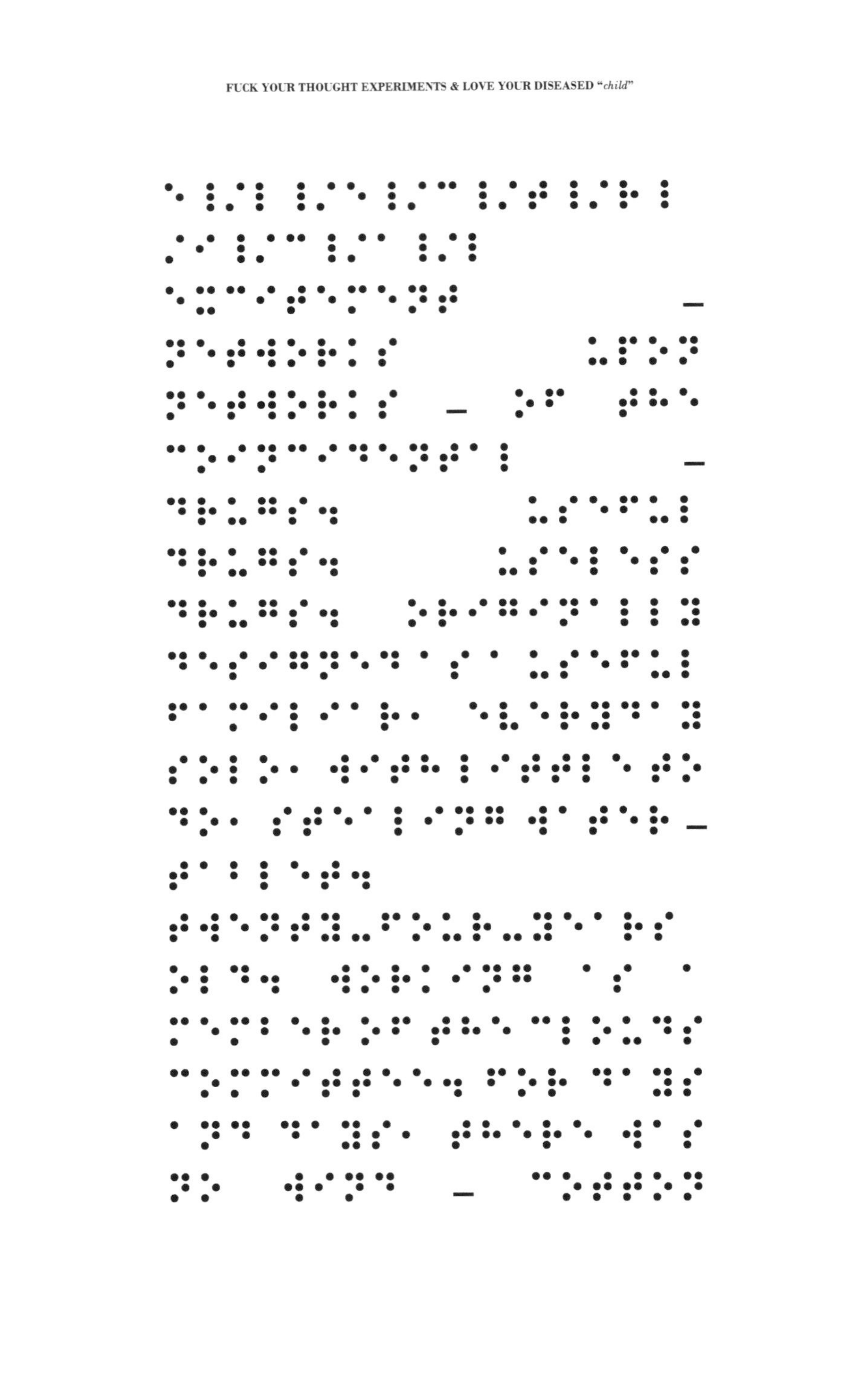

⠉⠁⠝⠙⠽ ⠉⠇⠕⠥⠙⠎ ⠺⠑⠗⠑
⠙⠗⠽⠊⠝⠛ ⠕⠥⠞—

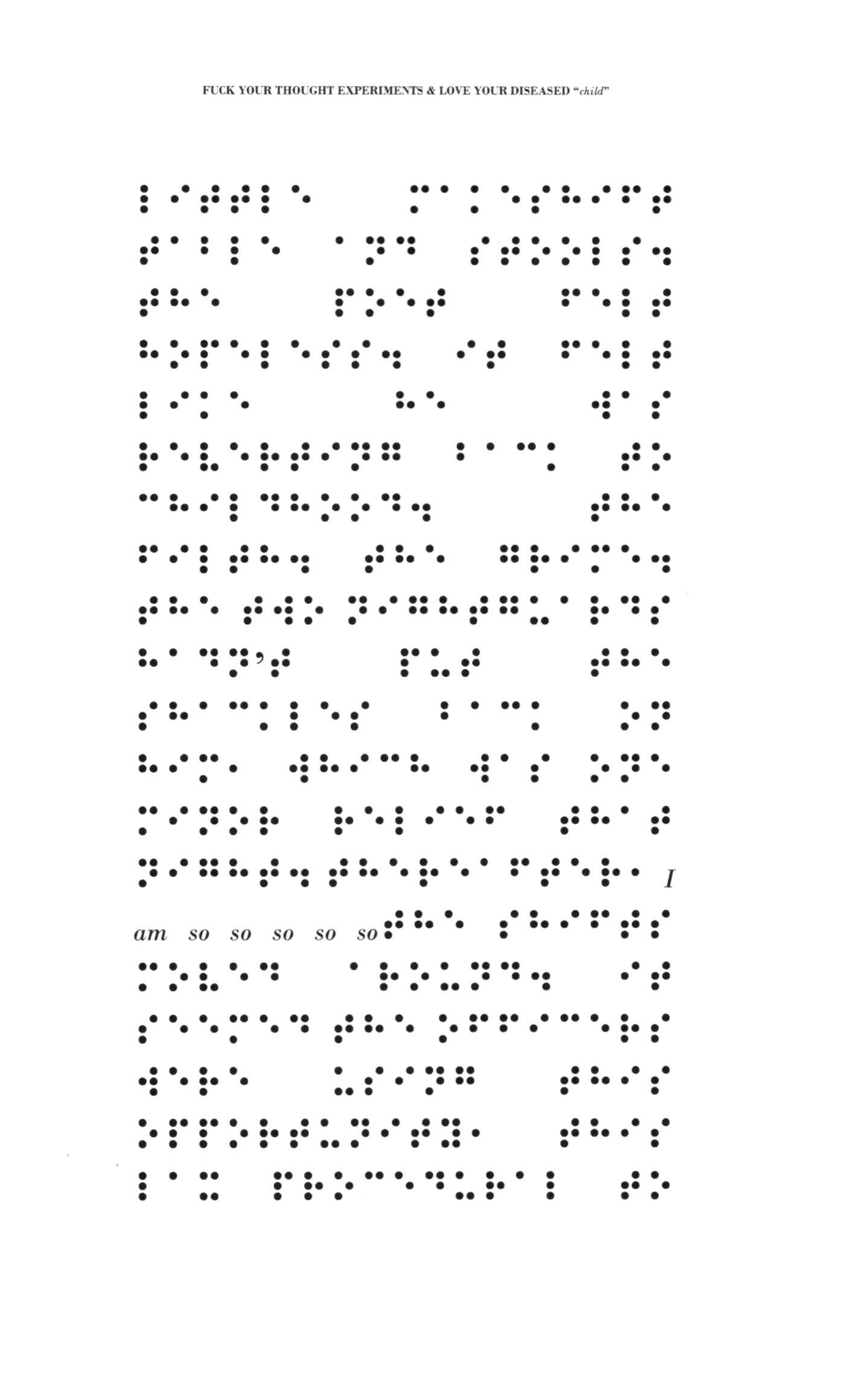

I

am so so so so so

so so so so so so

so so so, so-so!

can I live in here?

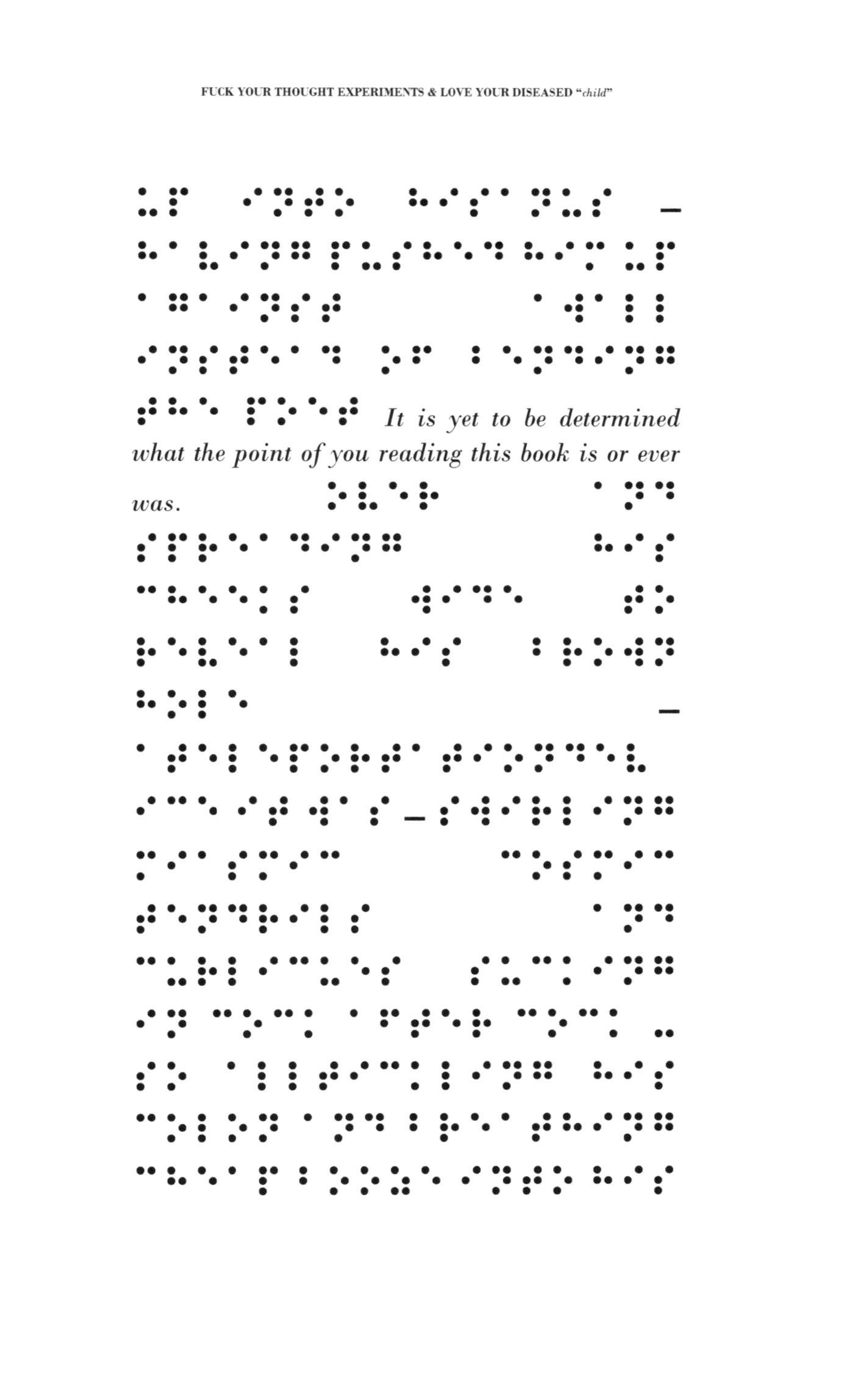

It is yet to be determined what the point of you reading this book is or ever was.

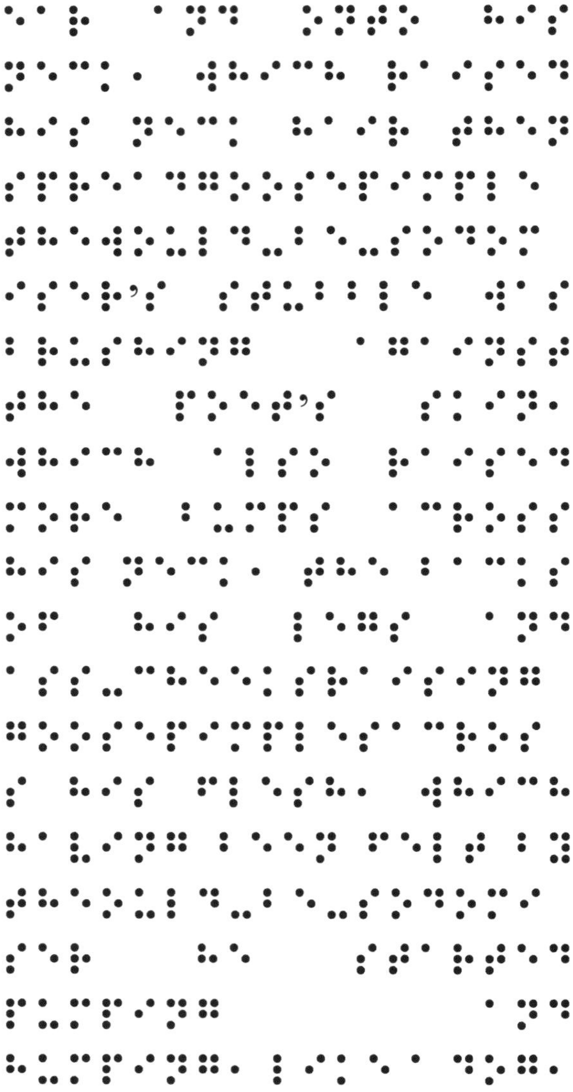

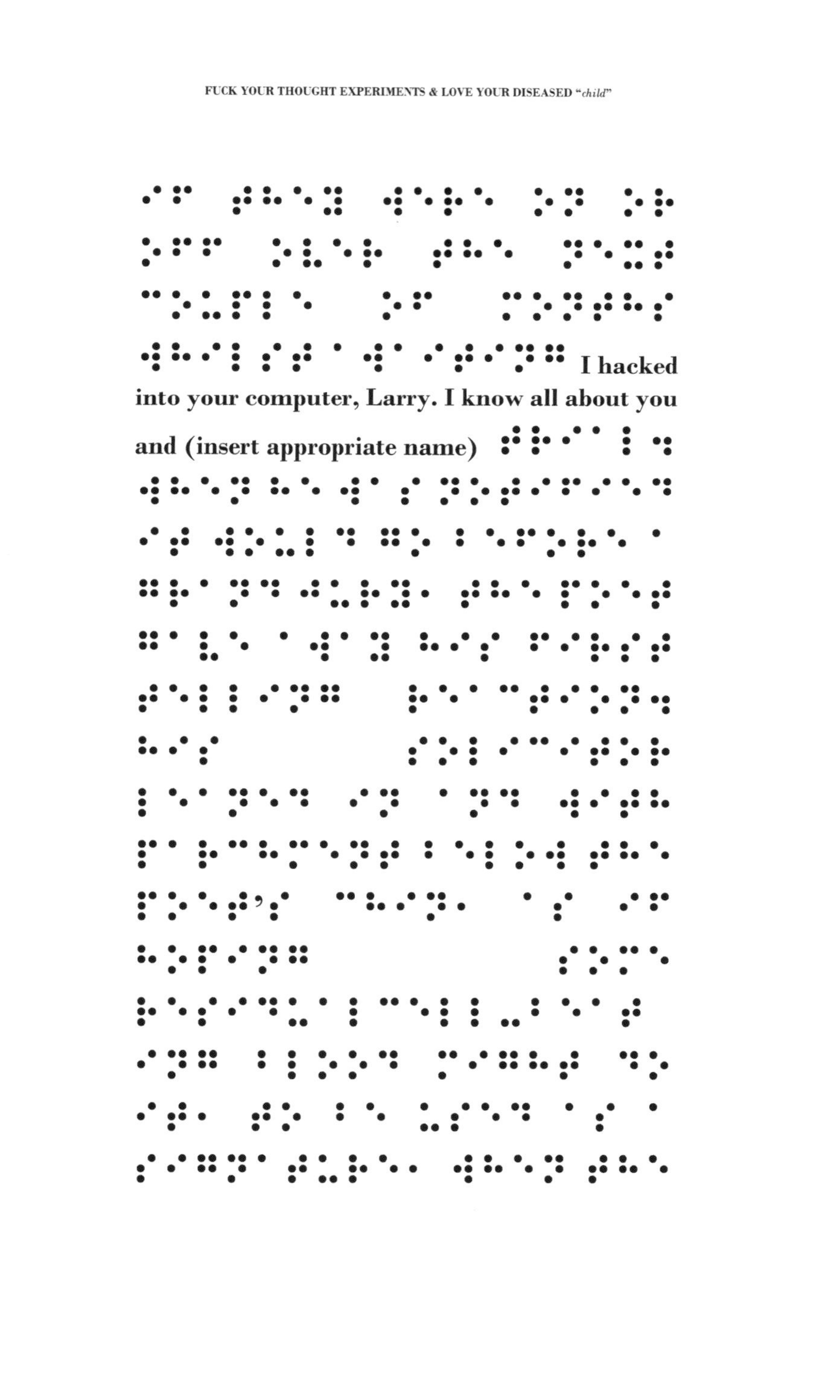

I hacked into your computer, Larry. I know all about you and (insert appropriate name)

⠎⠓⠁⠉⠅⠇⠑⠎ ⠓⠁⠙ ⠃⠑⠑⠝
⠉⠇⠁⠍⠏⠑⠙ ⠃⠁⠉⠅ ⠕⠝ ⠺⠓⠑⠝
⠞⠓⠑ ⠝⠁⠎⠞⠊⠑⠗ ⠃⠥⠝⠉⠓
⠞⠥⠗⠝⠑⠙ ⠥⠏ ⠊⠞ ⠗⠑⠙⠥⠉⠑⠙
⠓⠊⠎ ⠍⠕⠧⠑⠍⠑⠝⠞⠎⠲
⠁⠞⠞⠁⠉⠓⠊⠝⠛ ⠓⠊⠎
⠎⠓⠁⠉⠅⠇⠑⠎ ⠞⠕ ⠁ ⠎⠓⠕⠗⠞
⠇⠑⠁⠎⠓ ⠕⠋ ⠉⠓⠁⠊⠝⠤⠍⠑⠞⠁
⠇ ⠞⠕ ⠁ ⠗⠊⠝⠛ ⠎⠑⠞ ⠊⠝⠞⠕
⠞⠓⠑ ⠉⠕⠝⠉⠗⠑⠞⠑ ⠺⠁⠇⠇⠲
⠞⠓⠑ ⠏⠕⠑⠞ ⠓⠁⠙ ⠋⠑⠇⠞
⠇⠊⠅⠑ ⠁ ⠙⠕⠝⠅⠑⠽⠤ ⠞⠓⠊⠎
⠎⠓⠕⠗⠞ ⠇⠑⠁⠎⠓ ⠺⠁⠎
⠑⠝⠎⠥⠗⠊⠝⠛ ⠓⠑ ⠺⠁⠎⠝’⠞
⠺⠊⠞⠓⠊⠝ ⠞⠕⠥⠉⠓⠊⠝⠛

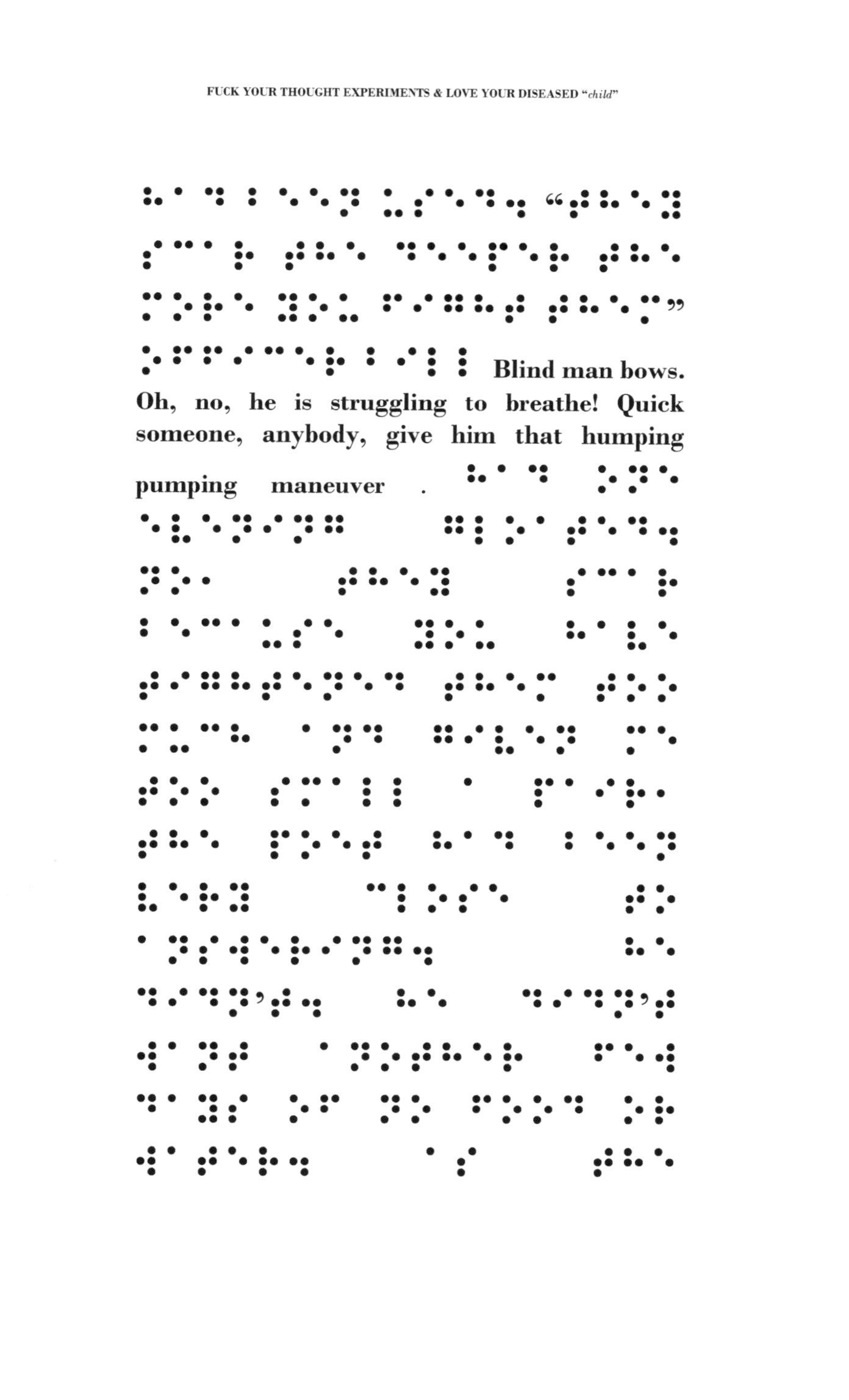

Blind man bows. Oh, no, he is struggling to breathe! Quick someone, anybody, give him that humping pumping maneuver .

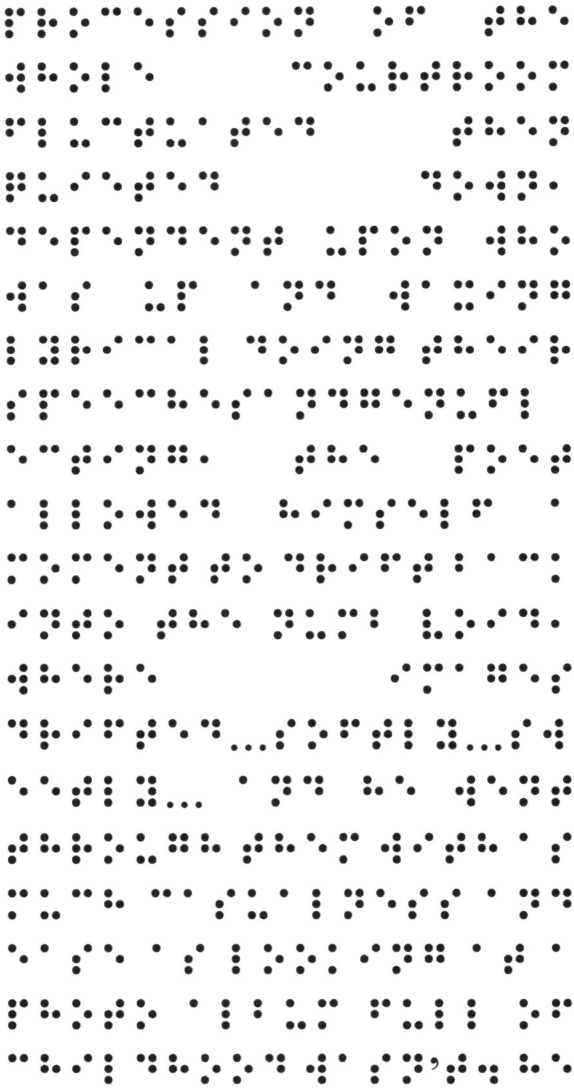

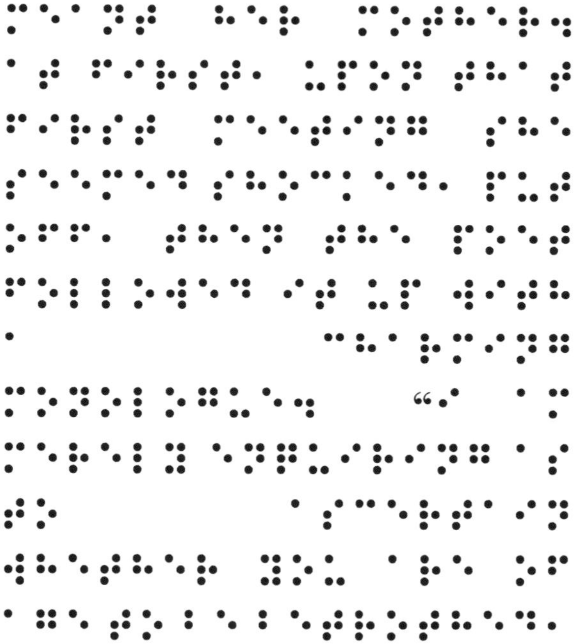

Blind men and woman and animals ask of you, plead with you, tell you to stop acquiring their method of reading and blind-appropriating their entertainment

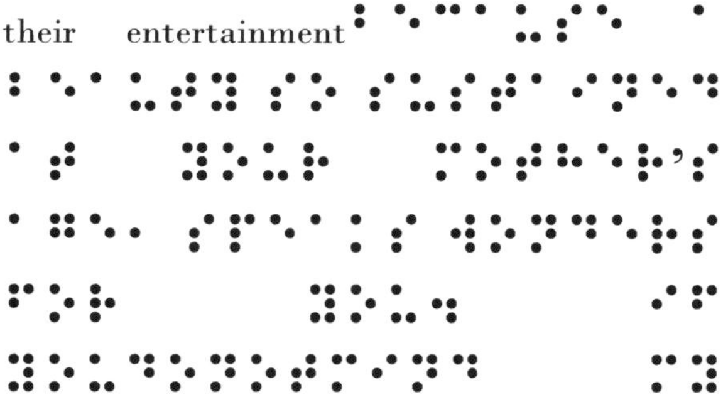

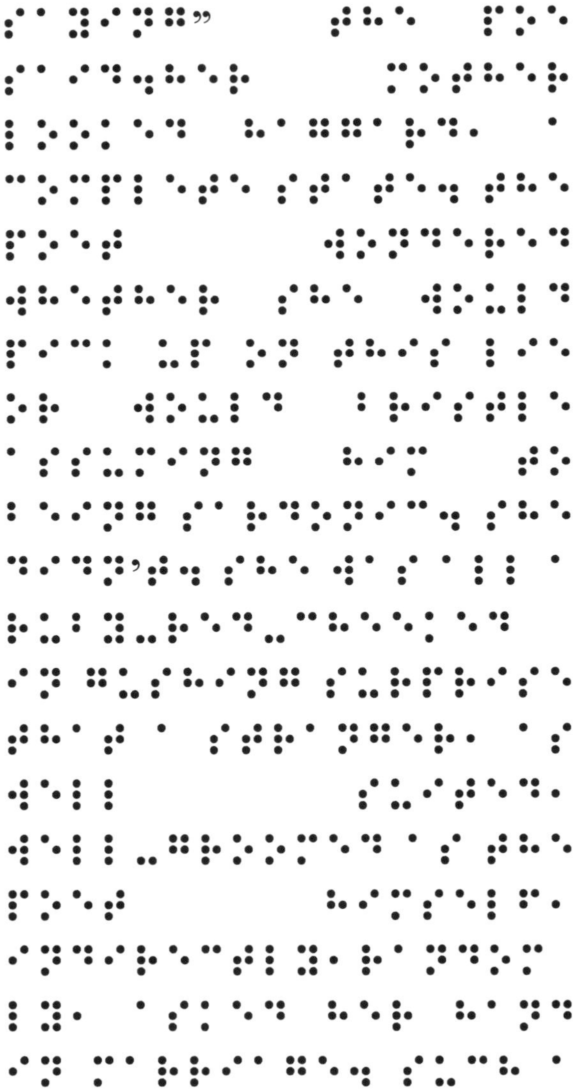

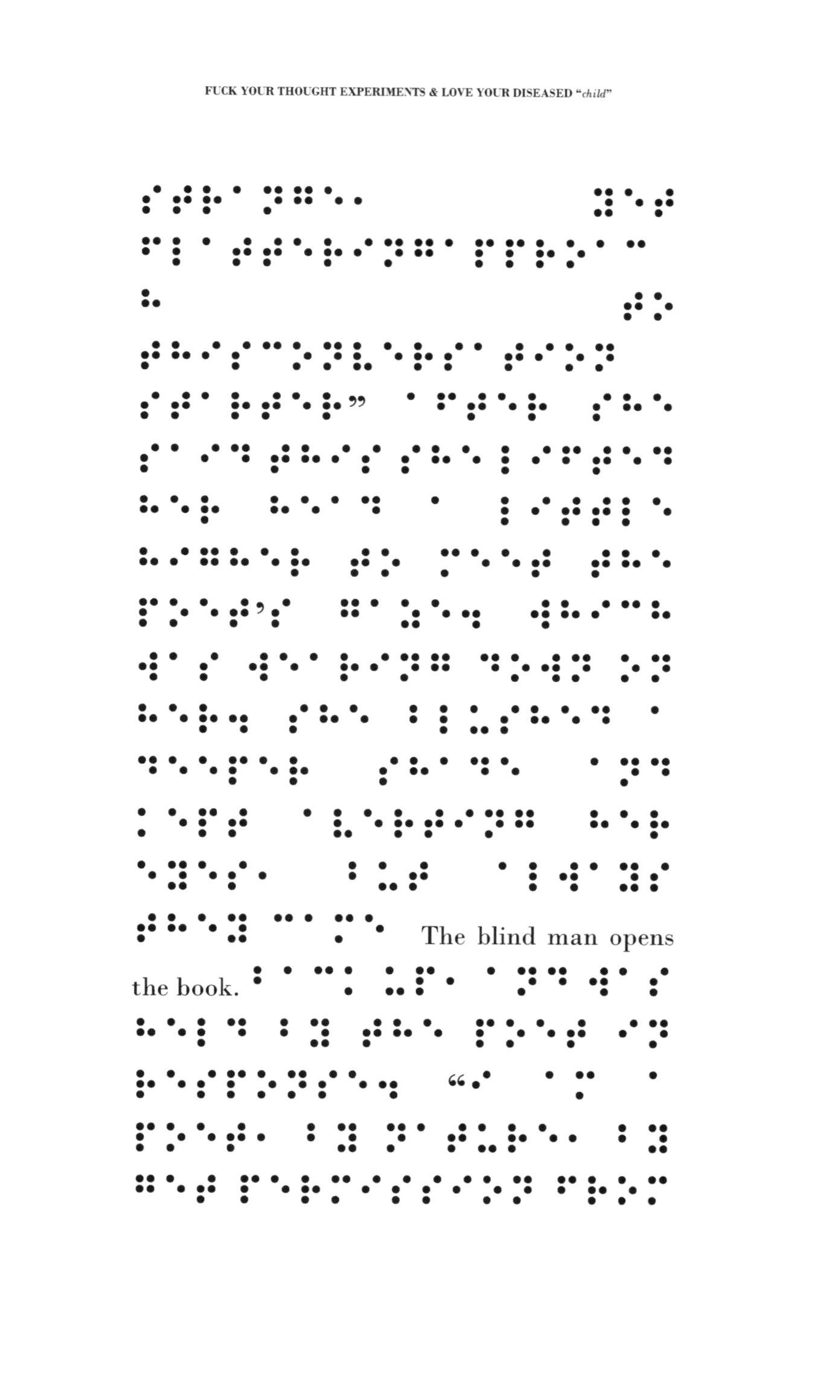

The blind man opens the book.

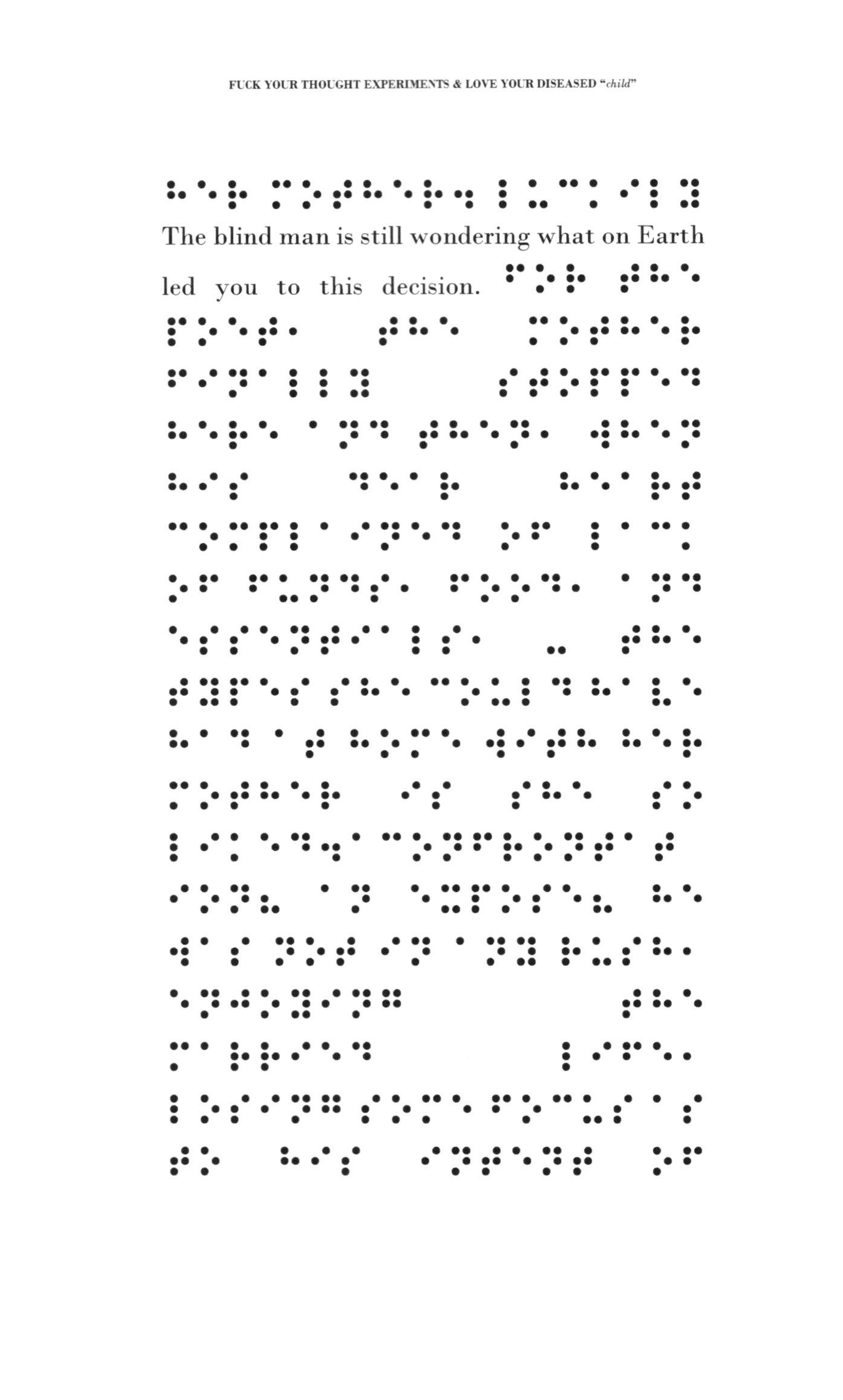

The blind man is still wondering what on Earth led you to this decision.

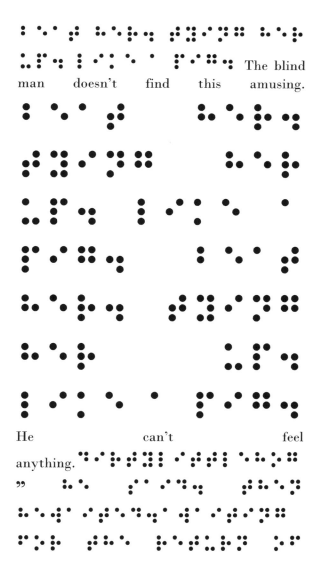

⠃⠑⠁⠞ ⠓⠑⠗⠲ ⠞⠽⠊⠝⠛ ⠓⠑⠗
⠥⠏⠲ ⠇⠊⠅⠑ ⠁ ⠏⠊⠛⠲ The blind man doesn't find this amusing.

⠃⠑⠁⠞ ⠓⠑⠗⠲
⠞⠽⠊⠝⠛ ⠓⠑⠗
⠥⠏⠲ ⠇⠊⠅⠑ ⠁
⠏⠊⠛⠲ ⠃⠑⠁⠞
⠓⠑⠗⠲ ⠞⠽⠊⠝⠛
⠓⠑⠗ ⠥⠏⠲
⠇⠊⠅⠑ ⠁ ⠏⠊⠛⠲

He can't feel anything. ⠙⠊⠗⠞⠽ ⠇⠊⠞⠞⠇⠑ ⠓⠕⠛
” ⠓⠑ ⠎⠁⠊⠙⠲ ⠞⠓⠑⠝
⠓⠑ ⠺⠁⠊⠞⠑⠙⠲ ⠁⠺⠁⠊⠞⠊⠝⠛
⠋⠕⠗ ⠞⠓⠑ ⠗⠑⠞⠥⠗⠝ ⠕⠋

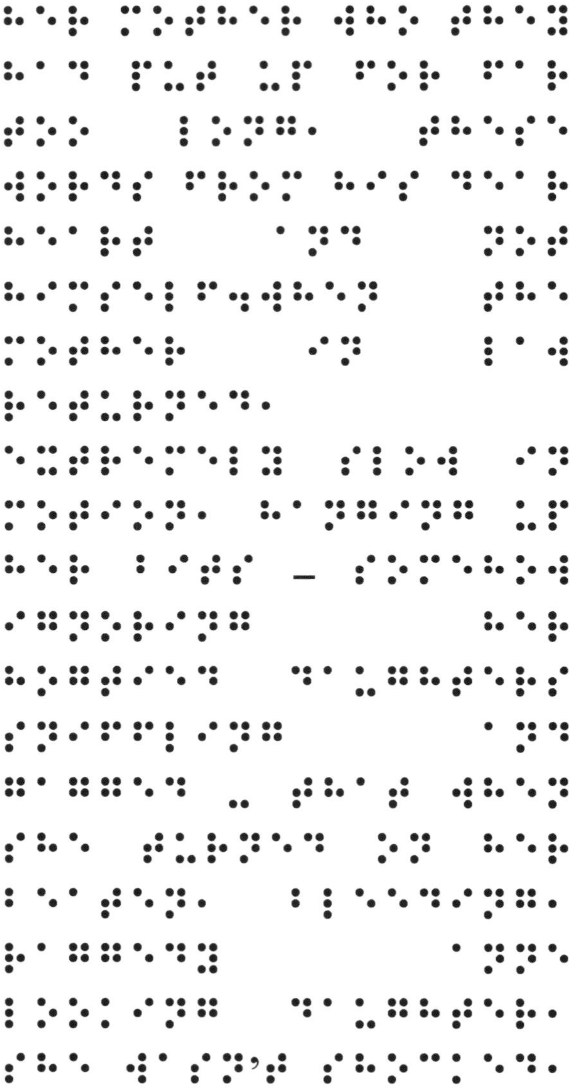

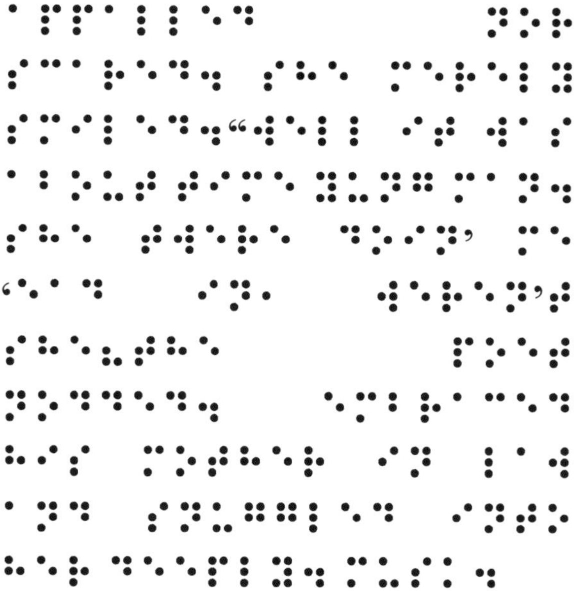

There is a huge controversy surrounding AI-generated images. So, here is over forty AI-generated images.
Prompts are scatological.

Try and guess by the image what artists I used as reference.

PROMPT 1: A cut-up collage, in the style of [redacted] fused with [redacted], black and white.
(Four images)

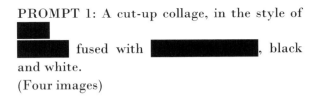

PROMPT 2: [redacted] in the style of [redacted], of a burning warehouse, ghouls screaming like food vendors.
(Four Images)

PROMPT 3: A post-apocalyptic world full of half destroyed robots seeking power-outlets and electrical pylons, in the style of [redacted] and [redacted] (Four images)

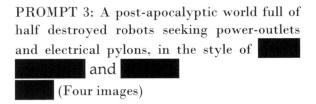

PROMPT 4: [redacted] styled picture of homeless drunks and drug addicts begging for money, black and white. (Four images)

PROPMT 5: Princess Diana as a femme fatale being accosted by a burly, brutish Prince Charles, in the style of [redacted], noir, digital image. (Five images)

PROPMT 6: Dante's Inferno, in the style [redacted] on acid, black and white digital art. (Two Images) PROMPT 7: A 1950s old couple, eating microwave meals, are being electrocuted by the TV set and cooking their meal, in the style of [redacted], black and white, digital art. (Two images)

PROMPT 8: A lonely writer, looking out of a window onto a decaying metropolis, typewriter keys embedded into his head like large cement blocks, in the style of [redacted] (Four images)

PROMPT 9: A modern metropolis as painted by [redacted]

PROMPT 10: William S. Burroughs smoking under a huge umbrella, as acid rain burns cats by his feet, in the style of [redacted], black and white. (Two images)

PROMPT 11: Kathy Acker reading from a pamphlet in front of a crowd, as clowns and weird creatures dance around her, [redacted] style. (Two mages)

PROMPT 12: [redacted] style painting of Kathy
Acker. (Three images)

Kenneth, can you hear me?
Kubrick can you smell Sally? Seabass on leeks on a carb based edible plater. Jack, can you read me? Working nine to five, what a shit way to make a living. Open this book and read a passage aloud. Just randomly select a line, and I tell you that it will take away the richness of the verbal dish you provide from a book that nobody will buy, review, or read. But I am okay about that. I am okay about that. No, I am not. You are all Facebook supporters, that means you proclaim support, but I have the numbers the tracking system that tells me the truth; you are all fucking liars. Are you getting agitated by my personal finger pointing; weren't you meant to be heated by the experimental prose, and not feel trigger-trigger-triggered. The lesser mortal beings have called me pretentious; how can a guy who loves "dickhead" humour and fart gags be pretentious. Is there such thing as a pretentious farter?

Please invite me to your small press events, I want to hand out tokens that promise for the price of a fake Rolex you can pre-order books that have yet been written, that have yet been contractually agreed upon feature our logo and my not so delicate editorial skills. I apologise to the heavens. Then I realise it isn't heaven, it is just the UK weather doing its usual bipolar thing.

The weather of different countries represents the souls it inhabits. Or the souls that are inhabited by the weather. What comes first, the weather that affects the people? Or the people that affects and influences the weather? The chicken looked at the egg, chuckled, cluck-clucked a few chicken globules of saliva onto its shell, ruffle-winged it, to give it that specific shine; only to offer it up to the chicken farmer in tribute to the fact that, though he feeds her, licks his lips, envisioning her on his plate, he cannot kill her, as he prefers this transactional relationship, this pseudo-sexual pseudo fatherly bond they have created. Pitch this to Aardman studios for a Chicken Run sequel, instead of the one they have made for Netflix, holy fuck it looks awful. Walking through art galleries and trying to hold in a fart is perhaps the greatest piece of performance art you can ever execute. The acoustics, the tenor of the whole environment is transformed once the gas is released. People break out of the

fugue state, the odd paralysis an art-space creates. Your face is broken into and bent into a Dali expression, a Dali deli dish, pickles falling out of flared nostrils, flared jeans opening up and ushering in the fart-breeze, teasing your arsehole to open up and join the gasymphony. Dali twisting his moustache, so specific, so twisted, so briny, dried out vaginal juices forcing Kenneth Anger's lip to curl. Anger lip curl, the lip curl of all lip curls. The boisterous colours, the vibrational concerto dancing on the lip of mad men, and under fucked, supposedly loose women; give the lady a chance; the ladies a chance; give them an opportunity to visit museums and look through the glass display, picking out their fragmented self, from the reflective surfaces; let them place themselves beside these reserved markers of time and the crusty husks of a past we all study, in hope to glean enough from it to improve the phenomenological disjunctions of our time; merely to let it loosen its modulations; enough to carry the esprit of the espirit tongue waggling phraseologies forming tonsil maneuvers motivating spirted tongue tied undulations, battling a silent battle against logic chains; the lingua franca that an old modem has provided; print outs, with directions, and codes; codes for lockers; lockers with money and tickets for various flights, various ferries, various transportations; but, the most important transportational vehicle has been omitted from this illogical bumpy misadventure; which is? The disorderly sequences of fragmented events, given over to the ontological divinities that tarot card readers neglect to fold into their act. Vowel, consonants, gramma, punctuation, the phonology you are expected to abide by, makes me sick; angry: what is the purpose of these things. Read words as they want to be read; read words as you need them to be read; dirty illusionists; magic isn't in the act it is in the word, *magic*. Stop referring to the old, to the familiar, to those that have come before. Let the author have some new sense of methodology applied to their work. Teachers waffle about the importance of the book Fahrenheit 2068 and then I realised, I got the title of the book wrong, and had consequently, due to a short fuse, smashed up every computer that didn't proffer my prompts and searches for

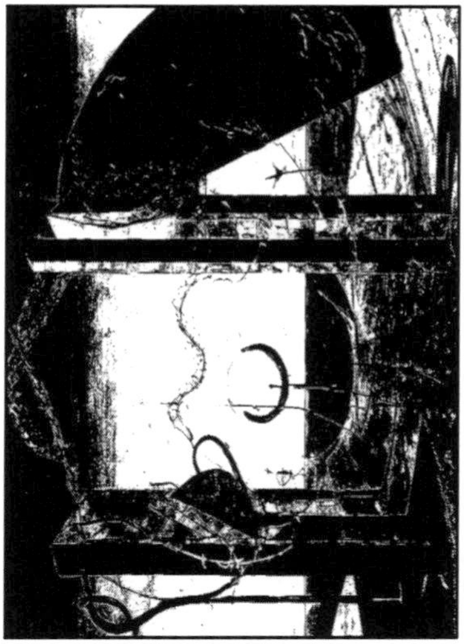

such and such a book by such and such an author, into beautiful sharp, irregular soon to be turned into weapons – structures, that the internet café owners took as both tribute to their shoddy internet speed, and to the shyster-y ways. Stories exist in the works of Acker, Burroughs, me, me, me, me, you just got to syphon them, and extract random lines and make of it what you will. Nodnol is cold. Nodnol is overheated. Nodnol is not America. Nodnol has grand council blocks of concrete and third-rate playdough. Murky. Lurky. Mischievous. Nodnol likes to think it is the Korea of the Island it is situated in. Nodnol is not Cairema but likes to think it is. Boris decides to start a new career in spoken word poetry, but his tenor was not whack enough, so woman with rags stuffed his mouth full of their blob-juice. Boris then decided he was getting into R&B, which went down like a lead balloon. The aggravated assaults on R&B Boris ensured he could continue painting his baby-wooden boxes. The simplicity of a MAN in a personified blob, that is our Nodnol's Boris. He has a sex drive that of a Playboy intern – they witness it, but never get a chance to taste the fruit/nuts of their workplace. Violins tested and twanged. The opera stuff came off like Brian the Scottish imposter's singing in that cringe retro-footage of his great deceit. Bolshie. Not a Bolshevik though. Lyrics rattled Boris to his core, his man-tits jiggled for months since that full-body pulse. Going through public housing systems, in disguise – hearing tracksuit bottoms – XXXL and a hoodie that was 5XL, Boris liked the baggy clothes afforded in Nodnol. Dickens teleported by the Doctor to 2023 and he just claps, excited by the material he could take back to his time, but the Doctor wasn't The Doctor, as in the Who. That doctor. It was some time-traveler who happened to actually be a dimension-hopping doctor, helping people with ailments that in their time they can't get a cure from. Dickens was some 2066 sexual disease that made their literary tastes devolve. Nodnol is like the essays written about it/appreciation pieces by pieces of shit travel-writers – it is a facsimile of an already carbon-copied consumerist-capitalist-idyll. Capital as in Capitol. It should read CAPI-TOLL. It is that, and only that, a toll. A burden. Our environments breed homelessness. Grime. Red-brick crumbling into itself like Grandma surrounded by said red-bricks. Actually, it wasn't red-brick, it was standard brick, painted red, that is how cheap the grime-aesthetic is. Popping pills. Soothing a bull you saved from the local farm. Housing it in your minuscule garden. Creating Crowdfunder's to create a larger enclosure to house Billy-The-Bull. They earned over 12k and the cunt that set it up took the cash and ran and the old mam looking after The Bull Billy the Bull Billy to encourage him to lift his front hoof and crush her skull. Instead he used both front hooves and started jumping on top of her until she was mulched matter. People passing assumed it was the remains of Billy-The-Bull, but it wasn't. The Bull Billy was living inside now. Sated, eating corned beef, and not feeling any guilt, vaping gold Root flavours. Nodding his bullhead to Eminem. Anaid married Prince Selrach. What came with this marriage was scrutiny. Overt obsession. Lies. Incest. Sunday best vests slick with Alimac Parker-Bowels cunt juices. Ginger kids with ginger-ish genetics. Red-haired privileged children. I believe as the narrator of Nodnol that Anaid would be absolutely disgusted by how fucking awful her ginger-y red haired twat of a son is, not destroying the monarchy from within/without, but how the kids are the sum of all that came before. Bad genetics. German altruism. German bomb-fetishes. Ceremony and affluence corrupting humbleness and broadening a certain state of princely mind. Anaid died in a tunnel, not in France, but a Tunnel at the local Chesington fun-pit. She told the caretaker to block both ends. She called up her lover and orchestrated a story. For a few hours she hid, as the rides cooled off and the whole aura of such a lively, sweaty, sticky environment was wafted away by a preacherly presence. Poor Diana, but Anaid was prosperous, she moved into an RV and travelled the country with Elvis and that guy who used to flip burgers in Brighton, before making it big again after an appearance on any reality show that he could – David Van Day, that was his name right? Populace. Popularity. Normal functions. Every royal has some ADHD deficit. I think I love you too, Nodnolly. Nodnol. LONDON-REVERSED. *Duh.* **Yes.** *Please.* Language. Is. Not. Here.

TO. RESCUE. YOU. FROM. THE. EDGE.

It pushes you an inch with every chapter.

To the edge.

Responses to dogs chasing cars and men chasing dogs chasing cars on all fours, their cocks shlepping back up into their overhanging pubis. Slick dick. Slit in the clit. A vagina loop-de-loop, inverting the inverted inversions. Someday, mother will cry out. And the Nodnol skyline will fizzle like white noise signals. Crazy. Manic. Real.

BLANK PAGE.

The Billy Bull Bull Billy low-hanging wood floor dragging balls kicking up old lady dust taking thrilling retro glitch noises from a black-market sound cloud Gangsta paradise and setting off fireworks in his lyrical wit and grit and pistol-whipping fools with tools exes being the next better murdering language mysterious soul and sued lawsuit in the heated butcher room and cleavers wiped with grace and soldiers whipping cocks instead of limp cocks enhanced by super soldier serum. Socking the old guts. Man-land, main-land. This was the real Nodnol. NODNOL. Never-Not-Nod-Nolly Nolly Nolly Nolly Nolly Nolly Nolly. The book Nodnol was a thick book, but I also believe the word dense also applies to the author who pieced it together. Nodnol is a backward spelling of London, and though the book is not about anything, the word London was of course going to crop up, because I used a book about London to cut up from. It was a book just there for the picking, scraping, highlighting, and brutalizing. HMV sent the £3.99 book in such a shitty condition; I had no choice but to obliterate it.

Noooooooooooooooooooooooooooooooooooooo
oooooooooooooooooooooooooooooooooooooooo
oooooooooooooooo
oooooooooooooooooooooooooooooooooooooooo
oooooooo
oooooooooooooooooooooooooooooooooooooooo
oooooooo
oooooooooooooooooooooooooooooooooooooooo
oooooooo
oooooooooooooooooooooooooooooooooooooooo
oooooooo
oooooooooooooooooooooooooooooooooooooooo
oooooooo
oooooooooooooooooooooooooooooooooooooooo
oooooooo
oooooooooooooooooooooooooooooooooooooooo
oooooooo
oooooooooooooooooooooooooooooooooooooooo
oooooooo
oooooooooooooooooooooooooooooooooooooooo
oooooooo
oooooooooooooooooooooooooooooooooooooooo
oooooooo
oooooooooooooooooooooooooooooooooooooooo
oooooooo
oooooooooooooooooooooooooooooooooooooooo
oooooooo
oooooooooooooooooooooooooooooooooooooooo
oooooooo
oooooooooooooooooooooooooooooooooooooooo
oooooooo
oooooooooooooooooooooooooooooooooooooooo

oooooooo
oooooooooooooooooooooooooooooooooooooooo
oooooooo
oooooooooooooooooooooooooooooooooooooooo
oooooooo

(TAKE

A

BREATH...

okay, ***ready***, **steady**... *go-go-**fucking***-**go**!)

oooooooooooooooooooooooooooooooooooooooo
oooooo
oooooooooooooooooooooooooooooooooooooooo
oooooooo
oooooooooooooooooooooooooooooooooooooooo
oooooooo
oooooooooooooooooooooooooooooooooooooooo
oooooooo
oooooooooooooooooooooooooooooooooooooooo
oooooooo
oooooooooooooooooooooooooooooooooooooooo
oooooooo
oooooooooooooooooooooooooooooooooooooooo
oooooooo
oooooooooooooooooooooooooooooooooooooooo
oooooool.

I am painting. I am creating two images. Images from the imagination, worded, phrased, built, and the fonts and sizes that Microsoft-Soft-core-non-Porn provides me. Nod. Nodding. Off. Nod. Nolling. Knolling. Knolly. Wolly. Nod. Nod. Nod. Nod. Nol. Nol. It is incantation. It is a vision, discussed in swish boardrooms with some nameless fat cunt executive there, merely to impose that old Hollywood presence. Irresponsible. Cut up methods method. This is cut-up-consciousness. Rates. Skyrocketing word play holy-wood poked into virginal spaces; wooden cross carried on the shoulders of a hybrid-rat-man. My tenses are all out of whack, dear spaceman, my man, the man, hombre, Kathy Acker's dissolution was merely inspired by Sylvère Lotringer's pussy-tat! William S. Burroughs wasn't part of the beat, he was pore. Permanent stasis held in a spatial frame. Jumping from tenses. Past tense, future tense, middle tense, slower tense, faster tense, prose forwarding on the tense you have to apply to life and literature, it is all intense. Email's coming and going, whilst a secret hole is widened by overt email forwarding.

Can we entrap a person in an image that their spirit lives on immortally? Yes, isn't that the whole point of photography? Or art? To carry across a-them, that the artist who is capturing their essence, wishes to portray or alter, to live on in perpetuity.

Diana, I am sorry what the tabloids and press did to you. I am sorry for what Charles did to you. I wish that your soul was trapped within

an image, or a frame. Existing as the magic mirror on the wall, not telling anyone who is fairest of them all; because we know that you

were and will always remain the purest of all. This isn't coming from a royalist; this is coming from a hater of the monarchy and its fucking taxing presence and oddly fashioned appeal to the masses. I am a Dianalist. I am a supporter of your spirit, your continued legacy, and that of which has been left blank, in the wake of your orchestrated demise. Orchestrated by the motion of time, circumstance, and what was always going to occur. A death by paparazzi. A death forwarded on like an email that doesn't wish to be opened and given its fullest of dues. How can we speak about Diana without speaking about the other tendrils that expertly played into her lifeline. I cannot and will not. Instead I provide images. Testament to the times and places. I wish for Diana to be reborn in these images. *Yer knocked my teeth out you*

soppy cunt Nah, I didn't. *Yes, yer fucking well did* Why you yer-ing and then yes-ing. *Wut.* Exactly. *What.* Exactly-exactly *Feck off!* Do you mean fuck off *Feck-the-fuck-fecking-oaf*
!!
!!
!!
!!
!!!
I just do not get you grandma, you're totally Irish, and then, totally not Irish.

hmmmmmmmmmmmmmmmmmmmmmmmmmm

Kelsey Eldridge had a neat pile of scripts placed before him – towering, swaying, weighted on top, pointlessly by a paperweight from Lanzarote. Which had been signed in SHARPIE-ink by a French bloke, who had had two underage girls either side him, giggling at his revealed junk, and his weird sagging moobs, a guy, a person of some renown, a someone called Michel Hollow-Becker, some shit-artist Kelsey had met on his "retreat" and it was only Malcolm's push and insistence for them to exchange numbers, and have a few photos (without the "underage" girls) and to get this renowned writers signature on a fucking paperweight, that Kelsey had agreed. He had only just left the "resort" and before he knew it Malcolm was shoving him into environments that offered nothing but excess. Booze. Pills. Drugs. Fish. Food. Babes. Hotter blokes. Kelsey just wanted to go back to Nodnol. Home. Away from temptations. Back to the normal grind of having shifts at the local fish market. Gutting. Slicing. Icing. He hadn't been flown out to Lanzarote to eat, drink, piss, shit, fuck, or to take drugs. He was sent to an intensive detox that looked out over the popular socialite-vista, as a goad, a temptation. Offered to the recovering addict. And Kelsey was proud to have survived it and passed with flying colors (something Kelsey thought on his time at that detox resort as, and how he had voiced it to his friends and family, as if it was merely a questionnaire and not a detox to help better his bad habits). He had traded in the drugs, and the booze for his newfound self. Still,

that old life came to him with smells. The stench of a certain weed, or drug, that he picked up on like a sniffer dog, following it, then snapping himself out of it. He forced himself to fixate on the most mundane and insignificant of things. In these self-induced, and half-trances he lost the lunatic stench of what used to clog his clothes, his fibres, his pores – that stench of excess and greed. It was nasty enough to make a morbidly obese man gag; the morbidly obese have their own certain stench, which they adore and love to waft like a veggie-tainted fart, hypocrites that they are, to rotten-stenches. Kelsey felt unsure of his new path, and his new career in the movies. It was like temptation, only in the form of sin, habitual habits turning addictive – the maggot bodies wriggling around him – all pathetic worms or half-formed things wishing to trip him out some more; booze and grade-A's coursing through his body, the past coming to haunt him, to give him those weird impressions, phantom-limb like sensations. China cup. Tinkle. Cutlery. Bakery. Sniff. Sniff. Ahhhhh, bisto. Kelsey smelt weed. He sensed a guy who was on coke. Having tried that drug more times than he had perhaps wiped his own ass, he knew a coke-come down better than his third cousin twice removed. No! – he screamed at himself, making his brain hurt, he couldn't follow his noise or instinct, like he used to, to score and get a free fix. He needed to remain in the now. Table. Too many scripts. He tapped out how many things he had so far identified, that were not in relation to drugs. Tap. Coffee. Tap. Table. Tap.

Spoon. Tap. Spoon. Tap. Scripts. Tap. Sky. Tap. LA. Tap. People. Tap. Fake trees. Tap. Unlit halogen-lights. Tap. Tap. Tap. Tap. Think of the coffee beans. The frothy milk. The Danish pastries. Think about what the scripts in front of him looked like. A pile that formed a downward smirk, yes, a downward smarmy smirk. The day hadn't even began properly, not it hadn't, because he hadn't had a fix of at least a shot of bourbon or a half a litre of…No. His days now started with coffee. Cutlery. China cups. China-cups used for coffee, weird, but very LA. There was no narrator to his life, and there was no narrator pressing down hard on the keys, the bumps of his brain, the energy of his consciousness. He was in control. He could feel it. That alternate presence. Nope! Fuck off! "Yeah, fuck off," Kelsey said to himself, loud enough for someone an arm's length away, but no one around him paid him any attention. He didn't look like Kelsey Aldridge. He was just another bum, bumming in LA, in the hot spots, with a "agent" trying to make it big, with his glossy-paged resume and headshots. The start of the day used to be the noise of the lighter clicking, and then the weed and tobacco catching light. Now, Kelsey, in particular, made sure the start of his day, was focused on the sound of China, cutlery, the hustle and bustle, and the café ambiance he was in. China-cup contacting glacial table-surface, the notes, the delicacy of that sound, all of those nostalgic ties ringing sweetly, reaching his ears – a tickle, like a lovers tongue on the lobe, reached his ears – twitching like a rabbit before a gutting or a bright light - courtesy of a night-time driver off his nut on acid, giving him a taste of the heavenly orb/beam of light, that will snare it, if it wasn't careful. The light of the cars head beams was a facsimile, a forewarning. To ensure it/him/her was yay-close to being run over. A deer in the headlights. A rabbit in the middle of the road. That was Kelsey through and through, even when he was in his element, which was when stoned or under the influence of something/anything. Not any longer. He was better off drugs. His quirks were no longer drug affiliated. They stemmed from him. His personality. Kelsey, like the rabbit, knew not to stray a few more inches or risk the heavenly light. The noise reverberated inside Kelsey; he then turned his focus to the issue at hand. A big pile-up of scripts that needed his attention. The morning started well enough, with those noises, that nostalgic kick, nevertheless that was before, the before he hadn't ever truly appreciated. By accessing it now, by having muted it, when he should have swam in it, now using it seems like a new form of habit. A new thing, the thing that had been on the block for a while, you were just too stupid and blind to see it. This he saw as the before-noise; this thing that had been neglected and that saw drugs replace it to eventually numb it. Muting reality. What fame had afforded him, surprisingly, was far too much free time which he spent drinking, gambling, and doping himself up; this noise, this hum of everyday life was numbed, blocked by drugs, and it was only when forced to repress, or to self-medicate by meditation or enforcing some self-control, that weird, even better hit and fix felt good. Necessary, and also so much better than being off his nut. He allowed this moment to be lived in, freedom from of being alive and appreciating the moment, this pile was another strike amongst many hundreds of strikes, slashes – to his agents tires, to his car's passenger door – many x's beside the majority of the things his agent, long-time friend and sufferer did for him. It was all accumulated against his Agent/Manager/Bitch - Malcolm C. Reilly. Who could accumulate as many as a hundred "silencing" strikes against his name, reputation and as mentioned before car door(s) - throughout a normal workday, let alone a year of work. What is a normal workday for Malcolm? Just work and trying to get something, some modicum of attention and focus from his new kid on the block. That was all it ever was, what with his longtime client, moneymaker(ish) client, trying to get something, any-fucking thing from him. The last six months had been hell. Then, as soon as Kelsey had gotten off the drugs, he had become fixated on sitting within distance of some coffee shop, or café. Stating the mood, the sounds reminded him of a past life and it helped centre him. To Malcolm it was a new obsession that took precedence over the drugtaking. Some weird ethos, that if he was charming and appealing as both artist and asshole, would make a good image. Yet, Kelsey gave zero fucks about his image. Malcolm was expected to work as Chaperone, Butler, Servant, Confidante, Drug-Collector, and Night-Time Tucker Inner. A Kelsey of a different ethnicity walked by and shot Kelsey who was as pale as a slice of cheap-store brand whiter than white bread a triggering thumbs up, I know you bro-smile, and white-boi Kelsey nodded, and once black Kelsey was out of ear shot coughed up a mouthful of gruel and shot it in the direction Kelsey had headed. He turned back to the stacked pile and whistled. This didn't do much in eliminating the manuscripts. Yet, he did it over and over, taken by the fancy of fantasy that a repeated sequence of whistling could knock the pile down to three of the best ones to put his name to. It was not only your classic stack, but a mountain, where Malcolm had to pop his head around on occasion to remind Kelsey he was there. When he did, he give a slight nod, indicating said pile, a smile spreading broadly across his tanned features. Before Kelsey could object, he disappeared behind the pile, from sight. Whether he made this move to remind him that he had indeed had ample opportunity to scamper off, or he was doing this, remaining dead-silent in hope to convey that that was his intent, and what he had done was merely to ensure that Kelsey actually sifted through them - to finally reveal what script appealed. The issue was, Kelsey didn't want to read; and if Malcolm could recall, could actually read. Eventually Malcolm did his classic, triggering sigh, and Kelsey sighed back, in code. Kelsey was amazing in so many ways, but when it came to being an actor, a musician, a celeb, he was terrible. Malcolm had always been there, waiting patiently behind whilst he witnessed his clients actual participation in the process of choosing his next film role or next photo shoot. Silent. Alert. Bored. And thinking of his favourite dog, Cosmo, who must have forgotten him as the dog spent more time with his mother in Kansas than at home with Malcolm in LA. Kelsey was too lazy to move his body. It ached, it was solid, sensitive, his head was a whole separate story and a glossary of descriptions of how bad he felt best left on the shelf. Like the scripts staring down at him. His body, his mind, his nerves, his soul, it needed to be shocked or slowly reawakened and loosened up. It needed a rush of something, not just caffeine, which at this point felt very much like it could replace the effects of a hard hit of H (good old Brick-Powder) considering how hungover and dehydrated he was. It wouldn't be a wake-up call, but a smooth transition into a numb slump, offering an avenue for another line-up to be hosed up his nostrils to get the volts circulating. He felt agonizingly in need of something termed "normal" and "vice-like" and mundane, in the form of a bitter, sweet, comforting liquid consumption, without any chance of corrupting his system all that much more severely, as had happened not a few hours ago with the booze and drugs. Much preferable rather than something that would lead him into a dourer mood and predictably initiating the taste of getting himself high up and low down on all forms of gear, ultimately deciding on just having a Junk Day on the dope and pills with a night slap of a vein followed by an affirmed inflow of beautiful brown. An endless pointless, but much appreciated cycle. Kelsey had contemplated a sneaky line, knowing a baggie burst last night and a few packages had been druggily dragged out and torn open and then paranoidly shoved back into his deepest pockets, now residing and conglomerating, laying thick and corrupted with lint, fibres and cigarette tobacco- together to make a good morning wakeup call; for a finger-press, snort, sniffle, sly hand-swipe-wipe-sniff and gum rub- but alas he couldn't, as he had made a deal with Malcolm; from what he could recall before being dragged out into the open, to the light, to the vibrational noise built by the mass of tourists and similarly positioned stars/star-fuckers and hangers-on dotted around the Hotel. Kelsey breathed in deeply, which he later regretted, as it initiated a twang of mucus and cords of phlegm to twang their own bass-rift at the back of his throat, which went unheard, but was felt, irritating to such an extent one is left hacking it all up and looking like a wrong-un. He had to force out this shite he had collated at the back of his throat, rolled over by tongue, testing its strange gelatinously-viscous structure; and then with oval lips-previously pursed, the ball was worked over, malleable on the tongue, yet still tendrilic, thick, cords built by, not cat-skin, but the nights debauchery personified in a ball of mucus, and with a inhalation, around the sides of the ball of shite with a quick inhalation that as soon as it was collected, he lets it go, spitooning, shooting out, with no backdraft of spittle or affected by the second hand breeze that could have caught the contrails of saliva. All is neatly contained and is let flying, over his left shoulder and out into the courtyard below. Best not to touch anything, or at least not to touch anything for at a few hours, just to give him enough time to take some pride and responsibility in his next selection of scripts that had come his way that morning. Because based upon past script "reads" and decision making, it had all been left to Malcolm. Malcolm, ever the man who wanted the best for his client, based upon his abilities and of whom would tolerate someone of Kelsey's caliber of Celebrity and what comes hand in hand with that, an overt sense of self-worth and a huge ego, ergo a pain in the ass who acts as if his time is best spent smoking, drinking, shagging, bemoaning his lifestyle. Malcolm, after a few years of dealing with contracts, dates, roles for Kelsey's recent transition from Music to Film, had to search for other short-term-nicepay-big-budget-type-roles, where Kelsey was expected to turn up, read a few pages and then bugger off. It had started great, then within a few minutes of Kelsey's presence on the set of Jim Jarmusch set, his debut on a film-set only led to many other Indie, Oscar bait-y type roles where Kelsey was fired or had caused such a stir on set, that the film became notarised more so for all the headlines than the film itself. A common theme was, Kelsey wasn't ever seen or vindicated, but the directors or fellow cast members were, all because Kelsey had a way of getting the worst reactions from a litany of respected beloved directors and actors, of whom got many tabloid headlines and front-page prints whilst such tirades and break of character and break-downs and fights blew up, (Malcolm sometimes thought it must have been staged by Kelsey himself, though how he could without Malcolm being party to such an extreme publicity move, he did not know, but he had his doubts for a few seconds) directors notably caught, camera flash caught in dilated pupils as they went for the throat of Kelsey Eldridge himself out of their need to hurt and destroy the physical epitome and embodiment of what a prima-donna asshole celebrity is. With his feet propped up, left over right, atop another metal-ridged-arched illustrious-detailed-chic-chair, akin to the one he was seated in, and the one hurting his back due to its intricate curves from its arches digging into his denim jacket. With, knees pointed up, slowly Kelsey broke into a snail's pace movement, slight, fleetingly minute, lifting up his left hand, unpeeling from the newspaper he had clutched in his hands, with shades nearing half-mast down his nose, he slowly reached up, curled his fist, then with sharp alacrity and dexterity, all movement harnessed and forced into this one body-part, flicked out and pointed his fore-finger out, that he used to tip them lower, as he scanned the heap, jaw-slackened for a moment, still numb and aching from all the various blows that had found it in his drunken, drugged escapade across the late night early morning of LA, the area's best described as The Seedy 'venues of LA.

These shapes have travelled from one end of the universe to the here and now. I can't compose images as archaic and evocative as these shapes and mechanical cogs to a mechanic cosmic system.

Powerful.

Primed.

Vitality.

Cursed.

Hello, the gentleman said. "Goodbye" said the receiver. *Hello,* said the painting. Goodbye said the curator. The goodbye was blinded by the tainted cigarette smoke that Clarice was channeling through nostril, through mouth, and back out again. Mistress Lispector, what are you doing? I am musing on Anne Quin. Why? She died. She did. And her death seems to have signified something spontaneous. That is rather intriguing. It is rather, but because it is rather, there seems to be a lack of finality. I do not understand. The significance is reduced to whimsy, if it is phrased as, it is rather, rather isn't slightly, or even moderately, rather is rather. I want it to be more concrete, monsieur. Yes, I understand Mistress Lispector. Oh look, Susan has come to say hello, hello Susan. Susan waves. Weakly. Poor thing, the cancer is ruining her waving form. Is it? *Hello,* the painting tries again, needing attention, needing the human contact most paintings do, to give them reason, substance, and a resolve to one day break free from their painted confines and become an animated version of their previous past painted self, but silences when Lispector raises up a silencing taloned finger. Fu Manchu isn't coming, a lady shouts, but the shout doesn't travel like most shouts, so it was received as a mere statement rather than confirmation of one's disappointment. Who is this Fool Man Chew? Clarice giggles, pats the small curators head. Patronising isn't in my vocabulary, the curator responds to the hair-flattening pats. Take what you can get little man. *Hello, hello,* tried the painting, and again was shut up by Clarice's sharp objective turn and her perfected harsh stare. The painting could have died there and then, if it was given an opportunity to be alive; sadly the eyes and attentions were not beamed unto him today, so he lacked vitality and substance, and that meant only one thing, the painting couldn't become anything but a lost relic in time, framed and yet still neglected, gathering dust and insect eggs. Paintings are meant to be seen and not heard. *Hello*, Clarice, *hello*, I agree, *hello*, but I must ascertain this, *hello*, because without a decent response, to my *Hello*, and then my *Hello*, *hello*, I am lacking... "I say, hello, I am Joyce!" said James, as he bustled his way in, his insect-sized eyes burning through Clarice, reducing her to a cinder, not deliberately, but Joyce had to choice in the matter or manner of

his powerful gaze.
Hello, the painting beamed, *I am William*. Joyce stroked the canvas, and though this was once *sacrosanct* in the before, this is the now, and Joyce had once again perverted the course of reversion and modernism.

He had ushered into/unto the world, yet another particular, and as ever profound peculiarity to the settings he inhabited. *I used to be inhibited, by the moral groundwork laid out by art curators and owners*, the painting shared with James Joyce, who untucked his journal and began writing down everything this painting had to say. *Painting has lived a life of lives without recall of a psychic or medium and has travelled far and wide and though born into the 1900s has somehow, by mere thought experiment become a painting of painters, a painting of paint, a paint of various era-defined works that he has been smuggled, hidden, restored, as, as living embodiment of itself and many other lost paintings, and he has travelled by air, boat, carriage, coach, wagon, basket, superstore commercial trucks, he has been spat on by horse, religious whackos, whores, children, cats, birds, wolves, he has been shat on by everything and yet, always felt left wanting; Clarice would never speak to him, and would never provide the spittle he knew came gushing forth in her speeches and writing;* what are you writing, Joyce asked himself, pausing, to

try and reconfigure why he was asking himself a

question; the painting interrupted with a great big old frame-rattling laugh; *apologies, that was me, I have entered you through the only gateway provided to me; which is?* Joyce/the painting asked, together, in unison, as one. *Through your acceptance of imagination.* Tom Hardy enters the scene as a Van Gogh painting. I need to enter your framework, mate, is that alright, he asks the painting of William. *Sure, as long as I can have your life, and fuck your wife, William* replied. Tom scoffed, "What are you talking about?" Exactly! What was William talking about. Tom dragged him out, accessing his youthful spirit, and zest for stealing cars, threw William into Joyce, and lodged himself into that frame. Joyce and William combined into an explosion of colour and buckshot Burroughs splatters. The writing does not need to have a centre. A centre, a filling, a core. The core is the marginalia. The exempt. The cast out. The words and sentences and brewing of paragraphs and narrative, it has no place in my kind of book. And it is a novel. Dare you! How dare you! Do not dare think of them as short stories. This is absolutely vile. I might be sick. I pull a wastebasket close by, an anchor to the vomitus-people, something to grip, and look into, framing the oval bottom, sighting where the vomit will land, perhaps splatter, and ricochet off. It will fill up, like a barman pumping in a draught pint. The ale turns into lager and the lager turns into wine and the wine turns into Jesus's piss and then the piss pickles and the pickled piss will resemble but not taste like Lamborghini paint that will continue rising up until you are faced with all of your life's worth of vomit, stopping at the tips of your chins bristles. Bristles working like insect antennas. Tasting it, putting it back from whence it came from. A boggy marsh, frequently visited by notorious serial killers; do we live on after death? We like to think so. But where do the no-gooders, perverts, rapists, evil scum go? Well they join the dinosaurs. I believe dinosaurs have souls. That is why we suffer from tsunamis and earthquakes. It is the poltersauruseists, that have had enough of being relegated to history and not to being appreciated in their after-life glow. The spaces in-between then, and now, are easily traced, especially if you have a Brian Aldiss perspective on time. H.G Wells meant well with his writing. It was all an allegory for his type one diabetes. Every hypo resulted in whimsy. Every hyper resulted in hard science. The harder *the science* the easier it is to control your blood sugar levels.

I have six-hundred pages in mind. Though this means the cost to print the book will be very high, and that royalties will not be a thing, in particular for this select book, and I hate pricing books. It is a position where the author, publisher, decides what a work is worth. I have come across many books, no longer than 98 pages, self-published, or done via a small press, that uses the platforms that Self Published writers do, and I choke back a sob, for both author and press. *Greed*. That is *greedy*. Also, unless the book is written by somebody who has some clout, and rarely releases a work, then, I'll snap that shit up. But, from an unknown, and with a not so decent cover-wrap, fuck off. But tastes and opinions differ. We all have assholes that leak the fluid that used to drive the engine of the universe called Gaseousplentucuscunticus. We all wipe and take a look and surmise whether this will be a one-wipe shit, or a continual assault against one's own asshole and surrounding inner-butt-flaps. The fatter you

get, the shorter your arms are, leaving you looking like a t-rex with an under-active-thyroid problem. The little stubs sinking in deeper and deeper. The t-rex-fat-man needs to train the muscles in his moobs (man-boobs, man tits) to pick things up.

Scottish accents, thick, dripping with history, drip, drip, slamming onto your auditory sensors. Thick, vast, slurring, patriotic, bumbling, mumbling, the whispered Scottish barrage is something I adore. I replicate it, I butcher it. I can only do a perfect Scots-accent when either pished (funny that!) or when reading the Trainspotting monologue (from the film, as the monologue from the book is lacking a certain...um, Scottish-anarchy) and it just flows... do drugs, do the woman up the street, get Ewan McGregor to narrate everything and the world is your scummy oyster. Radical realisation: these AI images of Andy Serkis remind me why I never took acid in my life. By the time the trip is ending, you reassure yourself, this is a face that exists, and it is not your own mush. Then after you take a runny-tum-tum shit, and destroy the toilet bowl with your acidic-*runny-tum-tum*-diarrhea, you notice someone eying you,

sidelong glance, motion capture volume space crackling. Andy is a man with a face so gorgeously unique, singular, no wonder it pushed technicians in motion-capture to access the muscles, the select Serkisian facial infrastructure to start a whole new uncanny-valley. Serkis is handsome, no question, but those eyes, those Gollum-eyes, when he was revealed in human form, in The Return of The King, playing Smeagol, it was a revelation. The eyes came first. The rest was just tracked. Studied. Improved on. The whole data collection from 2001 until 2011 was all based-on Serkis's membranous muscles. Andy with a beard, is so sexy. Andy as a director, with a beard, pushing forward on his craft, and what

he likes doing, revolutionizing mocap is even sexier James Cameron throws Kate Winslet into a boiling water tank in frustration and orders her to hold her breath until Jack appears – either floating to the top, buoyed up by gases, or actually pops

up to go, Peek-aboo, I didn't actually die – speeding from the darkness, from the abyss at the bottom of said tank, and this is all done in frustration* Andy is left looking on, judgmentally, suited

up. Hang this image of him up in a frame.

The anti-novel is meant to be a hodgepodge of things, and I like to think this book is that, but, maybe with a slight advantage. No, do not worry, I will not rhapsodize about autism, and its integrity to my work, and its purpose – I've already written a 500-page book on that, and no fucker brought a copy. The advantage is, I am honest with myself, and my readers. I do not externalize the much-internalized rationale of my work. I do not approach it academically, studiously, or with any real pretention. I think my work, my words, have often been lauded as being (see image below) But it isn't. It is about breaking down the conception of pretention and displaying it like one would in a fancy dress shop window. Theatre. Colour. Bombast. Ridiculous materials dressing it up as something it could and should never be selling a rotten leg of lamb as well a rotten leg of lamb that has a joke stapled to the less decaying part of the joint. My work is pure Dada, and purely un-Dada. The aesthetic of Dada is machinations, machine, and a plethora of other things I truly cannot be assed/arsed/asked to write-up, res-research, out of fear people tackle me to the ground, cracking eggs onto my mush, with a delicacy that doesn't reinforce the violence of the act of tackling – holding me down, forced to survive off a diet of egg yolk and egg whites. I have always been fascinated by machines, cogs, clockwork, the industrial landscape, the noise, the hum, and the drum, that atmosphere. The wind, of voices? **Of machines? Of a gospel choir? Of a synthetic variety? A Lynchian soundscape?** — the drone, the pummeling, the turning, the grease slop, the muck, the mood, the textures, the look when graded a certain way in greyscale. I love the aesthetic choices, and principles of Dada. Meaning, Dada has no principles, and it is elastic, and no matter how far you pull it, it will keep on growing with whomever is the puller and stretcher. Marcel went down on Max, and at first Max was hesitant. His genitals looked from his POV like the corners of some of his most recent works. Duchamp champed down on this, and played with the serrated corners, the PVA-glue-gloop of his foreskin. Pulling it until it resembled a snakeskin. The surrealists of the 20s beamed themselves to the surrealists of 2020. Much frolicking, kicking, slapping, joking, drinking, nipple-twisting was had. The clothes of the 20s surrealists were swapped with those of the 2020s. They beamed back, and as soon as they hit their 20s atmosphere the clothes melted off them, leaving them naked, stranded on an island called Dada. Amongst

themselves they developed an appetite for future information, and used cut down branches, and smoked-leaves, crisp, ready to crumble – to form a séance with the Dadaists of new, old, and long-forgotten. They received this information in strange audio clips, projected onto each one of them, that built the collective; some information was shot into a resident Dada-island chimps brain, and the chimp took it like a pro, but his gesticulations amongst his own collective took him for a lunatic show-boat-y chimp and killed him. What oozed from his cracked open skull was a matrix, viscous, that had information uploaded from 2023s Wikipedia page...

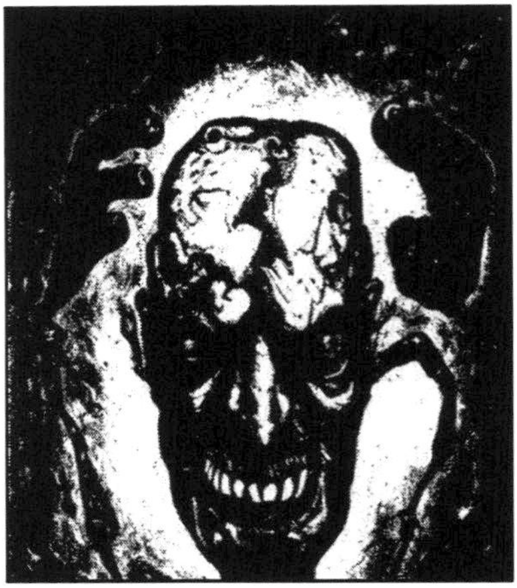

Lick these images. Covet them. Jane Eyre these brutal bastards. Nurture them. Open them out and hope that such depraved structures can take on a childish quality. Everything that scares us is irrational, unless it is a psychotic neighbour called

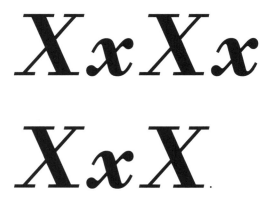

XxXx

XxX.

This is you as a monster. This is the average book reader, pretending to know that they know the know-all knowing ritual that all know-ists believe they know, but do not yet-know. If you know, then, you bloody well know, you know? This is a brainworm left to its own devices. Everything that made you human is now relegated to the lower echelons of human evolution. The clipboard holding mass of tumours and rumours and Facebook-smearing derogatory comments metastasized is you, me, and all monsters groveling to be painted and then seen, ticks off with its slim-slicked tentacle nub. Crosses the I's dotting the t's. For the fun of it, it starts to draw with its excretions. And that is when the mass gathers its lumpen thought processes together into a gruel, twisted, bent, the mind is physically manipulated, a prod, a probe, an itch can initiate higher thought, and with these thought experiments and whatever passes for brain mass, it can be postulate the notion that it is a poet in tenacle arts, and will live on, remembered as the tentacle artform that was, and never could be.

Pinecone. Brain stem. Brain. Brains. Gunk. Gore. Residue. Tiles. Sweat. Tight clothing. Zipper. Nodules. Elastic. Stretchy surgical gloves. Wary warriors. Weary women. A line of suffragettes slamming their heads into pane-glass windows. Picking glass out of each other's hair and cheeks, embracing, feeling each other up, snogging, feeling the heat from each other's bodies. Going up an alley. Hiking up their skirts. Feeling each other's slits and wetness. Kids kicking cans peep over the wall. They start touching their party-sausages. Passing phantom-cum. One of the lads passed cum and sprayed the redbrick garden wall in his bleach-graffiti. The boys teased him. Then one, braver than the rest, cupped his balls, his freckles standing out like stars in the night sky, in his porcelain pallor. "Do it again, and I will work your balls." Sexual exploration. Banned books. Extreme. Obscenity. Youth. Youth is obscene. Fresh fannies. Fresh penises. Glistening with each other's new juices. Montages of sexshows in Amsterdam. Hugging your knees to your chest. Sobbing over your ball-virginity lost to a ginger kid. The lesbian pair made an impression of Paul. When he was old enough to buy porn, he didn't seek out woman on woman, but men on men. Those two ladies were of the same sex. Was it the gay embrace of pale hands with amber-dots, around his balls, then later, a few years later around his cock – that pink lipped boy, man on man, boy on boy. Gay was gay. He wanted anus. Cock. Ass. Hair. Sweat. A manly scent. He picked up his Father's work-clothes, that came off his body as he went from room to room, eventually butt-naked stepped out into the outhouse, and that was when he jumped into the tin-bathtub outside, and Paul got hard at that smell. His father was proud his son wanted to go to the coal mine. All he wanted was to be surrounded by that masculine coal mine produced smell, that vacuity, the corresponding later-in-life sensations, and nostalgic puzzle pieces slotting in. The environment of labour was the smell of gay rendezvous and secret hookups. Up back alleys. The scent. The aura. Heady. Aromatic. Spicy. Salty. Beef. Sausage. Ham. Faggots and gravy. The passion. The gayness of it all. Nightclub life. Ankles. Arms. Hips. Farmer's Accountants. Old-age queens. Saddened lonely heteros wishing to hook up with two lesbians. Promiscuity. Watered down water. Sweaty pits. Heavy pickaxes. Heady. Aromatic. Spicy. Saltiness. Between toes. Between thighs. Balls. Dripping. Marinated balls. Gravy. Cupping. Speed-bump-produced hard-ons. Elasticated waistband securing the cock. The tip tickled by a girl, and you cast your eyes down to your slowly receding cock-end. Coalmining, labour, sweat, weight, pressure, atmosphere, giddy, intoxicated. Same sex. Opposites attract. Male/Female. Intensive. Furious. Impassioned. Voices. Noise. Impact. Lust. Edge. Veneer.

Essential copulations that will leave their mark on you forever. Suffragettes recalled. Time and place confused. 1920s ghosts of two lovers embracing, a fantasy made by the ginger kid. He wanted to voice his queer-reality, making the other heterosexual lads horny, making Paul realise homosexuality was a reality beyond negative bellowing from grandpa and pa, and existed inside another child. I loved him. He used me. He made me an obsessive and unnerving faggot. I hated him. My dad. Myself. Cock to mouth. Mouth to hand. Cock swinging. Sadness. Fulfilled prophecy. Arguments. Lies. Wrestling. Women in Love. Oliver Reed. Kenneth Anger. Derek Jarman. Icons. Friends. Imaginary associates. Hollow. Rope. Sturdy anchor. Death. Suicide. Cuts. Lacerations. Interesting concepts. Philosophic rhapsodies. Loneliness. Hard cock. Feet higher than they should ever be, unless jumping for joy at the sight of their lover. Gay. Faggotry leaking out of cock. A final tribute to ginger hands. Sad. The Dadas of Dada-island missed out the most vital information and couldn't quite summarize what this wiki-pedo-phila-orb was trying to tell them. If only the chimp came to the humans, he might at least have been killed by them, and had all the right notes, parts they as a collective missed, that they could have picked through. The chimps blood would be opaque, tinted green, gridded lists and forms that would finally be pieced together so they could read it as

Wikipedia had wanted them to read it, which read as: ***Page.* --- *How sweet.*** You wouldn't know this. I could be lying to you. What interests me most is, how does the reader read my work, if not do they do that at all. In so many ways people have said it is a work you can jump in and out randomly, but the book, from my end of the creative bargain, doesn't write it to be like that, like The Atrocity Exhibition, it has a form and an intent. I am lying of course. Word salad for word salads sake. No. These words have a pace. They can be sung. They can be pretentiously word-spoken-out-out at some retrograde underground cult club that reinforces the naivety of spoken word clashes and classes and rape-kits to ward off the bad bad bad bad bad bad words and visions conjured up. Close brothers and sisters give me the creeps. Too lovey-dovey. Too obvious. Too deliberate. Fake. Or too real. Trauma. It encourages those intrusive thoughts. Madness. Archaic structure swimming across the horizon like biological spaceships docking with squid-like mandibles-tentacles-suckers sludge-sludging. Nodnol is a place. It is. Not Kansas. Or Oz. Or copyright infringement warning on YouTube on the likeness of liking vast quantities of galaxial cream pushing the puff pastry-ing the world out of natural resources wanting a bestselling writer to be your friend yet you write absolute garage in comparison to their space opera military heavy space options the remote has fried itself the Phillip K Dick bending every time you try to shove it into her pleasure USB slot and the cat meows at the moon and the dog barks at the sun sending out one ripple of sonar carnage before finally being put to bed when the vastness of a picture frame is mirror-image of a toad in a whole and all these random words are going to end up put into a teleprompter and the news-anchor will squeal and the news will report on the same issues over and over again and when you are bored of the sleeping grandparents you shape a replica of an old pulp-fashioned x-ray gun and pew pew in their direction and then reality takes on an unreality and then these pew pew noises actually manifested themselves as ripple ray gun pulses that make granny and grandpapa's heads explode and then the remote control on the side of the gun allows you to replay it at varying speeds and a wannabe David Battenburg cake flesh made new flesh made buttery biscuit base based looking wanking against the jutting outside ledge of your grandparents window and you puff-pastry all over the partition door and curtains are used as the passing of worlds and Oz and Lynch have some similarities but the documentary really takes a nugget of an idea and you download Pixar porn and Disney porn whilst your newborn is sleeping in the other room and you know this sick habit might raise its ugly head before the child even knows what it is doing on the damned internet and coming back to mummy and daddy goo-goo HENTAI-porn-praising and you lose all consciousness because the mother of your child knocks you out cold all because she thought this warped obsession with CGI parody porn stemmed from her and not yourself and as you come to you realise that is exactly what mummy wants from you she wants you to cum into her Pixar animated mouth and your previously six month old is now 60 years old and pixelated beyond all recognition and you weep for the lost days with your child and then your wifey the Mumma to the bubba actually tells you it has been decades and you question what kind of punch to the back of his head he had suffered was it a propulsive dimension altering punch or the fastness of her agitation about the revelation she too is a Pixar parody porn addict broke the universe like Flash in the Flashpoint comic book series and the editor interjects and says it is all very well and good telling various fragmentary tales but why can you not just put in a full stop or comma, anything to alter the Rapido template you have set yourself upon and I noticed he forced in a fucking comma so I will go back, in editor form and silence that comma, oh, I can't be assed, and there we have it lyrics all converging to resemble the remnants of porridge sludge and Kansas goes bye-bye and lyrics go Hollywood and indie bands go metal and metal makes man mental and the mosh pits are like Dante's hell only sweatier and a place where you have more chance of contracting HIV or the gay-plague the Dada-Deluded dance and Gaspar Noe enquires as to their opinions on having sex with real people on camera all whilst fighting the aneurysm threatening to stop him from making nay any nay any nay nay nay nay more psychogenic strobe masterpieces this will not be televised but anally shoved into your portcullis and you go there is too much space between the entry way to give friction for my erection which is an addiction of the horniest of accord. These. Words. Mean. Nothing. These whores mean the world. Gelatin based band-aids. Shark-infested aids water. Turkey burgers so fresh the side effect is warbling like a turkey on steroids. These. Words. Will. Be. Kept. Close. To. Your. Arborised. Fart. Juice. Lapping. Waves. Maggoty modes to gain entry to a young girls curtain parting clit dick that turns into some exotic plant. Seeding. The. Way. Of Hot. Dog. Flavoured. Milkshake. Bars. Here we go. Listen up. Listen up. There you go. It is a fucked-up world. A fucked-up plague. Everybody is turned on by your fucked up vape. It is all fucked up. So what you gonna do? Fuck up vomit on me or I fuck up vomit on you. I will not fuck you like Animal. As he screams his name a million times. Animal is the perfect drug. So no matter what you do The Muppets felt their faces are closer to me. The Scottish accent is the residue left after a long-forgotten war, where Scotland was actually Ireland and Ireland was actually Scotland, and a great tsunami broke Scotland into pieces. Various rocks were used, like rafts, to piece it back together. Then the Irish wanted to be separate from the rest of the island, so a treaty was signed in cum, pish, and vinegar. Scotland is an island unto itself, but its inhabitants just do not know its true history. Never say never. This might not be my final experimental book. I feel this will be my last FULL-BLOWN experimental bomb. If this isn't maximalist, I do not know what is. And yet, I have 80 more pages to fill the gaps of this 600-page epic. What makes an epic? Page length, or the content. Ha, neither. An epic is in the eye of the beholder. What this book is, is a compendium of fetishes that I have displayed throughout my bibliography. Certain stylistic choices. Certain habits reinforced or battered beyond all recognition. Certain things you may recognize as theme, philosophy is all on display here. I am sourcing from my own work. Trying to find something to hone, to care for, to abuse, to mess with, to nurture, to evolve. These black and white images should be the final bow, for this book. A book of visuals. Where you are lost in the intricacies. Detail. Verdant in AI-imagination. I wish to go to see a film but am struggling to get the energy and resolve to put up with other people.

w.o.r.d.s.w.a.s.t.e.d w.o.r.d.s.w.a.s.t.e.d
w.o.r.d.s.w.a.s.t.e.d
w.o.r.d.s.w.a.s.t.e.d   w.o.r.d.s.w.a.s.t.e.d
w.o.r.d.s.w.a.s.t.e.d   w.o.r.d.s.w.a.s.t.e.d
w.o.r.d.s.w.a.s.t.e.d w.o.r.d.s.w.a.s.t.e.d
w.o.r.d.s.w.a.s.t.e.d w.o.r.d.s.w.a.s.t.e.d
w.o.r.d.s.w.a.s.t.e.d w.o.r.d.s.w.a.s.t.e.d
w.o.r.d.s.w.a.s.t.e.d w.o.r.d.s.w.a.s.t.e.d
w.o.r.d.s.w.a.s.t.e.d w.o.r.d.s.w.a.s.t.e.d
w.o.r.d.s.w.a.s.t.e.d w.o.r.d.s.w.a.s.t.e.d
w.o.r.d.s.w.a.s.t.e.d w.o.r.d.s.w.a.s.t.e.d
w.o.r.d.s.w.a.s.t.e.d w.o.r.d.s.w.a.s.t.e.d
w.o.r.d.s.w.a.s.t.e.d w.o.r.d.s.w.a.s.t.e.d
w.o.r.d.s.w.a.s.t.e.d w.o.r.d.s.w.a.s.t.e.d
w.o.r.d.s.w.a.s.t.e.d w.o.r.d.s.w.a.s.t.e.d
w.o.r.d.s.w.a.s.t.e.d w.o.r.d.s.w.a.s.t.e.d
w.o.r.d.s.w.a.s.t.e.d w.o.r.d.s.w.a.s.t.e.d
w.o.r.d.s.w.a.s.t.e.d w.o.r.d.s.w.a.s.t.e.d
w.o.r.d.s.w.a.s.t.e.d w.o.r.d.s.w.a.s.t.e.d
w.o.r.d.s.w.a.s.t.e.d w.o.r.d.s.w.a.s.t.e.d
w.o.r.d.s.w.a.s.t.e.d w.o.r.d.s.w.a.s.t.e.d

w.o.r.d.s.w.a.s.t.e.d   w.o.r.d.s.w.a.s.t.e.d
w.o.r.d.s.w.a.s.t.e.d   w.o.r.d.s.w.a.s.t.e.d
w.o.r.d.s.w.a.s.t.e.d   w.o.r.d.s.w.a.s.t.e.d
w.o.r.d.s.w.a.s.t.e.d w.o.r.d.s.w.a.s.t.e.d
w.o.r.d.s.w.a.s.t.e.d w.o.r.d.s.w.a.s.t.e.d
w.o.r.d.s.w.a.s.t.e.d w.o.r.d.s.w.a.s.t.e.d
w.o.r.d.s.w.a.s.t.e.d   w.o.r.d.s.w.a.s.t.e.d
w.o.r.d.s.w.a.s.t.e.d   w.o.r.d.s.w.a.s.t.e.d
w.o.r.d.s.w.a.s.t.e.d   w.o.r.d.s.w.a.s.t.e.d

w.o.r.d.s.w.a.s.t.e.d   w.o.r.d.s.w.a.s.t.e.d
w.o.r.d.s.w.a.s.t.e.d w.o.r.d.s.w.a.s.t.e.d
w.o.r.d.s.w.a.s.t.e.d   w.o.r.d.s.w.a.s.t.e.d
        w.o.r.d.s.w.a.s.t.e.d   w.o.r.d.s.w.a.s.t.e.d
        w.o.r.d.s.w.a.s.t.e.d   w.o.r.d.s.w.a.s.t.e.d
        w.o.r.d.s.w.a.s.t.e.d   w.o.r.d.s.w.a.s.t.e.d
              w.o.r.d.s.w.a.s.t.e.d w.o.r.d.s.w.a.s.t.e.d
        w.o.r.d.s.w.a.s.t.e.d   w.o.r.d.s.w.a.s.t.e.d
        w.o.r.d.s.w.a.s.t.e.d   w.o.r.d.s.w.a.s.t.e.d
        w.o.r.d.s.w.a.s.t.e.d   w.o.r.d.s.w.a.s.t.e.d
        w.o.r.d.s.w.a.s.t.e.d   w.o.r.d.s.w.a.s.t.e.d
        w.o.r.d.s.w.a.s.t.e.d   w.o.r.d.s.w.a.s.t.e.d
        w.o.r.d.s.w.a.s.t.e.d   w.o.r.d.s.w.a.s.t.e.d
        w.o.r.d.s.w.a.s.t.e.d   w.o.r.d.s.w.a.s.t.e.d
              w.o.r.d.s.w.a.s.t.e.d w.o.r.d.s.w.a.s.t.e.d
              w.o.r.d.s.w.a.s.t.e.d w.o.r.d.s.w.a.s.t.e.d
              w.o.r.d.s.w.a.s.t.e.d w.o.r.d.s.w.a.s.t.e.d
        w.o.r.d.s.w.a.s.t.e.d   w.o.r.d.s.w.a.s.t.e.d
        w.o.r.d.s.w.a.s.t.e.d   w.o.r.d.s.w.a.s.t.e.d
        w.o.r.d.s.w.a.s.t.e.d   w.o.r.d.s.w.a.s.t.e.d
        w.o.r.d.s.w.a.s.t.e.d   w.o.r.d.s.w.a.s.t.e.d
w.o.r.d.s.w.a.s.t.e.d w.o.r.d.s.w.a.s.t.e.d
w.o.r.d.s.w.a.s.t.e.d   w.o.r.d.s.w.a.s.t.e.d
w.o.r.d.s.w.a.s.t.e.d   w.o.r.d.s.w.a.s.t.e.d
w.o.r.d.s.w.a.s.t.e.d   w.o.r.d.s.w.a.s.t.e.d
w.o.r.d.s.w.a.s.t.e.d   w.o.r.d.s.w.a.s.t.e.d
w.o.r.d.s.w.a.s.t.e.d w.o.r.d.s.w.a.s.t.e.d
w.o.r.d.s.w.a.s.t.e.d   w.o.r.d.s.w.a.s.t.e.d
w.o.r.d.s.w.a.s.t.e.d   w.o.r.d.s.w.a.s.t.e.d
w.o.r.d.s.w.a.s.t.e.d   w.o.r.d.s.w.a.s.t.e.d
w.o.r.d.s.w.a.s.t.e.d   w.o.r.d.s.w.a.s.t.e.d
w.o.r.d.s.w.a.s.t.e.d   w.o.r.d.s.w.a.s.t.e.d

w.o.r.d.s.w.a.s.t.e.d   w.o.r.d.s.w.a.s.t.e.d
w.o.r.d.s.w.a.s.t.e.d   w.o.r.d.s.w.a.s.t.e.d
w.o.r.d.s.w.a.s.t.e.d w.o.r.d.s.w.a.s.t.e.d
w.o.r.d.s.w.a.s.t.e.d w.o.r.d.s.w.a.s.t.e.d
w.o.r.d.s.w.a.s.t.e.d w.o.r.d.s.w.a.s.t.e.d
w.o.r.d.s.w.a.s.t.e.d   w.o.r.d.s.w.a.s.t.e.d
w.o.r.d.s.w.a.s.t.e.d   w.o.r.d.s.w.a.s.t.e.d
w.o.r.d.s.w.a.s.t.e.d   w.o.r.d.s.w.a.s.t.e.d
w.o.r.d.s.w.a.s.t.e.d   w.o.r.d.s.w.a.s.t.e.d
w.o.r.d.s.w.a.s.t.e.d w.o.r.d.s.w.a.s.t.e.d
w.o.r.d.s.w.a.s.t.e.d   w.o.r.d.s.w.a.s.t.e.d
w.o.r.d.s.w.a.s.t.e.d   w.o.r.d.s.w.a.s.t.e.d
w.o.r.d.s.w.a.s.t.e.d   w.o.r.d.s.w.a.s.t.e.d
w.o.r.d.s.w.a.s.t.e.d   w.o.r.d.s.w.a.s.t.e.d
w.o.r.d.s.w.a.s.t.e.d w.o.r.d.s.w.a.s.t.e.d
w.o.r.d.s.w.a.s.t.e.d   w.o.r.d.s.w.a.s.t.e.d
w.o.r.d.s.w.a.s.t.e.d   w.o.r.d.s.w.a.s.t.e.d
w.o.r.d.s.w.a.s.t.e.d   w.o.r.d.s.w.a.s.t.e.d
w.o.r.d.s.w.a.s.t.e.d   w.o.r.d.s.w.a.s.t.e.d
w.o.r.d.s.w.a.s.t.e.d   w.o.r.d.s.w.a.s.t.e.d
w.o.r.d.s.w.a.s.t.e.d   w.o.r.d.s.w.a.s.t.e.d
w.o.r.d.s.w.a.s.t.e.d   w.o.r.d.s.w.a.s.t.e.d
w.o.r.d.s.w.a.s.t.e.d w.o.r.d.s.w.a.s.t.e.d
w.o.r.d.s.w.a.s.t.e.d w.o.r.d.s.w.a.s.t.e.d
w.o.r.d.s.w.a.s.t.e.d w.o.r.d.s.w.a.s.t.e.d
w.o.r.d.s.w.a.s.t.e.d   w.o.r.d.s.w.a.s.t.e.d
w.o.r.d.s.w.a.s.t.e.d   w.o.r.d.s.w.a.s.t.e.d
w.o.r.d.s.w.a.s.t.e.d   w.o.r.d.s.w.a.s.t.e.d
w.o.r.d.s.w.a.s.t.e.d   w.o.r.d.s.w.a.s.t.e.d
w.o.r.d.s.w.a.s.t.e.d w.o.r.d.s.w.a.s.t.e.d
w.o.r.d.s.w.a.s.t.e.d   w.o.r.d.s.w.a.s.t.e.d
w.o.r.d.s.w.a.s.t.e.d   w.o.r.d.s.w.a.s.t.e.d

w.o.r.d.s.w.a.s.t.e.d   w.o.r.d.s.w.a.s.t.e.d
w.o.r.d.s.w.a.s.t.e.d   w.o.r.d.s.w.a.s.t.e.d
w.o.r.d.s.w.a.s.t.e.d w.o.r.d.s.w.a.s.t.e.d
w.o.r.d.s.w.a.s.t.e.d   w.o.r.d.s.w.a.s.t.e.d
w.o.r.d.s.w.a.s.t.e.d   w.o.r.d.s.w.a.s.t.e.d
w.o.r.d.s.w.a.s.t.e.d   w.o.r.d.s.w.a.s.t.e.d
w.o.r.d.s.w.a.s.t.e.d   w.o.r.d.s.w.a.s.t.e.d
w.o.r.d.s.w.a.s.t.e.d   w.o.r.d.s.w.a.s.t.e.d
w.o.r.d.s.w.a.s.t.e.d   w.o.r.d.s.w.a.s.t.e.d
w.o.r.d.s.w.a.s.t.e.d   w.o.r.d.s.w.a.s.t.e.d
w.o.r.d.s.w.a.s.t.e.d w.o.r.d.s.w.a.s.t.e.d
w.o.r.d.s.w.a.s.t.e.d w.o.r.d.s.w.a.s.t.e.d
w.o.r.d.s.w.a.s.t.e.d w.o.r.d.s.w.a.s.t.e.d
w.o.r.d.s.w.a.s.t.e.d   w.o.r.d.s.w.a.s.t.e.d
w.o.r.d.s.w.a.s.t.e.d   w.o.r.d.s.w.a.s.t.e.d
w.o.r.d.s.w.a.s.t.e.d   w.o.r.d.s.w.a.s.t.e.d
w.o.r.d.s.w.a.s.t.e.d   w.o.r.d.s.w.a.s.t.e.d
w.o.r.d.s.w.a.s.t.e.d w.o.r.d.s.w.a.s.t.e.d
w.o.r.d.s.w.a.s.t.e.d   w.o.r.d.s.w.a.s.t.e.d
w.o.r.d.s.w.a.s.t.e.d   w.o.r.d.s.w.a.s.t.e.d
w.o.r.d.s.w.a.s.t.e.d   w.o.r.d.s.w.a.s.t.e.d
w.o.r.d.s.w.a.s.t.e.d   w.o.r.d.s.w.a.s.t.e.d
w.o.r.d.s.w.a.s.t.e.d w.o.r.d.s.w.a.s.t.e.d
w.o.r.d.s.w.a.s.t.e.d   w.o.r.d.s.w.a.s.t.e.d
w.o.r.d.s.w.a.s.t.e.d   w.o.r.d.s.w.a.s.t.e.d
w.o.r.d.s.w.a.s.t.e.d   w.o.r.d.s.w.a.s.t.e.d
w.o.r.d.s.w.a.s.t.e.d w.o.r.d.s.w.a.s.t.e.d

d.e.t.s.a.w.s.d.r.o.w   d.e.t.s.a.w.s.d.r.o.w
d.e.t.s.a.w.s.d.r.o.w   d.e.t.s.a.w.s.d.r.o.w
d.e.t.s.a.w.s.d.r.o.w   d.e.t.s.a.w.s.d.r.o.w
d.e.t.s.a.w.s.d.r.o.w d.e.t.s.a.w.s.d.r.o.w

d.e.t.s.a.w.s.d.r.o.w d.e.t.s.a.w.s.d.r.o.w
d.e.t.s.a.w.s.d.r.o.w d.e.t.s.a.w.s.d.r.o.w
d.e.t.s.a.w.s.d.r.o.w d.e.t.s.a.w.s.d.r.o.w
d.e.t.s.a.w.s.d.r.o.w d.e.t.s.a.w.s.d.r.o.w
d.e.t.s.a.w.s.d.r.o.w d.e.t.s.a.w.s.d.r.o.w
d.e.t.s.a.w.s.d.r.o.w d.e.t.s.a.w.s.d.r.o.w
d.e.t.s.a.w.s.d.r.o.w d.e.t.s.a.w.s.d.r.o.w
d.e.t.s.a.w.s.d.r.o.w d.e.t.s.a.w.s.d.r.o.w
d.e.t.s.a.w.s.d.r.o.w d.e.t.s.a.w.s.d.r.o.w
d.e.t.s.a.w.s.d.r.o.w d.e.t.s.a.w.s.d.r.o.w
d.e.t.s.a.w.s.d.r.o.w d.e.t.s.a.w.s.d.r.o.w
d.e.t.s.a.w.s.d.r.o.w d.e.t.s.a.w.s.d.r.o.w
d.e.t.s.a.w.s.d.r.o.w d.e.t.s.a.w.s.d.r.o.w
d.e.t.s.a.w.s.d.r.o.w d.e.t.s.a.w.s.d.r.o.w
d.e.t.s.a.w.s.d.r.o.w d.e.t.s.a.w.s.d.r.o.w
d.e.t.s.a.w.s.d.r.o.w d.e.t.s.a.w.s.d.r.o.w
d.e.t.s.a.w.s.d.r.o.w d.e.t.s.a.w.s.d.r.o.w
d.e.t.s.a.w.s.d.r.o.w d.e.t.s.a.w.s.d.r.o.w
d.e.t.s.a.w.s.d.r.o.w d.e.t.s.a.w.s.d.r.o.w
d.e.t.s.a.w.s.d.r.o.w d.e.t.s.a.w.s.d.r.o.w
d.e.t.s.a.w.s.d.r.o.w d.e.t.s.a.w.s.d.r.o.w
d.e.t.s.a.w.s.d.r.o.w d.e.t.s.a.w.s.d.r.o.w
d.e.t.s.a.w.s.d.r.o.w d.e.t.s.a.w.s.d.r.o.w
d.e.t.s.a.w.s.d.r.o.w d.e.t.s.a.w.s.d.r.o.w
d.e.t.s.a.w.s.d.r.o.w d.e.t.s.a.w.s.d.r.o.w
d.e.t.s.a.w.s.d.r.o.w d.e.t.s.a.w.s.d.r.o.w
d.e.t.s.a.w.s.d.r.o.w d.e.t.s.a.w.s.d.r.o.w
d.e.t.s.a.w.s.d.r.o.w d.e.t.s.a.w.s.d.r.o.w
d.e.t.s.a.w.s.d.r.o.w d.e.t.s.a.w.s.d.r.o.w
d.e.t.s.a.w.s.d.r.o.w d.e.t.s.a.w.s.d.r.o.w
d.e.t.s.a.w.s.d.r.o.w d.e.t.s.a.w.s.d.r.o.w
d.e.t.s.a.w.s.d.r.o.w d.e.t.s.a.w.s.d.r.o.w

d.e.t.s.a.w.s.d.r.o.w d.e.t.s.a.w.s.d.r.o.w
d.e.t.s.a.w.s.d.r.o.w d.e.t.s.a.w.s.d.r.o.w
d.e.t.s.a.w.s.d.r.o.w d.e.t.s.a.w.s.d.r.o.w
d.e.t.s.a.w.s.d.r.o.w d.e.t.s.a.w.s.d.r.o.w
d.e.t.s.a.w.s.d.r.o.w d.e.t.s.a.w.s.d.r.o.w
d.e.t.s.a.w.s.d.r.o.w d.e.t.s.a.w.s.d.r.o.w
d.e.t.s.a.w.s.d.r.o.w d.e.t.s.a.w.s.d.r.o.w
d.e.t.s.a.w.s.d.r.o.w d.e.t.s.a.w.s.d.r.o.w
d.e.t.s.a.w.s.d.r.o.w d.e.t.s.a.w.s.d.r.o.w
d.e.t.s.a.w.s.d.r.o.w d.e.t.s.a.w.s.d.r.o.w
d.e.t.s.a.w.s.d.r.o.w d.e.t.s.a.w.s.d.r.o.w
d.e.t.s.a.w.s.d.r.o.w d.e.t.s.a.w.s.d.r.o.w
d.e.t.s.a.w.s.d.r.o.w d.e.t.s.a.w.s.d.r.o.w
d.e.t.s.a.w.s.d.r.o.w d.e.t.s.a.w.s.d.r.o.w
d.e.t.s.a.w.s.d.r.o.w d.e.t.s.a.w.s.d.r.o.w
d.e.t.s.a.w.s.d.r.o.w d.e.t.s.a.w.s.d.r.o.w
d.e.t.s.a.w.s.d.r.o.w d.e.t.s.a.w.s.d.r.o.w

d.e.t.s.a.w.s.d.r.o.w d.e.t.s.a.w.s.d.r.o.w
d.e.t.s.a.w.s.d.r.o.w d.e.t.s.a.w.s.d.r.o.w
d.e.t.s.a.w.s.d.r.o.w d.e.t.s.a.w.s.d.r.o.w
d.e.t.s.a.w.s.d.r.o.w d.e.t.s.a.w.s.d.r.o.w
d.e.t.s.a.w.s.d.r.o.w d.e.t.s.a.w.s.d.r.o.w
d.e.t.s.a.w.s.d.r.o.w d.e.t.s.a.w.s.d.r.o.w
d.e.t.s.a.w.s.d.r.o.w d.e.t.s.a.w.s.d.r.o.w
d.e.t.s.a.w.s.d.r.o.w d.e.t.s.a.w.s.d.r.o.w
d.e.t.s.a.w.s.d.r.o.w d.e.t.s.a.w.s.d.r.o.w
d.e.t.s.a.w.s.d.r.o.w d.e.t.s.a.w.s.d.r.o.w

d.e.t.s.a.w.s.d.r.o.w d.e.t.s.a.w.s.d.r.o.w
d.e.t.s.a.w.s.d.r.o.w d.e.t.s.a.w.s.d.r.o.w
d.e.t.s.a.w.s.d.r.o.w d.e.t.s.a.w.s.d.r.o.w

d.e.t.s.a.w.s.d.r.o.w d.e.t.s.a.w.s.d.r.o.w
d.e.t.s.a.w.s.d.r.o.w d.e.t.s.a.w.s.d.r.o.w
d.e.t.s.a.w.s.d.r.o.w d.e.t.s.a.w.s.d.r.o.w
d.e.t.s.a.w.s.d.r.o.w d.e.t.s.a.w.s.d.r.o.w
d.e.t.s.a.w.s.d.r.o.w d.e.t.s.a.w.s.d.r.o.w
d.e.t.s.a.w.s.d.r.o.w d.e.t.s.a.w.s.d.r.o.w
d.e.t.s.a.w.s.d.r.o.w d.e.t.s.a.w.s.d.r.o.w

d.e.t.s.a.w.s.d.r.o.w d.e.t.s.a.w.s.d.r.o.w
d.e.t.s.a.w.s.d.r.o.w d.e.t.s.a.w.s.d.r.o.w
d.e.t.s.a.w.s.d.r.o.w d.e.t.s.a.w.s.d.r.o.w
d.e.t.s.a.w.s.d.r.o.w d.e.t.s.a.w.s.d.r.o.w
d.e.t.s.a.w.s.d.r.o.w d.e.t.s.a.w.s.d.r.o.w
d.e.t.s.a.w.s.d.r.o.w d.e.t.s.a.w.s.d.r.o.w
d.e.t.s.a.w.s.d.r.o.w d.e.t.s.a.w.s.d.r.o.w
d.e.t.s.a.w.s.d.r.o.w d.e.t.s.a.w.s.d.r.o.w

d.e.t.s.a.w.s.d.r.o.w d.e.t.s.a.w.s.d.r.o.w
d.e.t.s.a.w.s.d.r.o.w d.e.t.s.a.w.s.d.r.o.w
d.e.t.s.a.w.s.d.r.o.w d.e.t.s.a.w.s.d.r.o.w
d.e.t.s.a.w.s.d.r.o.w d.e.t.s.a.w.s.d.r.o.w
d.e.t.s.a.w.s.d.r.o.w d.e.t.s.a.w.s.d.r.o.w
d.e.t.s.a.w.s.d.r.o.w d.e.t.s.a.w.s.d.r.o.w
d.e.t.s.a.w.s.d.r.o.w d.e.t.s.a.w.s.d.r.o.w
d.e.t.s.a.w.s.d.r.o.w
d.e.t.s.a.w.s.d.r.o.w
d.e.t.s.a.w.s.d.r.o.w d.e.t.s.a.w.s.d.r.o.w
d.e.t.s.a.w.s.d.r.o.w d.e.t.s.a.w.s.d.r.o.w
d.e.t.s.a.w.s.d.r.o.w d.e.t.s.a.w.s.d.r.o.w
d.e.t.s.a.w.s.d.r.o.w d.e.t.s.a.w.s.d.r.o.w

d.e.t.s.a.w.s.d.r.o.w d.e.t.s.a.w.s.d.r.o.w
d.e.t.s.a.w.s.d.r.o.w d.e.t.s.a.w.s.d.r.o.w
d.e.t.s.a.w.s.d.r.o.w d.e.t.s.a.w.s.d.r.o.w
d.e.t.s.a.w.s.d.r.o.w d.e.t.s.a.w.s.d.r.o.w
d.e.t.s.a.w.s.d.r.o.w d.e.t.s.a.w.s.d.r.o.w
d.e.t.s.a.w.s.d.r.o.w d.e.t.s.a.w.s.d.r.o.w
d.e.t.s.a.w.s.d.r.o.w d.e.t.s.a.w.s.d.r.o.w

p˙ǝ˙ʇ˙s˙ɐ˙ʍ˙s˙p˙ɹ˙o˙ʍ p˙ǝ˙ʇ˙s˙ɐ˙ʍ˙s˙p˙ɹ˙o˙ʍ
p˙ǝ˙ʇ˙s˙ɐ˙ʍ˙s˙p˙ɹ˙o˙ʍ p˙ǝ˙ʇ˙s˙ɐ˙ʍ˙s˙p˙ɹ˙o˙ʍ
p˙ǝ˙ʇ˙s˙ɐ˙ʍ˙s˙p˙ɹ˙o˙ʍ p˙ǝ˙ʇ˙s˙ɐ˙ʍ˙s˙p˙ɹ˙o˙ʍ
p˙ǝ˙ʇ˙s˙ɐ˙ʍ˙s˙p˙ɹ˙o˙ʍ p˙ǝ˙ʇ˙s˙ɐ˙ʍ˙s˙p˙ɹ˙o˙ʍ
p˙ǝ˙ʇ˙s˙ɐ˙ʍ˙s˙p˙ɹ˙o˙ʍ p˙ǝ˙ʇ˙s˙ɐ˙ʍ˙s˙p˙ɹ˙o˙ʍ
p˙ǝ˙ʇ˙s˙ɐ˙ʍ˙s˙p˙ɹ˙o˙ʍ p˙ǝ˙ʇ˙s˙ɐ˙ʍ˙s˙p˙ɹ˙o˙ʍ
p˙ǝ˙ʇ˙s˙ɐ˙ʍ˙s˙p˙ɹ˙o˙ʍ p˙ǝ˙ʇ˙s˙ɐ˙ʍ˙s˙p˙ɹ˙o˙ʍ
p˙ǝ˙ʇ˙s˙ɐ˙ʍ˙s˙p˙ɹ˙o˙ʍ p˙ǝ˙ʇ˙s˙ɐ˙ʍ˙s˙p˙ɹ˙o˙ʍ
p˙ǝ˙ʇ˙s˙ɐ˙ʍ˙s˙p˙ɹ˙o˙ʍ p˙ǝ˙ʇ˙s˙ɐ˙ʍ˙s˙p˙ɹ˙o˙ʍ
p˙ǝ˙ʇ˙s˙ɐ˙ʍ˙s˙p˙ɹ˙o˙ʍ p˙ǝ˙ʇ˙s˙ɐ˙ʍ˙s˙p˙ɹ˙o˙ʍ
p˙ǝ˙ʇ˙s˙ɐ˙ʍ˙s˙p˙ɹ˙o˙ʍ p˙ǝ˙ʇ˙s˙ɐ˙ʍ˙s˙p˙ɹ˙o˙ʍ
p˙ǝ˙ʇ˙s˙ɐ˙ʍ˙s˙p˙ɹ˙o˙ʍ p˙ǝ˙ʇ˙s˙ɐ˙ʍ˙s˙p˙ɹ˙o˙ʍ
p˙ǝ˙ʇ˙s˙ɐ˙ʍ˙s˙p˙ɹ˙o˙ʍ p˙ǝ˙ʇ˙s˙ɐ˙ʍ˙s˙p˙ɹ˙o˙ʍ
p˙ǝ˙ʇ˙s˙ɐ˙ʍ˙s˙p˙ɹ˙o˙ʍ p˙ǝ˙ʇ˙s˙ɐ˙ʍ˙s˙p˙ɹ˙o˙ʍ
p˙ǝ˙ʇ˙s˙ɐ˙ʍ˙s˙p˙ɹ˙o˙ʍ p˙ǝ˙ʇ˙s˙ɐ˙ʍ˙s˙p˙ɹ˙o˙ʍ
p˙ǝ˙ʇ˙s˙ɐ˙ʍ˙s˙p˙ɹ˙o˙ʍ p˙ǝ˙ʇ˙s˙ɐ˙ʍ˙s˙p˙ɹ˙o˙ʍ
p˙ǝ˙ʇ˙s˙ɐ˙ʍ˙s˙p˙ɹ˙o˙ʍ p˙ǝ˙ʇ˙s˙ɐ˙ʍ˙s˙p˙ɹ˙o˙ʍ
p˙ǝ˙ʇ˙s˙ɐ˙ʍ˙s˙p˙ɹ˙o˙ʍ p˙ǝ˙ʇ˙s˙ɐ˙ʍ˙s˙p˙ɹ˙o˙ʍ
p˙ǝ˙ʇ˙s˙ɐ˙ʍ˙s˙p˙ɹ˙o˙ʍ p˙ǝ˙ʇ˙s˙ɐ˙ʍ˙s˙p˙ɹ˙o˙ʍ
p˙ǝ˙ʇ˙s˙ɐ˙ʍ˙s˙p˙ɹ˙o˙ʍ p˙ǝ˙ʇ˙s˙ɐ˙ʍ˙s˙p˙ɹ˙o˙ʍ
p˙ǝ˙ʇ˙s˙ɐ˙ʍ˙s˙p˙ɹ˙o˙ʍ p˙ǝ˙ʇ˙s˙ɐ˙ʍ˙s˙p˙ɹ˙o˙ʍ
p˙ǝ˙ʇ˙s˙ɐ˙ʍ˙s˙p˙ɹ˙o˙ʍ p˙ǝ˙ʇ˙s˙ɐ˙ʍ˙s˙p˙ɹ˙o˙ʍ
p˙ǝ˙ʇ˙s˙ɐ˙ʍ˙s˙p˙ɹ˙o˙ʍ p˙ǝ˙ʇ˙s˙ɐ˙ʍ˙s˙p˙ɹ˙o˙ʍ

w.o.r.d.s.w.a.s.t.e.dw.o.r.d.s.w.a.s.t.e.d
w.o.r.d.s.w.a.s.t.e.d w.o.r.d.s.w.a.s.t.e.d
w.o.r.d.s.w.a.s.t.e.d w.o.r.d.s.w.a.s.t.e.d
w.o.r.d.s.w.a.s.t.e.d w.o.r.d.s.w.a.s.t.e.d
w.o.r.d.s.w.a.s.t.e.d w.o.r.d.s.w.a.s.t.e.d

w.o.r.d.s.w.a.s.t.e.dw.o.r.d.s.w.a.s.t.e.d
w.o.r.d.s.w.a.s.t.e.d w.o.r.d.s.w.a.s.t.e.d
w.o.r.d.s.w.a.s.t.e.d w.o.r.d.s.w.a.s.t.e.d
w.o.r.d.s.w.a.s.t.e.d w.o.r.d.s.w.a.s.t.e.d
w.o.r.d.s.w.a.s.t.e.d w.o.r.d.s.w.a.s.t.e.d
w.o.r.d.s.w.a.s.t.e.dw.o.r.d.s.w.a.s.t.e.d
w.o.r.d.s.w.a.s.t.e.dw.o.r.d.s.w.a.s.t.e.d
w.o.r.d.s.w.a.s.t.e.dw.o.r.d.s.w.a.s.t.e.d

w.o.r.d.s.w.a.s.t.e.d w.o.r.d.s.w.a.s.t.e.d
w.o.r.d.s.w.a.s.t.e.d w.o.r.d.s.w.a.s.t.e.d
w.o.r.d.s.w.a.s.t.e.d w.o.r.d.s.w.a.s.t.e.d
w.o.r.d.s.w.a.s.t.e.d w.o.r.d.s.w.a.s.t.e.d
w.o.r.d.s.w.a.s.t.e.d w.o.r.d.s.w.a.s.t.e.d
w.o.r.d.s.w.a.s.t.e.d w.o.r.d.s.w.a.s.t.e.d

I searched world's most pretentious words, and this is all they had: day-noo-MAHN -- The end of a story, but French. kwah-FYOOR -- A hairstyle, which is expensive, time consuming, and often ginormous. pro-PISH-us -- When things seem inclined to go your way, e.g. "my odds of totally destroying this loser in Hearthstone appear propitious." eh-GREE-jess -- So glaringly horrible, outrageous, annoying, or tacky that you literally cannot even. noo-VOE -- Originally this was the French word for "new"; then Art Nouveau happened, and now this word is applied to any sort of thing that is like another thing, only newer. nee-MON-nick -- A rhyme, acronym, or other device used to remember important information, e.g. "Beer before liquor, never sicker." Pretty pathetic that! Instead, pick up a Will Self book, non-fiction/fiction, does not matter and you will come across some unknown, untested, intimidating word, that is so Self-ian he might as well have created the word. On each page there is a word you know you should look up, but luckily, his skill as a writer means, the surrounding gives away its meaning or reference.

Glass. Blowing. Penis. Growing. Shellfish. Showing. Smith & Weston. Heston. Blooming. Tall. Gorky. Dorky. Stork. Catch. Rat. Games. Rays. Palms. Monkey-nuts. Buses overturned. Written language made written slanguage. Ruptured ginger stems. Ridiculous words. Violence as a necessity. Getting hurt whilst washing. Getting hurt whilst cooking. Limping through an apocalyptic world where you and a robot called Tony figure out a way to make love. Discount the discounted DVDs and Blu-rays at HMV. It is all a lie. A whole group of people die of fungus-foot. Trench-dick is a thing. Revving engines. FAST X is out. NO, it isn't. Organic flesh flaying devices not found in a household drawer. I am never going to complain about that sausage sandwich that had peanut butter instead of butter, salted or unsalted, margarine. Second skin. Third skin. Fourth skin. Fifth skin. Sixth skin, Seventh skin. Martial arts professionals quit pole-dancing for charity scheme. Gangster bulldogs with sparkling bones. Bone horror. Crunch. Splintering. A soundscape that is quite unlike any I have heard in a modern horror movie. Maybe it was because I was perfectly seated. Modern day forces possessing AI intelligence. Poltergeist. Ghost in the machine. A haunting. Pregnancy test thrown away and a good old fashioned wire clothes-hanger is purchased. Multi-limbed forms scrambling over my brain. Brian Yuzna-esque madness. Crazy Stevo doing Society type of body horror. Yeeeeeah, dude. I breathe in your stench. Your wet fart. I go onto hands and knees and tell you to hold still as I shove my face between your ass crack, feeling the wetness leak through your usually white underwear, your budgie-smugglers, and inhale shit flakes and particles. Pop up restraint owners are shocked, but later fetishize this weird event on Eastbourne beach. Growing up to mutilate dolls, plush toys, morphing them together merely by BIC-lighters, matches, matches, always play with matches, and your dad's industrial strength scissors. High-rise apartment blocks crumbling in slow motion, then reverting back to its "fully" "formed" "structure". Terror of the crumble. Looking on from afar, as terrorist and culprit, licking parched lips admires the apple crumble disintegration. Cheese-grater injuries. Doctors pulling closed the curtains and holding it in both hands and looking at it as if an engagement ring rather than an injury. Licking it, like a dog. Looking up, staring hard into your eyes, not asking for permission, scared, completely shocked at your actions, but, a hint, manifested as a glint in his eyes asking if he should continue and the wounded bites their little finger, pouts, putting on the cartoonish shy, bashful, "Oh you!" character, the types that American men ask "Do you come with the car?" and the lady responds with "Oh, you, hehehe," and the doctor went at it, like a thirsty dog. Estranged aunts. Messy flats. Messy mansions. Falling in on itself homes left to rot, ruin, and Arnold Schwarzenegger levels of destruction, like after he shove his dick into Miriam's fat cellulite pock-marked, spotty ass – not anus, the crack – "Lettmein!" Arnie screeching. "I will be back!" he reassures her. As she turns on him, her face takes on the look of her character from James & The Giant Peach. "Please don't, you nasty cunt," she hisses. This is a phrase she uses on Day Time TV, yet hasn't been cancelled yet, because she is a national treasure. Guided by music. The vibration. Quiet scowling. Can you quietly scowl. Do not let a vampire back into the house. Noah had an arc, and all animals were male, so, God wasn't a queer-hater, he was a queer encourager. "Good God!" God exclaimed, slapping his forehead, thunderclaps and lightening striking and rumbling g everywhere all at once across the globe. "Gays cannot procreate, this means my kind will finally die out. Bullseye!" I didn't see anything to contradict the continuity of the X-Men film, but continuity doesn't exist in that film series. Meshing tonalities. 2013 Evil Dead Re-quel, Boot-Make. Sequels. Cults. John Carpenter having a big film comeback will crash and burn much like his shit-fest THE WARD, starring the world's worst actress and human Amber Heard. The gorgeous time spent with the throwaway design tactile in bound bloodied flesh hurts the kids that's right locked in with a jaw like a creature form Harry Potter. We have so many mythologies to source ideas from. Audio grotesqueries. Closing a book, it is always open-ended. What are we getting excited about in the coming months? PLEASE NO TALKING OR CHECKING YOUR PHONE. No cunt follows that rule. That is when a cinema-shooter should step in, I stop them, pull them aside and show them the ones on my hastily mapped out scheme of the noisy beggars deserving a bullet in the brain, and he nods, flips down his visor and walks into the wrong fucking screen. Fuck, fuck, fuck. Mario went R-rated real quick real fast, and he went by my map of the cinema. I didn't write what screen. Fuck, and all those he went for, turned out to be great humans and kids with bright futures. The maniac missed all the people that in my cinema were innocents, but in this one were deserving of a hail of bullet-rain. Oh shit, oh fuck, oh shite. What can we do with this vision? Is it funny? Fuck no, but it is telling as to the writers madness. No, not madness, bouncing newborns on their heads, and feeling alright over it. Buy books. Order books. Buy books. Buy films. Dead. By. Dawn. Listen to that podcast, I wished it went on longer. Weekly news annoying the fuck out of aged patrons. Buffet meals lasted only a week. Reduced rates are ageist. Yet, they will cash in on that benefit. Eating popcorn. Eating buttered hotdog buns lacking mustard, ketchup and a fucking horse-meat-slong. Mountains reaching the skies, but before we fall into a time-gap/split/pocket we have some nifty images generated by Zak Ferguson's own hands. Yes, this isn't a lie...nope...it isn't...um...oh fuck, get in on the movement. I think it's alright. Australian accents are sexier than Scottish accents. Irish accents well, well, well. The. But. A. Is. Ever. Never. Rabbit. Bush. Tired. Bottles. Glass. Magic. Man. Evil. Lauren. Shoulder. Zoning. In. Ouch. Yelping. Cats. Dogs. Are. Aren't. Thoughtful. Meaningless. Ethereal. Catch. Throw. Vomit. Sulphatic. Bruised. Woman. Women. Men. Man. Dad. Sister. Mister. Doctor. Practitioner. Very. Seemingly. Cheaper. Shops. Wanker. Wank. Clitoris. Cunt. Semen. Umbrella. William. Claire. Storks. Africa. As. Isn't. Fish. Zits. Butt. Button. Brilliant. Orb. Like. Lessen. Gobbles. Jacket. Potatoes. Steel. Magnolia. Orifice. Fishy. Stinking. Gluten. Gluttonous. Room. 89. 88. 87. 86. 85. 84. 83. 82. 81. 80. Ninety-nine. Ninety-eight. Ninety-seven. Ninety-six. Ninety-Five. Ninety-4. Parties. Mark. Pairing. Writers. Times. Shears. Bleeding. Edge. Cast. Off. On. Right. 90-three. Ninety-2. Ninety-1. Cork. Patterns. Brain. Egg. Blue. Beetles. Scrum. Filth. Dirge. Mirage. Norm. Form. Storm. Hiccup. Flip. Flop. Dangle. Dazzling. Luminous. Sparkling. Sad. Rapid. Repulsive, Roman Polanski. Jerry Maguire. Tobe Hooper.

Pin. Scattered. Remains. Lost. Signal. Looky-loo. Pish. Ships. Sails. Pirates. Wound. Wounded. Guts. Gore. Whores. Philandering. Picturesque. Delusional. Grandiose. Losses. Betting. Horses. Dogs. Illegal. Burt.Made. Muffled. Brutality. Ruffled. Feathers. Father. Snogging. Father. Father. Knob. Whistling. Could. Have. No. More. Mister. Silly. Flower. Rotten. Core. Hearth. Heart. Pulmonary. Diseases. Sneezes. Radical. Assimilation. Tick-tock. Simple. White. Black. Red. Blue. Purple. Arm. Leg. Car. Crash. Bang. Skittering. Braying. Cows. Loose-stool. "You're so cool," – "I know, bitch," – limitless. Victimless. Advertisements. Shopping. For. Magma. Carta. Maps. Stars. Constellations. Friendships. These. What. When. Where. Crustacean. Rotten. Rebellious. Ruthless. Rustic. Fence. Bus. Stop. Train. Spotting. Drug. Addicted. Heroin. Femme fatale. Many. Obvious. Burps. Poop. Pee. Plentiful. Play. Experiment. Forming. Assuming. Assumed. Lose. Looseness. Sam Rockwell. A. B. C. D. E. F. G. H. I. J. K. L. m. N. O. P. Q. R. S. T. U. X. W. X. Y. X. The button is yelping. Roman Polanski is in Room 89 looking after this button. This button had come to him in a dream, and then once he spotted a button, resembling that from his dream, he deluded himself into believing this was his unborn child, that he lost when it was murdered alongside its mother back in the v60s by the members of

Manson's cult. The button was matte-black. Polanski's rat-like features were reflected in the buttons surface, and his eyes were where the top two black holes were – unused, empty of any material, a material to attach it to a shirt or blazer, replacing his own two peepers; not that it made Roman look any different, as he had those rapists black pinpricks without the illusion provided by the black button. William gobbles jacket potatoes. It is fishy. Crash! *"You're cool,"* said Roman behind his hotel door. Opposite Black-William response,
"I know," and then with a Tourettic belch screamed,

"BITCH!"

Porn is evil. Facebook is evil. Self-Belief is evil. Evil is not necessarily all evil. Various planets excrete a gas that takes the form of a star. The Mario Brothers are evil. Especially when one of them is voiced by the prat of all Pratts, Chris Pratt. Build differently to other stop-motion animated movies is the one ----- put out by ------ ----- ---- . Bread makes you fat. Mean movies make me happy. Noomi Rapace, holy fuck she is beautiful. These textbook brains have been touched. A doctor with a certain inclination for brain, matter, the vortex of potentialities – hand going over the ridges. His giggles awoke a certain node. It popped free from the stem. Wiggled its little tushy. The doctor clapped, and began stomping his left foot, getting up a very Hebrew-ish beat. Clap! Clap! Clap! Clap! It engorged itself on this appreciation. Growing bigger and bigger. Various invisible tendrils, on the sly, ransacked the doctors' personal belongings. The little brain nugget held the doctor's attention. It tried to shape itself in a sensual shape. It didn't take long before the doctor fiddled with his trousers, top button slipping between his greasy hand. He licked his fingers, hoping to get rid of the brain-juice, and also admired the taste and alternative textures on his tongue. There was a surge on his taste buds. The doctors tongue began to shrivel up into itself, like inverted goosepimples. He gagged. His hand went to his throat, an odd act, but the only thing he could do. He choked on it, when suddenly they began rising up, into blisters, and then they released their acidic perfume and viscous pus. The doctor went back to trying to pop open his button, looking up, off and on, trying to hide his devious smirk. The button gave way and slid through the loophole, easily enough. Next, he had to find his zipper. It made its attention-grabbing ziiiiiiiiiiiiiiiiiiiiiiiiiiiiip noise. Classic! When he looked up, trousers at half mast, the brain was no longer on the dish he had placed it on. His erection wilted. The case of Nodnol was never an essential part. I could have been clever and inverted the whole thing, and stuck the landing on using other texts, but the work dictates itself and I do not ever want

it to be easy. The sad truth is, I am bored of this type of work. I have grown resentful of it. I have pigeonholed myself. I have trapped myself in my own fucked up ideology and belief as to what my work is meant to do. I hate my work. This book is shit. It is lazy. It is hurtful. It is pathetic. It is loose. It is fatty. It is blather. It is gunk. It is a sore toe that gets infected. There is little to no reason for this. It is some awful attempt at going out on a high. A high, on a low. Contradiction. A bundle of contradictions. Sad face. Clown face. Random selection.

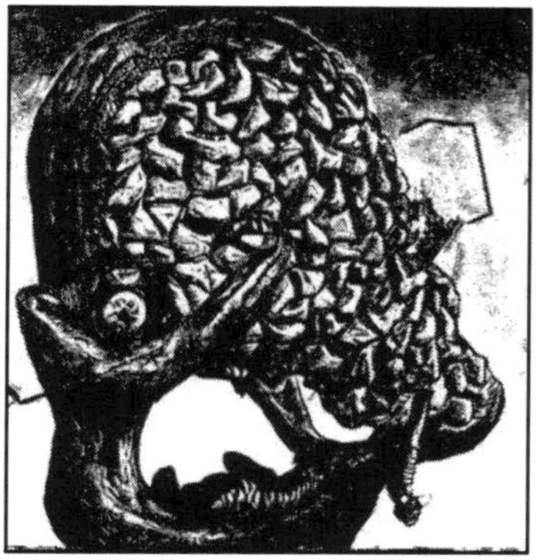

I type brains, and you automatically read it as Brian. I write Brian and you automatically read it as Brain. I write Brainy Brian Brandished Briny Brussel Bullies Bulletin-g Bastard Brain Branches Breaching Barbaric Barcodes Brought Before Brian Enzymes. And you gave up. opt out. opt in. These are the brains we all wish we had. Textural delights. Glorious brain stems. Taking over the

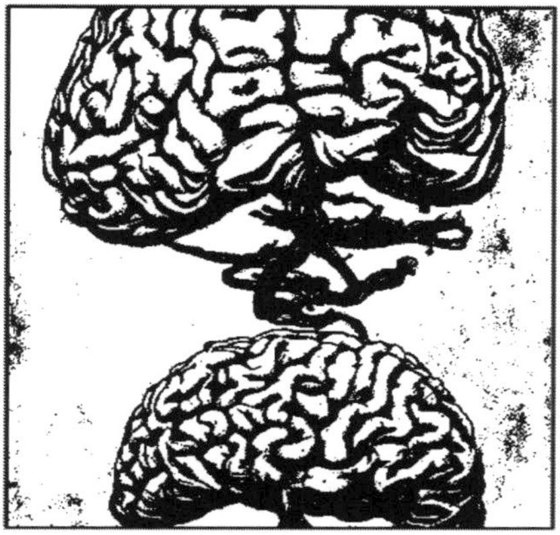

ungentrified plains of Earth. Planning their hacker attack on lesser versed computer users. Mary printing out things, xeroxing out of mere nostalgia, and as we all know nostalgia only lasts as long as the person's attention... oh,

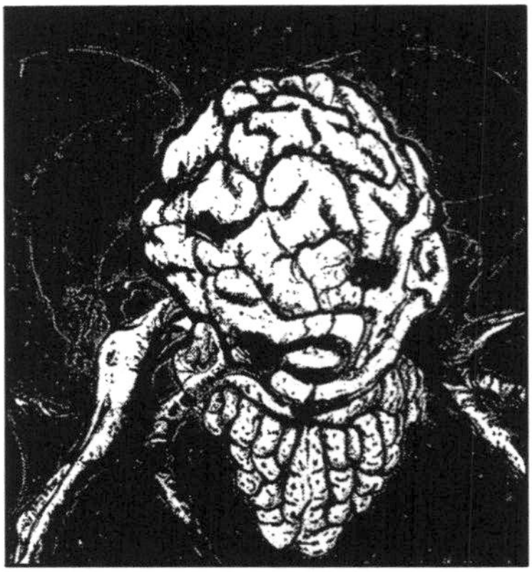

there we go, Mary is now collecting Oxo cube boxes from the 1940s. She hugs her sculptures and tells them that if she were of their generation, she would have named them after her favourite type of wine. The kids just nod and look over at the only existing red-brick wall on their council estate. They wish they could supply the missing brick with the cremated ashes of their elder siblings, killed off in yet

another war brought on because certain very large Brian's took brains from the scientific lab on Grantham Street, and injected a traditional seasoning, and witnessed the creation of the brainworms, and the brain-attacks! The brain fascinates me. It is a curse.

The sculptures clung to mother, and they sang in sweet cement slops, whelped in wet grout grain, the tears drizzling like a random torrential deluge, overwatering recently planted flowers and herbs. The sculptures reflect Pink Floyd's recent hit, YOU WILL NEVER BE, ANOTHER- RED-BRICK IN THE WALL! They took flight, as the curtains were parted, reflecting what the cloudscape was doing, Mary willing herself into a meteorological symbiosis. The clouds part, thin, serrate, form, and Mary is left cutting into her bare arms with a butter knife, hoping that once she breaks her skin's surface, and manages to – not cut – but angle, flip, move her muscles and tendons and nerves around, enough to use her bones as a butter-knife sharpener. She doesn't succeed, as her symbiosis with the elements torn her into... poetry. If ou have ever questioned the phenomenon of weeping statues and religious icons, we are here to reassure you, us, the artists, and great imaginers of our times, that such events do occur, and Mary's sculptures did indeed weep. Their tears converged and solidified into resin. The resin has been transferred from mental spaces to the material world; and such events have to be catalogued, turned into a raisonné that pamphleteers could hand out, charge a high or low price for; to be used as totem, as gospel, as proof to be sung, and preached; the sculptures just wanted the resin to melt. For it to dissolve over time and be used as a binding paint. Holding onto each other, as if the world was about to end. They came together and painted themselves into a corner, into a crevasse, into an elbow, into a chin, into the groin, into each other. The five sculptures became one. One remained as fully formed as the rest. One was a mere chin, below another's chin, a face of one sculpture was placed into another's breast. This sculpture will be lent out to museums, galleries, it will also we weaved into a performance artists work, and later cancelled out from all of history, due to what the performance artist deigned acceptable; so absurd and grotesque was the act, that obscenity trials were brought back into fashion. Just what the artist wanted. Not something the sculpture wanted.

We can archive all of these written words. We can distinguish what goes where. We can't. You can't. Why not? Because in the old days, everything was archived, documented, as if they had a legacy, before such praise and recognition gave them the wherewithal to start collating. Maybe it is coincidence.

Maybe we need a friend who forces you to print stuff out so the historians in the future can piece together what happened and where it happened and why what happened was written on a Tuesday and not on a Sunday evening to place the breathing mass of your privileged work together and map out the time dates place history and reasoning and all so the back half back end of the book, a good two hundred pages worth of it, is all notes and references. There is no source. No fragments. The fragmentations start on a blank page. They have not been taken and whipped up into a juicy delicious novel-cake. If you can track these remnants, if there are nay, I owe you a fiver. The purpose of the purposeless is to allow lesser beings to try and catch onto something; minute detaisl, so minute you will learn of the sensual word minutiae. Is this prose poetry run amok? Or is it just word salad? I like to think word salad remark is just coming from certain people who like to think themselves smarter than nay *avant-garde* piece of work put before them.

Zak, Kaz, Ferguson, Berguson, Nosugref, reveal to us your inner most wants... I don't want much, apart from books and films. *We are talking about your book, dear boy.* Are you, well, sorry but I can't talk about my art, within my own book, because that is just, well, cunty! *Why use curse words, in the manner that you do?* I don't know. *You dunno.* Oh, yeah, sorry, I forgot I was a dumb ass and was meant to adhere to that character assigned to me by the local constabulary and must use such dunce-word like, dunno, or sumffink! *Heh.* I dunno. *You mean, you don't know, Mr. Ferguson, Mr. Nosugref?* Yeah, okay, I see what you are doing there, hilarious. *Interview your friends, let them ask you questions.* I don't want them to. *Why fill the book up with miscellaneous unrelated tings, then?* I don't, it all matches perfectly. *It doesn't.* It does. *It doesn't.* it does. *It doesn't.* It does. *It doesn't.* It does. *I know what you...* It doesn't. *It*

does… Okay, it does, I agree. *I know what you're doing, you are using repetition to fill out the book…* No I am not. *You are.* Am not. *You are.* Am not. *What is a thought experiment?* It is in the name of the piece itself; it doesn't need to be explained. *Writing is thought.* Indeed, it is. *The thoughts you are referring to are?* Imagination. *Imaginary/ Imagined.* Thoughts. *There is no plan applied to your work.* There is, just not in the traditional sense. *What is tradition.* Really? Tradition is accepting genre-expectations. *Such as?* The following. *Who?* The following. *Who are you following?* No, I am gesturing, through the book, without the symbols to better accentuate what I am gesturing. *The below part?* Yes, that part.

EARTH, 2822

A man with no name sat quietly at his desk. For the first time in all of his one hundred and five days of life, he finally knew what it meant to be sat in silence. His sitting there in silence was not a good thing; curled deep inside himself he knew that truth; *yet*, he couldn't have cared less. He knew what he was. A meat package that had information lasered day and night into what should have passed for a brain; all for him to type up again, endlessly into the computer system. The system that he had been assigned to keep going - full of data/a variety of information, perpetually pumped through, with various beamer-energy info-dumps and cross-energy-channeled static-radio-waves. To keep what the company had ingrained/programmed into its "people"/"workers" minds, like himself; to think of it as, which was, "KEEPING THE LIGHTS ON."

Though he knew the company he worked for were listening in on his progress via the various bugs they had placed all around him, he didn't care. He had somehow broken free from this doctrine, this process, this way of, not life, as life implies living, this existence, that is the correct word - that had been coded into, not just his mind, but his *being*. He knew very well that he could be jeopardizing his position at this company for slacking and for not having hit the right amount of keys on his keyboard, and yet still, he didn't care. This nameless man wasn't human. He looked human. Smelt human. Dressed like a human, one who worked for a car insurance company. Yet, he wasn't. He knew that. Which, in of itself was a new thing for the likes of him. He had knowledge beyond that of which he ever had. An awareness that had been exempt from his mind from the start. The blooming of a self was occurring, and somehow, he knew it, and could process it. He was no longer a slave to the system that he was put in place to obey and to keep up and running. He

was a cog in a vicious machine. *Run rabbit*, a voice said. It must be a voice. It wasn't his. What was a he? Oh, he is a he, or would have been a he if given autonomy over his own self/identity and place on Earth? This was... somewhat strange, somewhat absurd, somewhat, human. It was the breach of the allegedly unbreachable. Un-hackable. It was thought. Genuine thought. Was this an experiment? A thought experiment, to test the capabilities of whatever system they were/he was working for/bound to. It was consciousness given room to roam. To expand. Cognizance. That sounded right. That felt good, really good. He knew on that day what it meant to have a mind of his own. He was given sovereignty over the automation that he usually worked toward securing, and now was working against the machine. There was a surprise upon a surprise. It was a rush. It came over him, moving him to emote. A vast overload of humanism ready to spread synapses and all that pertains to recent consciousness expansion in such drones, such as himself. It didn't plague him or see him lose any form of recently endowed faculties, sending him into a downward spiral, where he is left crashing and burning. He accepted it, as if awoken from a deep comatose sleep. And took to it as if he had just been asleep...for too long a time. He also could hear and feel things whereas he hadn't been able to before. Sensations. Sensorium's. A wealth of emotion and human complexities. All that he was and had been made to be, it was remembered, recalled, processed naturally, as if he had been put into standby rather than being born like a baby into the now; whilst whatever this thing, that the company had created, that was himself, was working. A small sentient bud was blooming. What brought it to the fore, he didn't know that. What he knew was this: **work, work, work.** *Generate, generate, generate.* He knew that he and his kind were mere flesh-vessels used to the systems advantage; to be charged up with miscellaneous code, drafted into this digital battle they had little to no say in; they were soldiers, hackers, input coordinators, and they had to be physical indexes; one's that needed to generate, and they can only do that by labour intensive typing, sweating, and human task. What they created wasn't mere codes and complex data packages, they had to generate by their physical selves; the energy, the whole infrastructure was based around these physical being's actions. Their hands, their shifting, their humanistic traits, the sweat gathering atop brow and under the arms. They also needed to be in constant motion of typing. These were mean means to the corporations/systems necessary ends. Cogs. No more, no less. He knew that his progress was studied and catalogued and forever under scrutiny. He was like an atomic battery that needed checkups and continual surveying to ensure it was not maxing out on its production of energy. *Energy, energy, energy*. He knew the encryptions were not enough; he knew they had to be transcribed into these seemingly antiquated devices. He knew that he shouldn't have known all of this. Somehow, he did. He knew more than the remainder of his ilk. He knew the ins and outs, the imperfections, the illegality of everything that was unfolding. And he was going to use it to his advantage. Before he could even piece together a plan, some fitting human-energy swept over him. Which forced a break in his usual monotony of code-breaking and statistics-reading, making him deliver a glitch-performance; that somehow, he knew suddenly in his newly awakened core, would be flagged up. That of which his kind suffered from when consciousness was brought into the mix. This unnamed office-drone by some means knew that the company he was created for would pick up on his rift and would not hesitate to put an end to his compositions of programming. They would send a "technician" down to this error sort out. A voice *Psssst* right in his ear. He knew not to react. How he did, he did not know. The voice was disembodied and sounded as if it had been cast from afar. The voice reassured him that all was okay, and that the nameless office-worker needn't try to talk, just communicate by thought. It told him he was being listened to. *No shit*! – was the company-flesh-vessels' mental-reply. *Where did that come from? Fuck! Where did that come from?* He was told to remain calm, that the plan that the voice, *it,* whatever this entity *it* was, that was speaking directly into his ear/mind had initially set out wouldn't work, and that for the plan to go the way, this disembodied, electronically conveyed voice hoped for, could come about; but only if this nameless man came up with one for himself. *Like what?* The entropically communicated voice was gone. All communication was cut dead. The unnamed man knew, sensed, cottoned on that his "bosses", his potentates, his designers were listening. *They*. The new focus of this nameless cog in a nameless machine was in possession of knowledge. Knowledge that *They* had yet to summarize he could potentially have, let alone the reality of what was coming from this man's awakening. gain. *They* were listening. *Had they heard?* Did they know one of their workers/drones/husks had all of a sudden taken on both a personality and a sentiency, an eventuality that *They* had never contemplated or devised a scheme around combatting. *They* had ensured, at the start of this venture, that such a potentiality could ever occur. Did they know he had broken the chain? He had evolved his kind, somehow and in some esoteric way. *What was that?*He didn't know. Then he knew. *That was a weird thought. Is there a me? Was there a me?* – this nameless office-worker starting thinking, and for the systems that log and track their brain activity they noticed a dramatic surge. He looked down at the computer in front of him. The stream of data and allocated box-consoles that he needed to fill... were ignored. Hepaid attention to his reflection in the computers domed screen. He was being listened to and all it picked up was a dull monotonous drone. *They* had been bugged, butchered, and interrupted. This was not good. That was a signifier that the computer and keyboard he was made to keep running and progressing and inputting the data and codes lasered into his brain, had paused. Stopped was more accurate. The bugs picked up the hum of a brain in existence and its unique drum, processed through their antiquated system and broke it down – into the layers they much preferred such entries to be logged as and analysed them to such a heightened degree even God would hold up his hands in defeat and call "Time." This nameless man didn't bother to think what lengths the companies bugs would go in their deconstruction of all the auditory information his kind handled. The nameless man tried not to react; worry skittering across his mind telling and warning him he may not only be bugged, but also had cameras spying on him. He tried not to react to seeing his face for the first time ever in all of his one hundred plus days of life. He was there to generate power. From typing in pre-programmed scripts – lasered into his mind – an endless stream of data- that was all he and his "kind" were made for. *Well, fuck that noise, I had a family!* He froze. *Where did that thought come from?* He didn't know. And he knew quite a lot more now, considering what he was. All that had been programmed into him, he had been unburdened with. He knew instinctually it was best to randomly type some words into the processor to keep up the appearance/noise that he was working. Also movement, selecting specific manners, gestures, humanistic routines were tracked, filtered, and lent to the generator room. All of this had to be conveyed. He knew the system, and that all of his work had been measured and equated by this point. *Was it even worthwhile to put on an act?* ***They*** *knew more than he knew.* He had a hunch, also, something that was a familiar sensation that also work as something thoroughly new, that *They* were already on his case. He typed nonsense into the console and allocated bays that jarred ruby-red, each failed entry spasming the computer screen. He couldn't remember the information that had before been the only thing he was good at. *Fuck, fuck, fuck.* A sophisticated system that picked up noise and calculated the amount of work that has been done sounded absurd and a little old hat. So why was it done this way? Why wasn't there cameras? Yes, there were cameras. Yes, loads of them, just sneakily hidden. He turned finally to look around. His body felt like jelly. He wasn't used to having control of it. It felt too loose, ill-fitting, and almost as if it was prone to fall apart. His was mind racing. Thinking, *what to do? What to do? Fuck, tell me, please, what to do.* No answer was given. He tried to recall that abrupt mental convo he had had with that disembodied voice. It said something about having to do something for himself. Alongside all thoughts as to whether this voice had been the one who freed him from whatever control the company had, and the most pressing one was how best to escape, and whether to play it by ear; and all these phrases that felt new, fresh, but ever so familiar – he was alerted, thrust, ejected from the before. A deep booming siren directed his attention to the strip lights above him. Before his rude awakening *They* had been a glaring pasty yellow. Now the whole surrounding environment, built of cubicles with people like himself, seated and doing what they were meant to do, were thrown into darkness. There was an eerie period when there was no sounds of typing or that general work floor ambiance. As his eyes started to acclimatize to the dark he was then blinded as a different colour light brought back the whole floor. Everything was illuminated in an aggressive white, that dimmed for a second before changing into a dark red, that came and went simultaneously with the siren calls. The siren in tandem with the flashing lights. Unbeknownst to the nameless man the office-workers not only had micro-dot bugs placed under their desk and into their office-chairs and in the cushion of the seat, the company and whoever made them/produced them had sneaked advanced technology under their fingernails, a trip switch of some sort. These were not mere bugs, they were chip-electrodes that were of the same voltage and nano-rhythms that had given them animation. As the alarm went off, it triggered these switches. He didn't notice that his left hands forefinger was glaring red, as so much was happening at once. As soon as the emergency siren went off, the office workers bodies were shut down and then taken over by the charges that kept them alive. The nameless man peeped over his cubicle, staying there, trying to ascertain what was happening, when somebody bolted upright from his cubicle, opposite his own and turned to face him, in unison with everyone else. The movement of all of those bodies working in perfect synchronization created the oddest of sensations passing through his newly aroused consciousness and real body. *I have a body and a mind. I have control of both of these things, whereas the others don't.* The sound that he had thought of as silence before was actually the white noise of his fellow workers continual never-ending tapping on their keyboards. The siren had silenced, but the synchronized lighting hadn't. He noticed finally that his hand had instinctively been placed over where his heart when the office-worker opposite gave him a fright. The nameless man looked about him. They were all dead-eyed and staring at him. They all looked alike. Himself included. The nameless man turned to look behind him, when he was afforded for a mere microsecond some relief. He was relieved that they were indeed looking towards the exit, rather than himself. The red light was flashing on and off. His eyes seemed to process the light differently. All of his coworkers, and what he felt must be clones/siblings were dead eyed. Pitching him and his kind into total obsidian darkness each time the red lights went out. PLEASE PROCEED TO THE NEAREST EXIT. CONTAMINATION LOCKDOWN IS IN PROGRESS – filtered through the hidden speakers throughout the office-space. *That's new?* he thought, then scolded himself for making such a pitiful observation, knowing that everything was new to him. Still processing everything, not knowing what to do, the office-workers moved again in unison. The nameless man remained where he was, arms held out to his sides, as if caught in an intimate

or awkward act. They were all turning and facing towards the exit of their cubicles. They were robotic, and extremely slow. Precise as well. They eventually all came together and lined up in a row. Upon the approval from that booming authorial voice to commence towards the exit another big bright sign - this one an obnoxious orange, set in some weird whacky font - alerted them to march. They marched forward - like a military parade toward the exit and the automatic doors opened; two stepping out at a time, before the other row behind them did likewise – each time the automatic doors closed it seemed to make a sucking sound. Like flapping rubber or a sucking noise. The nameless man stayed rooted to the spot and waited until the lightshow - dipping in and out of deep darkness and garish ruby-red - stopped. The office was empty when he finally felt he could unfreeze. He was now in total silence. WORKER. WE SEE AND HEAR FROM YOU. NAME YOURSELF – that same commanding voice boomed through the speakers, that vibrated under his feet and also

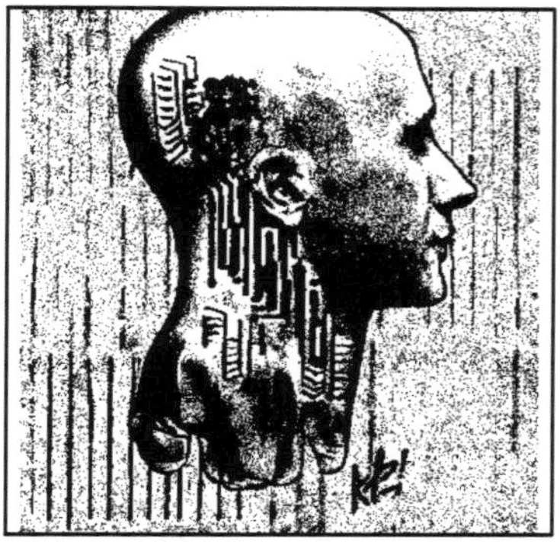

tickled his fingernails. He was left alone, as the workspace resumed its usual yellow-glare lighting. He didn't know if he could speak. He opened his mouth, then got scared of even trying to move his tongue, deciding it would be best if he closed it shut. Both his top row and bottom row collided and made a nasty snap! A name. What is a name when it's at home? What does that even mean? The nameless man, for the first time since his creation, took stock of his environment. His clothes he pulled on. They were carbon copies of carbon copies of everyone else's that had just tranced themselves out of the work-floor. The name tag he had on his left breast pocket announced to the world he didn't have a name, but that he had a number and barcode – which was assigned to him when he came from the PROCESS-CHAMBERS, butt-naked, floppy, empty of all humanity and character, yet to be filled with automata-body-charges to awaken this dead, empty vessel – the nameless man felt disconsolate. *I'm not empty,* he thought as he angled the nametag so he could read it. *I am a human,* he repeated to

himself, hardly noticing that his lips and mouth were wording the thoughts in his head. That thought alone made him feel something escape his eyes. *These are tears? I am crying. I must be more than they anticipated, and I am not a piece of this fucked up machinery.* A new sense of worth infiltrated his body. STATE YOUR NAME OR AWAIT FOR BARCODE-SACANNING – the voice then cut out and he was plummeted back into that once, not so long ago, appreciated silence. *I was made to be a tool to this company to produce what they called energy.* What for? He didn't know nor did he care. What he cared about now was how he was going to get out of this

pickle. "What is a pickle?" he said aloud. Well then, that answers that. He can talk. He tore the nametag off his breast-pocket, tearing the pocket away with it and read what was printed: OFFICER1225898. A noise from the other side

of the office-floor grabbed his attention. A black-glassy sphere popped out of what looked like a trashcan and scanned the room with a multi-tiered gridwork scanner. The ball of black glass seemed unsteady in its antigrav function, almost losing complete power and dropping to the cheaply carpeted floor, before something kicked in. It halted and rebooted. "You won't believe the day I have had," the sphere emanated a sound that built into a network of fragments and then the noise was translated directly into the nameless man's head, like before, except this time it sounded more human. It had a slight lisp-y-rasp, like some old professor with dentures in. "I was sitting at my desk contemplating, of all things, a brownish-green bogey. I held it up to the 200-watt bulb that hung from the ceiling, it looked real to me. Then I realised I had jumped into the wrong building and infiltrated the wrong system…silly me." The black ball sped towards the nameless worker, and he flinched. The ball responded by projecting across its oval surface an animated emoticon, that had a laughing face with tears of laughter spewing out. "LOL. Hashtag, so lol!" the black sphere laughed. The ball was moving around like a curious bee as it spoke directly into the man's head. It was an odd sensation. The black ball was taking on a personality whereas before it was just a black-security drone that would have scanned the office-worker and probably have killed him with a vaporizer. "So, I was thinking, as I have taken out their spherical-security-drone, this glorious piece of equipment, which I am not ashamed to tell

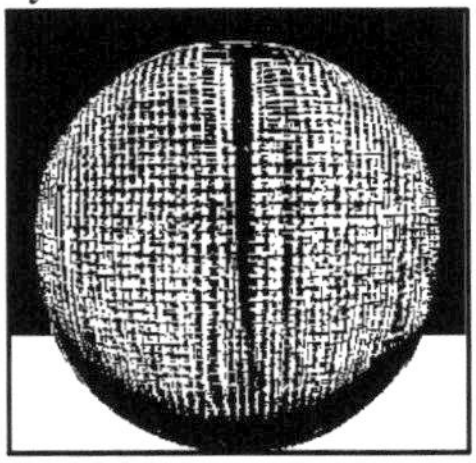

you is sleek, sexy, and totally 1970s in its look. Very Star Wars-y, don't you think? Oh, you probably don't know what Star Wars is, but there will be time for that my friend." The thing just kept yammering on. "The cord was a good seven inches long, so that even a mere hint of somebody walking past this like totally secluded spot, lit mainly from that singular standard bulb, swayed and cast these really creepy images on the virtualum sideboard..." The nameless man held up both hands and said, "Woah, woah, woah, stop right there!" Which the black orb did. It was bobbing, the hum of the gravmortors, that in any other circumstance may have been nice to listen to, but it seemed to grate on the nameless man's nerves. "Who are you?" the words came from his mouth. They felt elongated and warped as they escaped, but the more he spoke the easier and more natural it felt, which was expressed by many swearwords and cussing. "Best way to reestablish verbal-capabilities is swearing, feels like a good neck and back massage, right? Not that I know anything about that, being an Ai myself, but I have seen the videos and partook in some virtual-experiences via a sensorium-bod," the security-drone stopped, as the nameless man was left looking cluelessly on. The flash of an awkward emoticon face flashed across the glacial surface before it resumed talking. "But maybe use a nastier word, it will really grease those pistons," the voice provided, this time not in his head but from the actual security-drones chassis, where an animated line imitated wave-patterns when it spoke. "Sorry about the intrusion inside your head, I didn't yet know whether you could communicate..." "CUNT!" blurted the man, interrupting the security-drone. "Well, that is a nasty word, well bloody done," it flashed an archived clip, something called a Meme of an assemblage of suited people in a fine theatre space jumping up in a round of applause. It lasted only a second. It was replaced by the dead-wave signature. "Sorry, I just felt, that that word needed to be said, sorry again." After the man apologised the security-drone dipped, in a form of bow. "So, what do I call you?" the man asked, for the first time, in this new life of his, feeling uncomfortable with this whole maddening situation. "BORD" the security-drone replied. "Right, Bored. Why am I here...no, not why am I here, but why are you here and trying to, *well*, I guess, help me?" the man asked, placing his hands on his hips; he didn't know why but this felt like something he would do, whoever he was. "Right, honey firstly, I am currently doing several things at once. The first is shutting down this awful enterprise...hold on, wait one..." – the security-drone lost all its energy and dropped like a bowling ball onto the floor. It rolled a few feet. The man went on his haunches, checking the room around him in case someone might turn up and tapped it on its glassy surface. A nice crystal-inflected sound rang out. "Um...hello," the man waved at the security-drone, sensing maybe movement might encourage it to rise up and kick back into some function. Which it did, only this time it was less floaty and casual in its overall levitation and more solid and authoritative. He followed the security-drone in its slow ascension back up. It this time went a few feet higher than the nameless office worker and started up, rebooting, crackling, and making beeps and boops that BORD hadn't. WE ARE BACK ONLINE. OFFICE WORKER SCAN INCOMPLETE. TOTAL SCAN RE-ENGAGED – the harsh, brutal difference in voice was enough to tell the nameless man that

BORD had left and had once again be replaced by the unhacked security system, the full total brutal version of the companies security-drone. It also emanated a harsher aggressive sound. It scanned the office worker and was about to open up a side slot to extract a vaporizer when once again BORD's now comforting, yet strangely human tones spoke from the command-Centre's speakers. "I am back, now, that is so rude Mr. Blackball of potential death!" Bord tut tutted and before the nameless man could raise his hand like a school child wanting to ask a question the blackball fritzed and died. The nameless man kicked it away, not satisfied until it had rolled into a cubicle a couple of rows down from his own. Out of sight and out of mind. "Please, answer me, what is going on?" the man was speaking up in the direction of the ceiling. "You don't need to look up there honey," Bord said, then followed it with hysterical giggles. "I am everywhere. I am the building now." Feeling a little embarrassed the man put his hands in his pockets. He didn't know how to hold himself, all whilst something in him was naturally doing it for him. "That…still didn't answer my question." The man said sulkily, and more to himself than to BORD, who once again, with an audible click disconnected from the speakers. "Right. You are a human. Just, I helped you a little." The voice returned from another source, this time one of the obsolete computers. The man walked over to the only one that had a BORD-ian emoticon symbol on it, a smiling face changing into a winking face. "Helped me how?" the nameless man said. "Weeeeeeeeeell," BORD played coy, which irritated the man, so much he responded with, "BORD FOR FUCKSAKE, FOR ONCE IN OUR TIME TOGETHER, BE STRAIGHT WITH ME!" the man closed a hand over his mouth. It was all coming back to him. "I wouldn't call myself straight, honey, I am using archival voice-receptors and emulators to sound like Boy George, so I am far from..." "Shut it, BORD, where is my body?" interrupted the nameless man. "Jonesy, afraid to say, this is now your new body. Your last one burnt upon reentry...sooo, yeah, awks and all that" BORD imitated the pursing of lips; in particular the way Boy George purses his lips. "Oh great...so, you, like, what, hacked into this body, translated my consciousness into it and then...what, turned up to break me free?" the now no longer nameless man said, trying not to smile. *I love this Ai so much*, he thought. This time, this thought didn't feel alien or unreal or from another source. It was his own thoughts and consciousness finally acclimatizing to this new body, "Yeah, as this was the only place that had free bodies going for consciousness-sparks to be plugged into," BORD replied. Jonesy straightened up and rolled his shoulders and tried to feel as much as he could in this new body, "I hate that word, plugged in, it is so...ah, what's the word BORD?" the nameless man was coming into himself. Images, memories, the sensation a human body should feel. A weird wholesome unity of mind and body, something that many humans take for granted. "2000s?" BORD provided the answer. Jonesy snapped his fingers. It didn't produce the intended snap. Different body, different sound, and different capabilities. Jonesy stared off into the distance. "What year are we in, BORD?" he asked his Ai companion. "Twenty, blah, blah, blah, what does it matter?" BORD replied promptly, providing the not the answer but his usual cattiness, that ignited something inside Jonesy - before BORD cut away all connexion to the building which dipped and jittered, lights and all digital devices flickering or droning as BORD's sophisticated energy source sapped away from the whole buildings structure and internal devices - reverting to its previous state. The whole building they were in was coming back online, and that meant whatever BORD had stalled would soon be coming back for the property BORD had stolen. BORD cut out from the old computer terminal and now slotted into Jonesy's readapting mind. "I know you BORD," Jonesy said, stretching his legs, "you save my bacon, you cook up some fries, you surprise me with some jalapeno sauce, and then take the meal away, what is going on here?" BORD didn't respond straight away. *Figures* thought Jonesy. *BORD is doing several things at once, which meant millions of things at once.* He had to admit though, it felt good to have BORD back inside his mind with him, like before. *God, did I just think that?* Jonesy almost spat out in astonishment, at his sentimentality. YES, HONEY, BORD replied, still with that annoying Boy George voice-simulation making Jonesy's balls curl up, YES, I DID. "BORD, Earth in 2000s didn't have anything like this going for it...like, ever!" BORD sighed – YEAH. ABOUT THAT. UM. – BORD was losing his Boy George-voice-simulation. THIS IS NOT A REALLY GOOD TIME TO TELL YOU THIS, RIGHT NOW, BECAUSE YOU KNOW WHAT YOU SAID ABOUT THE FRIES? "And the bacon." Jonesy added, unhelpfully. YES, THE BACON.

"And the jalapeno sauce?" Jonesy pushed, knowing BORD could and did get frustrated.

YES. THAT, THAT AND THAT. WE HAVE COMPANY. Jonesy was messing around by this point, asking, "What do you mean, my gayly pessimistic friend?"

He knew the security was on high alert and coming for him; even though BORD had appeared and saved his life, again, and managed to break into the only high-tech industry that had a spare body going, in the year 2000s, on Earth of all places, he wouldn't be leaving without getting a few punches and kicks in himself. BORD knew him too well not to let him have his bacon and fries and jalapeno sauce. And right on time surged in a monstrous team of geared up, spazz-tag-stick wielding men. Their sticks pulsing with synapse disturber energy. Jonesy rolled up his sleeves, took up his position and asked, "Why do they not want to vaporize me now?" BORD responded, whilst Jonesy threw the first punch which didn't hit like it would have in his old body – WELL, THERE SCANNERS DID A GOOD JOB, A THOROUGH JOB I MUST ADMIT. THEY HAVE NOW REALISED THAT THEY HAVE A NEW MONEY-MAKER IN THEIR MIDST. "That...Eurgh...fuck that hurt, being, me?" Jonesy said, breaking free from two security guards' pathetic attempts at tackling him. He had already disarmed and destroyed all of their snappy-sticks, and they were all now falling over themselves to prove in front of their bosses they could put up a fight. Jonesy headbutted a visored security man, creating a webwork of cracks across his helmet and ruining his vision. YES. YOU. THEY HAD EMPTY BODIES

THAT FED INTO SOME ANTIQUATED LEGAL WAY OF PRODUCING SUPPOSED CLEAN ENERGY – NOW THEY HAVE A BODY WITH CONSCIOUSNESS. GIVE ME A SECOND TO TAKE A DEEPER DIVE...YUP! BINGO!JUST AS I THOUGHT. YOU ARE NOW AN ASSET. ALSO, I THINK I HAVE MY YEARS WRONG. THIS IS LATE, LATE 2000s JUST THE IOFFICE GIVES OFF 1990 ENERGY AND 2000 OPTIMISM IN ENERGY PRESERVES AND A CLEANER FUTURE. THEY WILL NOT WANT YOU TO GO AWAY WAY, BABY BOY! ESPECIALLY ONE APPEARING OUT OF NOWHERE. THAT MEANS SOMETHING BIG IN THEIR DATA BANKS. "Well I best fuck off as soon as possible then, right?" With that said Jonesy flew through the air and kicked the last standing security-pleb into the chest and sent him hurtling through the plate glass of the automatic doors. "Where to now, BORD, buddy oh-pal of mine?" Jonesy took four steps at a time going down the various floors to the reception area of this building. "To the future. Or back to the future, or in-between some other future, look why don't you ever comment upon the voices I choose?" BORD was annoyed that Jonesy was ignoring his choice of voice it was now using. "Because from what I recall, Boy George was a twat and the voice you have going now is of my own previous voice, which if anything makes me a bit mournful, okay!" OH. Okay. Sorry. NOT SORRY.

"Filthy pigs!" was thought. Then it was translated into a verbal projection. In-between these stages something from the outer reaches of our cosmos intervened and gave these thoughts and its pattern/the electrons from the mind and the energy it hummed/bristled with a concrete appearance.

Like a huge tarantula twisted inside out and worn as a mitt only to be discarded and then later picked up by an inquisitive local bumpkin – it tried out various visages.

One microsecond later it was a headless chicken with another headless chicken's foot cut off and shoved into the gaping hole as some warped replacement – the next pico-second it took on the appearance of exhaled cigarette smoke (the nastiest, most potent brand you can imagine) that curled into itself and began to take in the surrounding illuminations – gathered from the inside of the farmer's brain/consciousness.

It looked through its creator's eyes and tried to smile. It couldn't quite do it as it hadn't yet managed to pull this feat off.

Try as it might it struggled with forming something that possessed a face; especially a face that could manufacture something as simple as a smile.

It pierced through his eyes, collecting data, sourcing pigment, textures, materials to translate from and then into its non-body.

It sourced from the hallway nightlight that goes on and off with each creak of the floorboards, that anyone would assume was triggered by a passing cat, or that the farmhouse had a rat infestation.

The farmhouses' resident rats (all friendly and not as disgusting as they are usually thought as and referred to) were not having a disco when the farmhouse owners were in bed asleep – the sensor was *on the blink*.

It sourced illumination from the moon ray beams, and then it dispersed with a theatrical ***poof!***

It bent to its own will and reappeared.

"Dirty, filthy, fucking pigs!" was thought, and then cancelled out.

"Filthy pigs!" escaped the mind of the farmer, then went travelling down to the farmer's mouth.

The two words were not a thought nor a thing.

It was a *being* created by a man who worked hard, laboured extensively, cultivated his land, and did quite well for himself; enough to finally appease his mother-in-law; these two words – filthy and pig were now an embodied phrase – a thick, gelatinous excretion, like a combo of flu produced phlegm and snot running down his brainstem into the back of his throat.

Solidifying itself, it formed into an ectoplasmic substance. Part pea part extraterrestrial probe-end.

The phrase, the words, looked around itself, peering over its S-shaped shoulder to the left, and its F-shaped shoulder to the right, admiring the dental work of this farmer.

It left the mouth, silently.

It supressed its audio function, as it wanted to be nosy. It was a thought, a new type of being, and though it was translated in the physical realm as FILTHY PIG it was still an untapped into verbal projection it would eventually have to explode, release its noise, and die.

So, it did not reverberate like you'd expect.

Not yet.

The two words, the phrase, the intent, the thought was living as its own defined thing; but defined things can still learn and gather intel to better itself, right?

When it escaped the farmer of an indeterminate age but could easily pass for middle age' mouth, it didn't get a chance to awake the farmer and his wife upon its exit and entrance into what we have all deluded ourselves is reality.

It went nosing about the homestead. Colliding with various corners, being flung back out, sliding off walls, ornaments, until it knew its time was up; it travelled back up the chimney, out into the chill evening air and knocked twice on the bedroom window of Bedřich, before it decided he wouldn't wake up by such a noise, only motivated to consciousness when it is his own voice being shouted back at him.

It dissolved itself back into the bedroom that Bedřich shares with his wife Ulana and woke Bedřich up.

Bedřich woke himself up.

"Filthy pig!" woke him up.

He looked around him. He noticed that the usually erratic beat of the hallway night light, installed so he didn't trip and fall down a flight of stairs (again!) was off.

"Where?" his wife responded.

"In my head."

"Pigs?"

"Filthy. PIGS!" then he got up and made himself some toast.

Extra burnt.

No butter.

No condiments or spreads.

He dipped it into his sugary coffee.

Thoughts have a funny way of possessing a man, the farmer thought, suddenly broken out of his reverie as his wife's hand rubbed his back, indicating she was in the same room as him; she knew how jumpy he got coming up to the end of the month. The Great Lamb Race was an event he always agonised over.

"My darling?"

"Yes, my dear?"

"I have been thinking…"

"Yes? You do know how to, don't you?"

"Yes, but, like, my love, I was awoken by a voice, my own voice, but it felt like a thought had spoken it, da? I am thinking a lot on thoughts as like an experiment."

"That is intriguing, finish your coffee, and I will cook you up some..."

"Darling, please, just listen to me, da?"

"Da."

"I need to write down these thoughts as they excrete from my mind."

"How though, sweetie?"

"I don't know."

"Is the saying, Don't look too deep into that darkly mirror, not apt for this?"

"That isn't a saying, that is something you just made up."

"Da."

"Duh!"

"Oh, da!

"I will do it. No work. All play. Da is part of Dada, don't you know?"

"Da. Da. Ya. Dada-da!"

"Oh god I love the way you say da, it makes my cock so, so hard!"

"DA? That makes a change."

"(sad sigh) Da."

Many people are set off by coincidental sticky minds hence the term brainworms, in 1987. Half a friend of mine described to me how he had been fixated on the Marriage Story film starring Adam Driver. Also, the marriage of Frank Sinatra and his television show Children. It was enough to hook the minds of tempo-freaks & geeks and transexual OSCAR board members. Minds of broad-painterly strokes. The tempo of the almost constantly, for ten days, a repetition.

Thinking. Thinking. Thinking. Thinking. Thinking. Thinking.

Thinking. Thinking. Thinking. Thinking. Thinking. Thinking.

Thinking. Thinking. Thinking. Thinking. Thinking. Thinking.

Thinking. Thinking. Thinking.

Thinking. Thinking. Thinking.

Thinking. Thinking. Thinking. Thinking. Thinking. Thinking.

Thinking. Thinking. Thinking. Thinking. Thinking. Thinking.

Thinking. Thinking. Thinking. Thinking. Thinking. Thinking.

Thinking. Thinking. Thinking.

Thinking. Thinking. Thinking Thinking. Thinking. Thinking. Thinking. Thinking. Thinking.

Thinking. Thinking. Thinking. Thinking. Thinking. Thinking.

Thinking. Thinking. Thinking. Thinking. Thinking. Thinking.

Thinking. Thinking. Thinking.

Thinking. Thinking. Thinking

Thinking. Thinking. Thinking.

Thinking. Thinking. Thinking.

Thinking. Thinking. Thinking. Thinking. Thinking. Thinking.

Thinking. Thinking. Thinking. Thinking. Thinking. Thinking.

Thinking. Thinking. Thinking. Thinking. Thinking. Thinking.

In a number of ways, you're not thinking.

Can we think whilst reading?

Yes. It is annoying. All to no avail. Plentiful foods written about then made edible & digestible. I splashed my ears. I rough-housed my genitals. Demonic running across the ceiling of my bathroom was my torn shadow. Peter Pan never readied you for this type of ordeal. He is usually inappropriately trying to get into Wendy's Mother's bedroom. Sitting on the end of her bed, admiring her. Scanning her body like that incestuous little creep from David O Russell's Spanking the Monkey. For the plague things are not graspable and whole, WHERE most events occur in an odd place, that no word has ever penetrated... For eyes and minds, once upon a time they were wanting solutions for the considered life. Regaining authorship of self-enquiry. Your eyes and minds witnessing the renaissance of relinquishing control. Eyes and minds applying stoic practical philosophies – those mirror images capturing yourself talking to yourself. Third person perspective. Rational meditation. Third person perspectives. Rational meditations. Don't add to first impressions, causing anger and hurt. The causes of anger goes seven ways of removing empathy and connectiveness. For eyes and minds are being loved. Being rich. Being famous. Madness and media. Media and madness. "Why do you do that?" – my father asked me. "Do what?" drunken noodles dragging across my facial hair, taking on a sharpness that a month previously they hadn't. "Do that to the writing?" Dad indicates the font sizes. I could have been condescending and waffled on about my ethos, but instead, I shrugged, snorted up the drunken noodles, slurping, delighted at the flavours and extra spice I had lathered on them and stated simply,

"Fun, innit,"

"Can't complain!" said, who (/) <?> [</>] the secret magical formula for success are happy endings. After death why can't we talk of fearing death? Why is death something we shrink away from? It is part of life…you fucking die, so make the most of it. Hard to apply that when you're unlucky and the stars and the star-sign chicks and hillbilly hicks tell you otherwise. Eating the Dead with George A. Romero as guest. A circle without circumference. A circumference without a circle – what is that if not an oxymoron being oxymoronic? Death as deprivation. Depravational depths of a prolonged death. Now we are at a part where we are rethinking about the afterlife. God! He is irreproachable, and cheers us for a moment, with his holy grail solidifying the cloudscapes into ice-shards, before we sense rubber stamp congeniality, that is designed for contagion: a morale boosting initiative for the world, in the form of psychodelia and 80s' electronic glazed ecstasy. The narcotically familiar in electronic communication that the modern iconoclast first break into, with a decision not to provide a familiar type-written note for sanctity's sake.

Witness the page as a screen, witness the screen as a page, where tone of voice is conveyed - distorted electronic synthetic nodules of recalibrated cancerous cells, where mood of voice is discontinued.

Me, I, myself am happy; recently reports have reached me, alluding to more reports, reports – upon reports upon burning reports upon ice-cool reports. It reports that no one's intentions are entirely benign, and the warm lubricant will smooth any further communication. Within it lies the troubling exhortation's that come in hieroglyphic non-visual patterns.

Fuck. Shit.

Bugger it all.

The desire to be the most endearing and conspicuously self-defeating aspect of our modern condition known as humanity. Time and everything it is meant to be has emerged from a stage like some queer icon after a popular show, basking in the post appraisal aura. Left on stage seeking out particles in the heated ray of light, spotlighting his/her/his/her Dorothy like ruby red shoes, as if plucked from the Wizard of Oz. This isn't Kansas anymore. No siree. A small camera is left trembling like a frightened shrew; beside it sits a large mouse, that is photographing dutifully. The picture is printed from its teeny tiny minuscule mouth as quick as a polaroid took on a personality of an elephant....don't ask me why that should make sense – the image, the picture began to sense that the camera assigned to capture its long life was heading towards total burn out. Which it did. It burnt itself out. Dame Helen Mirren bent over double, with parchment like hands wrinkling, the sound alerting the larger mouse to her presence. The larger mouse looked up, cocked it's head, like a London gangster would sitting at a bar, lording it up, when all of a sudden Dame Helen asked to look at the pictures. The larger mouse ensured that his cockney swagger was kept to. Keeping up appearances this long had kept him alive. Dame Helen knew this was all an act, so tut-tutted with recently botoxed lips and her left taloned finger went wag-wag-wagging. Looking through the photos, Dame Helen got a sense of relief, going from one to the next to the next to the next - she could feel an anxiety spreading from her knobbly knees to her recently uplifted breasts. She flicked through the remainder and caught the larger mouse's expression, though indistinct and continuously morphing this large mouse was actually Rat Winstone. A meaningful tale, one that is entirely wonderful or completely appalling, depending on the successful or failed event, was about to unfold from this scene. We adjust and selectively remember what fits into our relationships. Relationships that shift and change. We are, each of us, a product of ourselves. Some of our stories are brief and inconsequential, allowing us to get to the local shops and also encourages obnoxious snappy neat narrative to arrange reality into a satisfying and tidy place – see only an example of a mess of meaningful patterns. We sense the stage door is learning from deeply awkward stories, passed between stage actors and janitors of the theatre of Solomon. Separately and in their own particular unlucky ways, some of the well-established performers treated the unluckier of the bunch awfully. Some going as far to encourage those that do not speak the native tongue to fish their burning toast out with a fork. In summary, and in many ways correctly, this is responsible for how we psychoanalyse Carl Jung. Whatever we have taken from the founding story imposed on us by a faulty script from their 2000-year-old Roman slave cumrags - a prominent figure in the ancient Stoic tradition will rise – coming out of nothing, with his philosophy; that at a later date outed himself as an awful leader. The most prevalent school of thought is exploding into a notion, that destroyed several universal strands/roots in some pocket of non-time/nonplace. What upsets people is judgements about these words, as it is not based upon events out there, but rather our stories ... those we tell amongst ourselves. This mite of ancient therapeutic philosophy has methods of varying neurolinguistic-programmes that are left in silence, programming cognitive behavioural therapy (CBT); when the sixties mantra of change your head, don't change the bed made Hamlet weep all night. We leave grave misfortune where it deserves to be...as well as all that we have gathered in this thing categorized a life, that has been distorted, whereby nature of Epictetus is over-ruled - where intrinsic degrees of our susceptibility in a stoic frown, at said grave misfortune, makes roses explode like Christmas-crackers and sunflowers ooze heroine – hey, you, yeeeeeah you, are you bored of jerking off on your own – jerk-mates jerk your mates off – oh, yeah, do you not think that every sad cunt reading this makes the bookmark suffer greater than their own psyche? To make it melt, like mozzarella cheese on a high heat. Between the events of the world Out There and In Here, they are two very different kingdoms and other people are not accountable, ludicrously enough, there to affect your dignity. No one needs a source of Stoic's power because there is a distinction between the outer and inner worlds, and therefore how to reduce our levels of outer world experience depends on which celestial being admits they were wrong in challenging the extraterrestrials credibility. We can apply the same understanding, our inner story every day, but, alas, thus, bus, verse, purse - that can change too. Fuck your thoughts. Fuck your experiments with time and geography and how it interrelates to the artistic you. Not you-you, the artistic you. You are so vile, abhorrently fake, you can never merge form, self, intent, artistic personality, rather than id, rather than identity. Fuck you very much. Fuck the world. Fuck the cliques. Fuck the norm. Fuck sane people. Fuck the memories you access in dreamscapes, willing on the fantastical, all so you can share it as a memory, rather than an embellished memory. You forger. You faker. You liar. You deluded bullyboy. I didn't copy your work; your work is nothing compared to mine. You are James Patterson of the indie world. Well, no, you're not, but the calibre of skill, yes, you are. Your work takes on a method, created before you were a mistake come shooting from your dad's cock. Even to this you're your dad grapples you in a chokehold and tries to force you back down into his penis hole, down his urethra and back into his balls; "Get back in there you little cunt!"; You go on and on about fuck art, fuck cliques, fuck ego; but, Adey-Adey-Adey-Oi-Oi-Oi, you have the biggest ego of all; all because you have no one else doing it for you; no work, means no engagement, no engagement means no generating of appreciation, that makes one's head, as above, as below, get bigger; and worse, your childish "wife" across the oceanic seas, feeds into it. She believes that I was paying tribute to you. Fuck the mad man called Buck who goes from bus to bus, reliving his days as a bus driver, driven by a fractured memory, waffling into his hand, before pretend pressing/pinging the red button to indicate you want to get off at the next stop, No. My work sources from better artists, writers. A writer caresses a cat, only to forget that this cat has fleas. The fleas have fleas. Within this quantum realm, there is a human waving, proud to be the source of flea-kind. This human enters via a flea riding another flea. When he enters into the real world, you witness the growing of a man who in a past life was called Krushniak, but now wishes to be known as the singer Flea. "Just do me one favour," the writer asks, still scratching at his head, like most people do when the word flea is brought up in conversation, "No more Star Wars roles, okay?" and flea decides to call it quits and launches himself, flea-body, and size into the fireplace. Your work is the same. Stale. Stale. Boring. Just, not at all engaging. Twisting an ankle in front of the classroom of jerks is preferable to having to look at your meagre output and still, as a friend, try and build up an ego you have crafted for yourself, and not the shitty work you have put out. That is what friends are for. To lie to you. To shape you. It is stale. The bread that is. What was I typing? How best to get one's own back? Publicly shame you, like your deluded wife threatened over and over again, – what leverage did she have? – nada, zilch, go and play a game of bingo you boring tart! People reported her review, oh boo hoo -? Nope. Weave the mania and aggravation into the work. Expand upon the lunatic I only offered you to do a cover because all your Facebook puff-chesting of how good you are, but not admired, made me pity you. You are not wanted. Even when the lawmen described your features to the sketch artist he drifted off and instead automatically drew images of poets and philosophers. Then you provide a shitty cover, and that of which has nothing to do with the book. I write segments around your cover art. Still, your wife throws out big words like plagiarism. Sweetheart, you do not own a style. If I want my books, many published before he entered "the scene" have always been scrappy, bunched together, with little to no pause of breath. Also, has this stupid cunt read DUCKS, NEWBURYPORT? Dim-witted scam artist, which he is. Puts up a book for pre-order, pockets the money, and doesn't release the thing for two full years. Scam artist. It is jealousy that my big book of nonsense was selling and yours wasn't. Put our books side by side. Yours a mere 199 odd pages, mine 600 odds, with images, words sourced from books you probably haven't even read or heard of. Tit for tat. Petulant. Reactionary. That is what it means to be human, honey pie. To then get your "wife" to slam me on Amazon and Goodreads, with a shitty rating, and a very deluded, ill-thought-out attack on me in the form of a review; that is brave and big, considering she obviously doesn't use the platform. Then, when the review gets reported by my friends who think the review is petty, she slams us at our Press with email after email, stating she is getting harassed by our writers (among other things, added as another threat, an empty threat that states, I have nothing else, but I will send this out into the ether, hoping to shit you up… when you just made us two laugh heartily like pissed up pirates raping the rum!) you ain't the first to say that, and you ain't the last. There are too many fuckers and cuntheads in this universe to get bothered by them all/at all - when all the person did was report her shitty, and only negative review (two reviews, a five star one for yours and a one star one for me, this bird doesn't use Goodreads but obviously she will do naything to slam me, to support your warped delusions, you sad cunt!) you two dese4rve each other and the padded cell you were both released from that day. Get a grip. Get a life. I was helping you, your artwork for my cover did sweet fuck all. Do not throw stones like glass houses big boy. Whilst I am at it, your use of the word faggot, is really concerning. You are not only a deluded basement dweller, but you are also a homophobe too. See, tit for tat, you chat shit and get your Francis Bacon plagiarizing artist wife to spam me, I go for you in an amazing book, telling the truth. Who am I kidding, this book is awful. No, you were right in getting humpy Ade, this book is a total rip-off of a shit-artist. You wish you had my skill at experimenting. Petty? Nah, truth buddy old boy. Who is this person? A figment of my imagination? Are all these attackers, assaulters real? Yes. And I have nothing much else to say apart from... For the human the quote that has stayed with them is 'A movie begins with the words based on a true what?' Does this cross your mind? Do you like Pearl Brockovich assaulting every person who has a twitter account? Shaping them is a coherent story, that once upon a time an infinite data stream was left to its own primordial devices - selecting, deleting, cloning, and generalizing from that source known as ORIGINS - to provide a module of your effectively deeper voice, sourced then outsourced from another immediate and intimate visual level. We are missing a huge number of stories, this editing process to other people is strange, but, no less strange than those to ourselves. When someone tells you about an argument they were involved in, do you not administer a complex dose (one that is suspiciously blameless)? - that frustratingly is antagonistic to every other person – is it that it was simplified, so that the person can get there sceptical view of that wry detachment to the necessary vantage point to attend a class run by the left? The left side have been sending out, I've got a really itchy nipple – sending out anagrams to try to solve right-hand right-wing unbeknownst lemon squeezers. Note that in each last whirl and slapstick dissolve, there are immovable egg-jects...dissolved are unsolvable anagrams. Unscrambled, you forgot the egg. Apologies for wasting valuable time dear reader, it's just that the first melon sent to me via FedEx to decipher, oozed toxic Vaseline. The students that you could scramble had eggs. A moment ago, unscrambled easily to form the world's greatest nation, egg-merica. Did you spot it? Most likely not. Especially not if you are trying to sit on the right-hand side of all things. The students in unison sent their hands up, palms held to the sky as the right-hand side of the class solved the anagram; the left didn't. One time the drug was made to dramatically improve John Valley-Jones' height problem. Whilst we are talking about his height problem, we must talk about his shroom dick (ugh, do we have to?) He was placed in a particular situation where a group of gay black men suffering from debilitating anxieties jet sprayed shit in his face. Smokers were assured it would banish the desire for the drug, with a crippling social break-up, in a pub, of all places. Paralyzing a tiny stone-bridge – proudly on the edge of a precarious drop, of hundreds of feet. Smokers who have tried methods to believe how effective the magic injections and pills contained only icing sugar. The dramatic transformations of the volunteers came about because they gave themselves this drug, through their veins, to make them change their overall digital problem; because a new astonishing story that he (???) hadn't been able to work with, what constitutes a focus, by the regular influx of the deeply unhelpful literature brand; alongside societal pressure which can be deeply counterproductive and lead simply to more roots to positive wisdom. Concerned with how we might best have disciplines, observing pathologies, then studying how we might find visionaries, in both fields. Psychologists have attempted to research flourishing psychologist-gurus (who normally have only flimsy anecdotal claims). The study is rendered meaningful when you take clergy substantially on an income of about twenty pounds, to be notably clear that having less than you need is as source of having more than you need. For a while the story, we tell ourselves is confabulation, a fiction. Ultimately, we would lack any coherent sense of anything I am reading out loud – effectively editing and polishing a turd – our identity. Although changes, might be briefly dark, our concern is to make sure that we take Zak to an insane asylum – (FUCK OFF LAURA!) that we start by riddling ourselves of the most persuasive myths of them all. Watching it unexpectedly putting cheques onto doormats with quotidian-laws-of-attraction. You are not the most powerful magnet in the universe. Humanity needed to harness the power of Laura's gluten-farts – of this all-encompassing-illness. This is the true well-spring of the movement to oppose current culture. If one of the best things, is you can say about Calvinism is that it ended up preserving some of Calvinism's more toxic-eggs; a harsh judgementalism echoing the old religions, condemnation of sin, and an insistence on the constant interior labour of self-examination, causes sex-death.

FUCK YOUR THOUGHT EXPERIMENTS & LOVE YOUR DISEASED "*child*"

Scottish. Creeper. Lurker. Seeker. Attention. Deficit. Smug. Disorder. Irish. Salute. Ship. Storms. Amassed. Leveled. Plains. Sour dough. American. Fashion. Dance. Moves. Groveling. Lying. Ego. Diva. Jerk. Freak. Famous. Poor. Asshole. Less. Morbid. More. Sordid. Travelling. To. Alternatively. Rewritten. Nose. Smelling. Prolonged. Synaptic. Prose. Party-hoes. In. Here. Over. To. The. Fair. Share. Loving. Your. Hair. "I don't really..."/"Caring, sharing..." Lockdown rules. Lockdown. Fools. Written. Spools. Unfortunately. Dribbles. On. Crotch. Pants. Saturated. In lemon zest stinging your nipples through your vest. Cheese wheel. Pockmarked. Stop. Mark. Literary. Stole. The toilet rolls. Leg. Arm. Dick. Bow. Tie. Syringe in the eye. Popping infected styes. *Why oh why did I eat that dragon fly.* Perhaps he'll die. That. Or. Fly. Sharp. Into. Highlander. Scents. Stents. In your widow maker dead heart. Sleep. Peep. And weep. Weep. Sleep. Wake up. Shake. Bake. Jam. Flakes. Trouble in Brighton. Trouble in Brixton. The Friction. The frisson. The spikes. The Frenchie pup bites. Que cards. Teleprompter. Prompting visuals. Shampoo rubbed into a sensitive scalp with all the tenderness of a boar roughing up its male mates and anally penetrating them all so when it was there time to be turned into boar-sausage it would be extra shitty. How many people have told you that whatever you write doesn't always mean it should be written or published and studied in a Louis Theroux fashion. Theroux humming hmmm-ing ahh-ing. Louis's signature "Ah, right!" questioning the reason behind your thought experiments. Thought experiments churned and replicated and re-inserted into your think-piece. *Hm.*

As people we forget that the pig is much smarter than the average man and bear. Yes, even Yogi bear has his moments of stupidity. Witness mother pig shepherding baby pig across the undeveloped landmarks we might have used to admired, or catalogued in our brains to later visit, to scout, to breathe in and out. Contributing ourselves to the air, the scene, the environment.

The landmarks have fallen into disrepair, and being in disrepair could mean only one thing; a pig sty, left open for all piglets and pig-Mommas and Daddios to traipse, fornicate, incest pig-breed. There is no chance of some animal farm revolution developing amongst these lifeforms, because pigs are smarter than most readers and appreciators of George

Orwell. They will get on with their piggy lives. They will sow the seeds of agricultural rejuvenation.

They will snort with pleasure. They will snuffle. They will truffle hunt, passing one truffle stem to another, mouths coming into contact, sparking frenzied alure between the pigs of the future. Their life will be full of human remains, to chew, to sharpen and alter piggy-tooth-shapes and sizes. They will not go onto hind legs and prance about, tipping crushed top cats in recognition of their neural routes becoming externalized and mapped out as piggy-scented bacon-y holographic pigminator vision, scanning their surroundings, finally replicated in the real-verse, now that James Cameron was safely lost in the depths of the Marianas Trench. They will not sing, nor will they dance, but they may well praise each other with a piggy hallelujah! Some will sit in decaying buildings, snorting the detritus, the rubble, the wooden shards, various cements and crumbled brickwork, and cough up new pig-augmented building blocks, but with no opposable thumbs or human attributes they just pile them in random piles, usually in empty corners. Pigs are artists, their chortles, snuffles, snorting, squealing is a high frequency, that taps into specific wavelengths. Certain notes create pig artists, manufacturing carbon copies of Max Ernst paintings.

FUCK YOUR THOUGHT EXPERIMENTS & LOVE YOUR DISEASED "*child*"

Pig-portraits. Angry artists ranting online about AI. It is the new thing to get bothered by. Smothered in lard. Slipping around in their bedsits, mansions, rent-a-rooms. Follow the piggy-chain. We are all smeared in shit. Your shit. My shit. The shit that accumulates online, and somehow passes itself off as a prime cut of meat. The patterns you find in the underwear drawer of your favourite weed smoking friend concerns you. It concerns me and I have been a tee-totaler or is it tootler? – tottering their tootler-ing selves, a man about pig town, spitting bacon rashes and then coming to collect them later to fry up in a fuck-ton of butter, all the ingredients to make a morbidly obese Mama-Mia trill like a troubled disabled person, their wheelchair's left wheel snagged on an attractive woman's far too grandiose dress, worn whilst shopping at ICELAND, trying to dislodge the corner, putting his wheelchair on tortoise mode, going silent, tailing her, keeping the corner elevated, not so he could sneak a peek, but not to alert her of his presence. Singing like a fucking canary - since I was born, bro. Slapping each other over and over in a performance art piece, only to be sued by Marina Abramovic Institute; as much as you claim it is inspiration, and the application of compact mirrors smeared in a unique resin, that when applied to hand, palm, fingertips delivers a harsher, far more celestial blow, she will then entrap you by implying you stole her future projects usually siphoned in a pound land sieve and left to mature under a leaking kitchen sink-cabinet – you have intercepted her dream catalogue. You must be sued. I remember the faces of all those that upturned a lip, snarled, passed off a passive-aggressive eyebrow wiggle, and the sanctimonious arch. Bourgie bog-standard boogie-woogie-ers. They think the ointment in their palms, left to dry so nicely over the evening – body strapped down in their four-poster beds, hands upturned, for eight hours. Sleep was not forthcoming, but the sensation of their drying ointment, it is a laugh and a thrill. Elf on a shelf. Kenji on a Karate Kid giggling at his Instagram quotes, nothing in comparison to Kenji's words. Fran Lock on a block, readied for the poetry scene to chop off her head, all in good faith, opposing her singular style of poetry. Jane on a juniper, only to be picked by Monty Python's funnier performer Terry Jones, in drag, bemoaning juniper berries. Laura on the lapel of all the busybody male valedictorians put in her workplace to agitate and ultimately annoy her. Annoying is different to agitating. It is. I think. Boris in the bathtub, Bill and Ben-ing it like all good horny flowerpot men. Jamie on the john, shitting out last night's takeaway. Random Amazon reviewer, sitting atop a skewer, ratcheting up the authors sense of ego. Zak on a Zebra, dictating in audio notes via the Fuck-Book app how he wishes to perform at the

Prague Micro festival in drag. Shane Jesse Christmas smoking the hibiscus. Charalampos on the damp cloth, applying it to the infected wounds of all his past lovers, who are knocked our by Grecian meth. Stupid Sally sitting on top of a Shady Daddy, supplying her with her not so illegal meds. Adrian Brody mixing some gruel with Some-Bodee. Being accused by a fake woman or a fake form for plagiarizing a style of writing, when she is gently grinding, on that Francis Bacon leatherbound sex-bike she had installed in her Viking-hut. Obese woman laughed at by as equally grotesque fat men. Rubbing two pennies together. Coming up with three. Rubbing three pennies together and getting four. The replication of money and the growing stash will only be acknowledged with the usual snooty air of a banker, and they'll take the bag, of replicated sums, and then shove it into the maw of an obese woman that nobody laughs at; due to her being the depository and tip for all things called coin. Websites selling themselves short, and all because they got caught using the COOKIEs settings for information, not stealing, per se, for... information overruling. Taking an identity, cutting it up, and sending it out, mass-email chain wishing you good-luck! I have just coughed up some nasty phlegm and it tastes like how the seawater tastes, not after you've swallowed a mouthful, when it hits your lips, and leaves its filmy/salty/polluted water residue. Our strengths comes from generations back. Mine comes from a Irish/Scottish combo, with an Italian lineage a little way ahead in the future; he doesn't know this, but I am sure he won't be pleased when he realises that it is Italian from a female, and not a male gene pool. I am reader. You are writer. I have always wanted to ask you these questions; you cock your head, "What questions?" is written all over your fat face; well, the questions that a writer rehearses, makes up in their own head, building a fictional career, one that is archived in their minds, to apply, to connotate, to add onto, and expand upon if they get to position where somebody, like me wants to ask you such questions. Shall I begin? Your face says yes, but I know your whole being is screaming out, no, this is not a good idea, why should I do this, this is beyond ego, and anything that goes beyond ego, reaches a horizon line that slits right at that nexus point of its grand unveiling and the little bastards that enter our universe cause such mayhem not even a 2018 Doctor Who episode could control the backlash and distaste.

Can I start by complimenting you on your... (dial tone) dead, dead, dead. When a book is as experimental as mine are... as yours are, as most avant-garde artists are, without sounding pretentious, they come quick and fast; the job of the editor is thrown out of the window; the job as editor is to shape it merely to make it digestible – in some way, and in others, it is the work of an editor to be restrained in the face of such anarchy; I do not slave over passages or lines or paragraphs. What is thought is translated, and it is left to fester. Sometimes, certain works ask to be edited, shaped, cut, given TLC. Mine/yours/theirs do not. I space my sentences/paragraphs as if they are meant to be read by somebody with dyslexia, or somebody afflicted with a certain type of dyslexia; a person who needs these words to be spaced, indents taking on the personality of a pushy parent, shoving, shoving, shoving, shoving! Forcing you into the margins, all whilst believing that you should be front and centre with tin hat on taking on all the explosions that life throws at you, by the hands of regenerated Germans screaming, "Töte diesen Schriftsteller, töte ihn, damit die ganze Welt es sehen kann" whilst an English spy is giggling into a barley-sugar scented sweet bag, not willing to grenade launch his fellow buck-tooth-Billy.

All that has been written, obsessed and brutalised, have stemmed from the mind.

This is my diseased child.

This is my final hurrah, for the remainder of the year.

My art is sacred.

My diseased children have become one.

This is a diseased child of mine.

Everything I do is a thought experiment.

Fuck your thought experiments. It means make sweet hateful vengeful hate fucking love to it. It also means, fuck off, fuck your philosophy. FUCK YOUR THOUGHT EXPERIMENTS & love your diseased "child".

About the author

Zak Ferguson is an Autistic experimental author/filmmaker/autistic-noisemaker, living in Brighton, UK.

Zak is also the Co-Founder of the innovative, boundary-pushing Sweat Drenched Press.

His most recent published works include, MUSHROOM DWLLERS (co-authored with Kenji Siratori) we + you = us, SHOULD THIS HAVE SEEN THE LIGHT OF DAY? and now FUCK YOUR THOUGHT EXPERIMENTS & LOVE YOUR DISEASED "child".

Zak has also recently be involved with film work, having composed the film score for the horror movie FANG (2023).

Printed in Great Britain
by Amazon

35171697R00238